THE

CHAPEL

OF

RETRIBUTION

The

CHAPEL

of

RETRIBUTION

GLENN BURWELL

Somewhat Grumpy Press Inc

Copyright © 2023 by Glenn Burwell.
Cover photograph © 2023 by Corrine Chan, used by permission.
Cover design by Marcus Burwell.

All rights reserved. No part of this publication may be reproduced, stored, or transmitted in any form or by any means, electronic, mechanical, photocopying, recording, scanning, or otherwise, without written permission from the author, except in the case of brief quotations embodied in critical articles and reviews. It is illegal to copy this book or file, post it to a website, or distribute it by any other means without permission.

This novel is entirely a work of fiction. The names, characters, locations, and events portrayed in it are either the work of the author's imagination or used in a fictitious manner. Any resemblance to actual persons, living or dead, localities, or events is entirely coincidental. Any public figures, institutions, trade names or organizations that may be mentioned in the book have not endorsed this book, have not made any payment for mention, and are not otherwise associated with the book, author, or publisher.

Published by arrangement with Somewhat Grumpy Press Inc.
Halifax, Nova Scotia, Canada.
www.SomewhatGrumpyPress.com
The Somewhat Grumpy Press name and Pallas' cat logo are trademarks (registration pending).

ISBN
978-1-7776898-6-5 (paperback)
978-1-7776898-7-2 (eBook)

First Printing, March 2023

"God Almighty first planted a garden; and, indeed, it is the purest of human pleasures."

"A man that studieth revenge keeps his own wounds green."

Francis Bacon

PROLOGUE

Vancouver, British Columbia, Thirty Years Ago

The boy bounced downstairs early one morning after showering, to get some breakfast before school. He walked by the den, then slowed as he saw his dad sprawled on the couch in front of the television, seemingly asleep. The television was off. There was an empty glass on the coffee table paired with an equally empty pill bottle.

"Hey Dad, did you sleep down here last night?" No answer. He went over and shook his dad's arm. It felt cold. No response. He started to feel ill. He walked slowly back up the stairs to his parent's bedroom, uncertain what was wrong. He stopped at the partially open door. "Mom, Dad's not moving."

"What do you mean?" came a groggy reply. "Where is he?" Then came a louder reply as his mother woke up. "Where is he?" she shrieked. The boy started to cry.

"He's downstairs in front of the TV. He's not moving, Mom."

His mother ran out of the room and down the stairs. Then the screaming started. "Call 911, now!"

His mother cried and quietly moaned that day, not understanding what happened or why. The boy surely did not understand what happened to his father. The call to the police, the arrival of the paramedics, the questioning looks from their neighbours, all of it a living nightmare. Then nothing for a while.

He stayed home from school. The neighbours avoided talking to the remaining family. Their friends did not know what to do any more than the boy and his mother did. Grief counselling was a thing for the future, and there wasn't much family left to help console them.

When the banks came calling, the boy's mother slowly realized that their whole life had been mortgaged by her husband. She had no idea whether it was stupidity, bad luck, or something more sinister. The bank foreclosed on their home while all the other family property, including a shopping plaza and a few older apartment buildings, was somehow not theirs anymore. Instead, it belonged to someone else.

After his mother explained things to the boy, he considered this and realized that someone had tricked his father. He made a vow to himself to find out who had done it. Then he would exact revenge for his family.

~ 1 ~

Vancouver, Present Day, October

An all-out brawl was taking place in the boardroom of the Visitor's Centre at VanDusen Botanical Gardens. Brawl was perhaps an overstatement, as there were only two men dressed in suits taking part, but they weren't holding back. They also weren't experienced fighters, so most of the jabs and haymakers missed their mark. They quickly tired and when one of them had the other backed against a wall and lined up for a knock-out punch, then missed, putting a dent into the drywall, the fight stopped.

Blood was dripping from the puncher's hand onto the faux wood flooring. What didn't stop was the swearing and name-calling. Some of the remaining people in the meeting were huddled together close to the window wall overlooking the café's outdoor eating area, hoping the bad dream would come to an end while the others remained sitting around the table, vaguely amused by the spectacle. The Garden's manager had seen enough. "I'm calling the police." With that, he left the room.

A director sitting at the table, one with more of a sense

of entitlement, looked at the man who had punched the wall, adding, "So we'll send you the bill for wall repairs, right?"

The man laughed and shook his bloodied hand so that some drops flew onto the suits of those closest to him, disdain tugging at the corner of his lips. As he watched the manager leave the room, he calmed down enough to decide it was time to make himself scarce.

The two combatants were both part of the development community in Vancouver but couldn't get along with each other. The man who had dented the wall, damaging his knuckles in the process, was Samuel Greene. He had been on the board of directors for VanDusen years earlier but had been voted out when his true character surfaced and was found to be wanting. The other combatant was Nicholas Ng, also a developer, who had essentially taken Sam's place at VanDusen as a director. The board was continually looking for ways to fund-raise and tapping into the development community had seemed like a good idea. Developers always appeared to be awash in money, at least, it seemed to follow them around. The Garden's manager had been having doubts about this strategy for some time; this was just more evidence supporting his thinking.

Over on Cambie Street, at one of the two Vancouver Police Department headquarters, the manager's call was received, logged, then transferred to Steve Christie, head of the Investigative Unit. This wouldn't normally happen, but the VanDusen Botanical Garden occupied a special place in the hearts and minds of Vancouverites, not to mention its location smack in the middle of old Shaughnessy where some of the wealthier Vancouverites rested their heads at night.

After the brief discussion, Steve thought the situation called for tact, not brute force, so he called the detective responsible for this area, Robert Lui, to his office. Robert was not his favourite officer owing to Robert's penchant for frequently taking his coffee at a café up Cambie Street, seemingly missing a fair portion of each workday in doing so.

After hanging up the phone call requesting his presence, Robert stood up in his own small office, stretched with his arms overhead for a moment while he looked out at the collection of nondescript commercial buildings spreading east into the distance, then sighed and headed dutifully across the floor to Steve's larger office. His room sported west-facing windows with a much better view than Roberts'.

"There is a disturbance over at VanDusen. Sounds like a fight between two gentlemen who should know better. Please go take a look." With that instruction, Steve's eyes dropped to whatever he had been studying on his mostly empty desk. Robert shrugged his shoulders, turned, and left without saying a word, making sure to close the door behind him. His best guess was that discretion was the order of the day, otherwise, wouldn't a patrol officer be sent to attend? He descended to the basement to grab an un-marked car for the short ride over to VanDusen.

* * *

Robert was on the tall side, thin, and of mixed race; the product of a Cantonese father and a Caucasian mother who had been raised in Vancouver. The mixture hadn't done his looks any harm. Women were continually attracted to him despite his own family, or maybe because of it. It was difficult to know, not that he spent much time thinking about the subject. Robert had been born in Hong Kong but had spent his teen years growing up in Vancouver. His father, Ethan, had been a top-rated chef in Hong Kong. He had cooked for people on both sides of the law, including triad members and officers in the Hong Kong Police Force. The complexities of doing this eventually forced Ethan to the decision that it might be safer for his family to be in Vancouver.

Robert joined the police force, both because he wanted to be a detective and because the force wanted more people from racially diverse backgrounds. Being a 'halfer' was a helpful factor in his hiring; he was an oddity before mixed-race people became somewhat more common in Vancouver, if not in the police force. Working his way up the ranks to investigator was more difficult. He took a lot of crap along the way, and it was a miracle that he had made it this far. He did not get along with Steve, feeling that Steve's capabilities didn't come close to matching the requirements of the position he occupied, a judgment quickly formed after he had joined the investigative group.

Robert had been wondering lately whether leaving the Special Enforcement Unit had been a rash move. It wasn't just his seemingly ill-qualified boss. Instead of travelling the Lower Mainland investigating the latest gangland shootings, he was again back at a desk at the Cambie Street offices of the Investigative Services Unit, where he had previously worked on more pedestrian cases in the Major Crime section.

Robert had liked the excitement of the gang chase, but truth be told, the gang members weren't the brightest, and most of them couldn't even shoot straight. Finding enough evidence to bring the gang cases to court, however, was difficult. The police could usually predict who was going to target whom as they knew most of the players, but the actual gunplay was not predictable, and the gangsters had taken to setting their cars on fire after the action to help obliterate forensic evidence. As far as Robert could tell, it seemed to be nothing but a boon to local auto traders. This appeared to be the new equation; one shooting equalled one burned-out car. It was always a stolen car, because as dumb as these gangsters were, they weren't quite so stupid as to torch their own cars, although Robert bet that the first few times, this was exactly what happened.

He had grown tired of the media circus surrounding the gang unit and wanted more normal cases, if such a thing even existed, which he doubted. One thing was certain: all the money pouring into the city was not helping things. Port cities always had drug issues, but the extra people and money arriving in Vancouver over such a short time exacerbated the existing problems.

These excuses were but the rationale he needed to hide the real reason he had left the Special Unit. He felt like a coward, but when he had received the death threat against his family two months earlier, it didn't take him long to figure out that no one was really going to protect his family, nor did he want his children living in fear. The picture taken of his two kids on their way home from school, and then mailed to him at the precinct office, drove the point home. He hadn't told his children about any of this, nor did he plan on doing so.

He had seen the results of the gang wars, even the results of mistaken identity. The young gangsters just didn't give a damn—they killed just as easily as opening a beer. Being a police officer was dangerous enough, without the extra threats that came with being on the gang detail. Many officers dreamed of the day they could operate out of uniform, as detectives, going undercover, or being on special operations such as those with the Special Unit, but with this came danger. Most of the younger officers seemed to embrace it or ignore it, with the protection of the force at their back, or so they thought. Robert's understanding came from age and experience. Not everyone could be protected, and while retribution by the police force would come, it might very well be too late to save anyone who had become a target of the gangs. The threat of retribution only worked on people who took the time to think. Thinking strategically didn't seem to apply to most gangsters, hence their relatively short life span.

* * *

He sighed again as he drove out of the garage. Another waste of time was his best assessment of the assignment.

As he drove south on Oak Street, he spotted the turnoff to the Visitor's Centre at VanDusen and decided to drop his car right by the front entry, despite signs suggesting this would be frowned upon. Regular parking was farther south on the grounds, but Robert had decided some time ago that he was past being 'regular' in this city of far too many rules.

He ambled over to the entry and went into the long, echoing foyer, which seemed to lack any straight lines. Robert was no expert on architecture, but he liked a straight line or two just so you knew what was what. He walked up to the members' kiosk, showed his badge, and asked for the manager. One of the elderly women behind the counter turned and opened a door behind the kiosk and went inside. A middle-aged man of vaguely Mediterranean appearance came out and greeted Robert.

"Hello. Thanks for coming, but the troublemaker has already left."

"And he was?" Robert assumed it was a man.

"Samuel Greene. A past director on the board, but now, just a nuisance."

"What happened?"

"We were having a special board meeting when Sam barged in and started accusing one of the directors of some malfeasance."

"Who is?" It felt like dragging a confession out of a child.

"Nicholas Ng. He is a developer in the city, as is Sam, and must have done something to upset Sam. They got into a fight. It was disgusting."

"Can I talk with Mr. Ng?"

"He left as well."

"Fantastic. Always pleased to be of assistance." With that sarcastic comment, Robert turned and walked back the way he had come, shaking his head. He then had a thought, so he wheeled and caught the manager just before he closed the board room door. "Do you know what they were fighting about?"

"Not really, but it seemed to be related to Eden Gardens. That's about all I know."

"Okay, thanks. Wait a second, Eden Gardens?"

The manager smiled. "Sam Greene set it up supposedly as competition to VanDusen, but it really is a very shoddy piece of work. Don't waste your time."

That opinion was clear, so this time Robert kept walking, all the way to his car. Why would two developers be arguing about Eden Gardens, and to the extent of getting into a fight? Kind of puzzling, but since no one had been hurt, Robert was already pushing the event to the back of his thoughts as he closed his car door and made his way back to Cambie.

Once back at the office, his caseload being on the light side for once, Robert thought he'd do some online research into Eden Gardens. He was curious about a competitor to VanDusen and the man apparently behind it. On reflection, he thought he remembered perhaps being there ten years earlier for a summer festival, but details about the place were hazy. After reviewing a few websites, he concentrated on the City of Vancouver's.

He learned that the City of Vancouver had put one of

their money-losing public golf courses on the east side up for sale, golfing as a leisure activity having one of its cyclical downturns. At over two hundred acres, the sale attracted sizeable attention from the development community. There wasn't much detail on the unsuccessful bids, but Robert imagined they would have involved a lot of housing, maybe just solely housing with no imagination brought to the table. It seemed that the winning deal had involved hiving off some of the land for a public park to be donated back to the city, and another piece for both market and social housing, leaving a garden attraction totalling roughly one hundred and forty acres. This was some sixty-five acres less than the original golf course, but still well over twice the size of VanDusen Gardens. The odd part was that apparently Samuel Greene's involvement with the winning group had been shielded from the public until recently.

Robert then found an analysis written by a newspaper reporter around the time the metamorphosis was taking place. The article commented on the residential portion of the deal. It supposedly was put in place to provide an endowment for the operation of the Gardens once it had been set up, though the financial arrangements were complex. A second piece reported on the design and intent of the Gardens. The designers modelled various areas after famous classical European gardens, with the scientific and horticultural aspects downplayed. 'More flowers, fewer trees' was apparently the motto. There was even an article about poaching members from VanDusen to come over to Eden Gardens and join the newly minted Vancouver attraction, gifts and promises apparently being used in this pursuit. As far as history was concerned, this seemed to be the extent of information publicly available.

Robert did some light digging into Mr. Greene's background. Samuel seemed to have led a very successful life by anyone's standards. There was scant information about his start as a developer, but as his career blossomed, he put together condo project after project and successfully sent them to market. Although not alone in this type of success in a growing city such as Vancouver, he seemingly excelled at it. Some of the properties he owned were situated on the west side of Vancouver, and these were the ones he first exploited. Robert knew that the east side was historically to be avoided, that is, until so much money had funnelled into Vancouver that eventually land costs forced people to consider living in areas they used to look down their nose at. Samuel sat on the east side properties until their value rose so much, he started developing them.

Robert found Sam's home address, noting that it was in Southlands on the West Side of Vancouver, not to be confused with the West End of the downtown peninsula which was the former home for Vancouver's wealthy, nor with West Vancouver, an entirely different city, but equally prosperous.

Nothing Robert found explained why Samuel would be in dispute with another developer, but supposed that it was a competitive business, and maybe disagreements were more common than generally known. He doubted he would hear anything further about Eden or Sam.

~ 2 ~

It was a Tuesday night in October, actually early Wednesday morning, and traffic along East Hastings Street was slow. It was always slow; both because of the 30 km/hr speed limit, and the reason behind the limit, which was people wandering into or across the street at any moment, traffic or not. This was human tragedy on display day and night, winter and summer, whatever the weather, in the poorest neighbourhood in Canada. Drug use was rampant and on full display.

The thin traffic included an old brown panel van heading east. Its rusted fenders and bumpers were splashed with mud obscuring the rear vehicle plate. The van drove on Hastings at a snail's pace past a church, dilapidated convenience stores, and single room occupancy hotels where the poorest of the poor resided along with numerous bugs and more than a few rodents. It passed ground zero for drug use in the area; a storefront location staffed by community workers that allowed users to shoot up in relative safety using vetted drugs. Along here, people were camping on the sidewalk with their meagre belongings gathered around them in tattered suitcases or dented shopping carts.

The van slowed down even further before signaling to turn right at Dunlevy Avenue, then quickly right again at the lane. It was now in behind the buildings that fronted Hastings Street. On the south side of the lane, the edge was like a fortress; with concrete walls, garage doors, steel railed gates and a surplus of razor wire strung along the top of it all. These buildings were the beginnings of Chinatown just to the south of Hastings, but appeared to have the defences of an area at war.

The van stopped in front of a passed-out man slumped against a block wall that was inset off the lane, his legs sprawled in front of him. The rest of the alley was deserted. A large rat, or a small dog, ran away down the rear of the building. The occupant of the van leaned over; grabbed a bottle and a rag, looked up and down the lane, then got out of the van quickly. He stumbled a bit as a powerful stench of urine smacked his nose. He looked up the lane again. With no one in sight, he bent down and smothered the man's face with the rag. The man didn't seem to be all that alive anyway, from whatever he had shot into his arm. The works were sitting on the pavement beside his legs. The rear doors of the van were opened, the seemingly lifeless man picked up and thrown in. The doors were slammed shut, the engine started, and the van headed back west to Main Street. Thin rain started to fall, increasing the misery of the area.

* * *

Later that same night, Gorbi Preshenko, who had passed out down at the end of the same lane after drinking too much, was awakened by the drizzle. He went to look for his friend, Stan; he considered Stan a friend—he wasn't sure how Stan thought about him. Stan usually popped his drugs up near the midpoint of the block. Gorbi was short and portly, at least as portly as you could get when you didn't eat very well. His round cheeks sported a stubble of hair, trying to pass as a beard. When he got to the usual crash spot for Stan, all he found was the works for injecting whatever he was doing that night. No sign of Stan, which was weird. Usually, after Stan did his thing, he would pass out for a while. Oh well, he'd meet up with him tomorrow morning at their rooming hotel or the Carnegie Centre on Main Street. This was where they could get some coffee, for free on occasion, and get out of the weather if it was raining, which occasionally happened in Vancouver. He hoped Stan was dry, wherever he was.

***

The next morning, Gorbi yawned and opened his eyes in the single room on East Hastings Street that he called home. He slowly got up and shuffled over to look out the grimy window at the grey skies, then turned and went back to brush his teeth in the sink beside his small television. The television didn't work after the powers that be stopped broadcasting over the air, and the rabbit ears didn't have anything to catch. He hung onto it anyway, in case things changed. Wondering where Stan had been the previous night, he headed down a couple of floors to check on him as soon as he got dressed.

Gorbi arrived at Stan's door and knocked a few times. There wasn't a sound from beyond. He assumed that Stan had already made his way over to the Carnegie Centre. It was still raining softly, but he decided to head there to catch up with Stan and shoot the breeze.

The Centre was a former library, one of many libraries built throughout North America's cities in the early 1900s, benefiting from the largesse of the American philanthropist, Andrew Carnegie. When the library was completed in 1903, it was situated in the centre of the downtown business district, the present social conditions of the east side not even a glimmer on the horizon. It was now located right in the midst of one of the poorest neighbourhoods in Canada. It also happened to be one of the oldest buildings left in what is a very young city, so eventually qualified to be a heritage structure worth preserving. A small community library still graced the site, but the main functions of the building had changed into a supportive social centre for the local community.

Gorbi entered the front doors of the Centre and was met by the familiar smell, redolent of a fifty-year-old locker room that had never been cleaned. He walked by the front desk, manned by an unsmiling security man, who was probably having trouble breathing, then went around the corner to the canteen to get some coffee. His eyes darted around, all the while searching for Stan inside the Centre.

Lynette, who worked at the Centre, smiled at Gorbi and got his coffee. She knew Gorbi was a former sailor from one of the merchant fleets circling the globe, ferrying goods or materials so that countries could eat or make things. She also knew that Gorbi was on the wrong side of fifty and couldn't expect to find other employment except menial labour, despite the best efforts of the skills training class on the second floor of the Centre.

"Have you seen Stan this morning?" he asked Lynette, while drumming his fingers on her desk, waiting for an answer. He checked out the exterior deck where some men were sitting in the mist, smoking. He could hear the trumpets of a band playing in a back room, likely a Salvation Army Band trying to rally the troops or win some converts.

"Don't think so, Gorbi," Lynette responded.

Hmmm, thought Gorbi, this was unusual. He went over and took a seat next to a couple of other men he knew. One of the 'boys' was playing solitaire on the scarred wooden table, laying out the cards deliberately, as if he had all the time in the world. Despite all the drug attention this area got in the media, Gorbi was old school, which meant that he liked a drink or two. Everyone inside the Centre seemed to have a story involving problems or bad luck, but as far as Gorbi knew, most of the people who frequented the Centre had alcohol as their demon, not drugs.

"Have you guys seen Stan this morning, or last night?" Gorbi asked, as he scratched at the flaring eczema on his arm.

One of them said they had seen Stan wander off Hastings heading south last evening, probably to the lane where he usually shot up. But no one had seen him this morning yet. Gorbi decided to wait before telling anyone about this. People wandered all over the area in a daze, and Stan could be close by without knowing it.

Gorbi eventually left the Centre and killed some time by trying to bum change to buy a bottle. After a couple of hours at this in an area where most of the people were in the same financial situation as him, he made his way back to the Centre, not a dime richer for the effort. He had also walked most of the places where Stan usually could be found, but there was no sign of him.

Gorbi went back to the canteen to talk with Lynette. She would be more sympathetic than the security guy manning the front door. The Picton event from several years ago was relatively fresh in Gorbi's memory, when women were systematically kidnapped off the street and ended up on a pig farm in Coquitlam in tiny pieces. With those horrific events in his mind, he knew people tended to react more quickly to a missing person report than they used to.

"Hey Lynette, do you think you could call the cops and tell them Stan is missing? I've been all over, and he isn't anywhere."

"When did you last see him?"

"Earlier last night before it started raining, I think," he said hesitantly.

"Well, that's not very long ago, is it? You look around? Wasn't he in his room?"

"Nope."

Lynette thought about this but, given that Gorbi was in better shape mentally than most of the people who came through the doors, and seemingly sober this morning, she gave him the benefit of the doubt and did as he asked.

Because the call came from the Centre and not from Gorbi, the admin assistant at the police station logged it in and gave it credence. The assistant also said the expected: "Most of these things sort themselves out in a day or two, particularly in your part of town."

"I know," said Lynette. "But I trust the guy who told me, I think." One could never be totally sure of anything in this neighbourhood.

"Ok. We'll let the patrols know and keep an eye out. Can you get a photo or something like a description, so we know who we are looking for?"

"That could be a problem, but I'll see what I can find." Lynette couldn't think of how she would do this, but she'd give it the old college try. Very few people had pictures of themselves or the means to take them in this part of Vancouver.

***

A day later, Thursday, at Eden Gardens, the gardeners were at the service building preparing for their day. It was just past eight in the morning and rain was holding off. The swallows and crows were chirping about something important.

Strange, Rollie thought, I don't remember leaving that wheelbarrow outside over by the barn. The workers were fastidious about taking care of their tools and equipment as a rule. Everything had a place and was in that place at the end of each working day. Marty, who was their supervisor, ran a tight ship. Carelessness was sometimes cause for dismissal, or at least punishment. However, if you worked hard, Marty was your best friend. Seeing a piece of equipment left outside was disconcerting. Rollie asked the others if any of them had left the wheelbarrow out.

"It was left inside the barn last night, I'm sure of it." Nate said.

"Were all the doors locked?" Rollie asked.

"Yes, all the doors and gates locked up."

Rollie was troubled by this news. He would double check everything tonight when they were done with the day. "Is anything else out of place? Take a look around before we get going for the day and let me know. And no need for Marty to know unless there are more surprises."

"So let it be written, so let it be done," said Nate.

Rollie rolled his eyes. Nate was a movie buff and loved quoting old movie lines. *The Ten Commandments* was one of his favourites. "Good grief, just take a look, will you?"

~ 3 ~

Eden Gardens had been carved out of a former well-treed golf course, similar to how VanDusen Gardens had evolved, and contained many collections and hundreds of plant species native to North America. For the visitor, there were a multitude of follies, ponds, pavilions, formal and informal mini gardens to enjoy. There was a large maze, which you entered at your own risk, considering what might be inside waiting for you. Also on the grounds was a restaurant, the Restaurant of Earthly Delights, which was reputed to be a decent place for a full-service meal.

Bernice and her husband William were in their mid-seventies and had recently become members of Eden Gardens. They came from old Vancouver money in Shaughnessy, rooted in a time a hundred years earlier when three-quarters of the area's residents were on the social register. Bernice and William were attached to the past, to a time before Expo 86 and all the changes the exposition brought to Vancouver, thrusting it onto the world stage for good and bad. They were also members of the VanDusen Botanical Gardens and were gardeners themselves, even volunteering on occasion for events at either Gardens if their friends asked them for help. The couple were hesitant at first about also joining Eden Gardens, conservative to the core, but they had no interest in the scientific side of gardens, so Eden was proving to be a great match. A second factor influencing their decision to join was the neighbourhood surrounding Eden. They were pleasantly surprised at how well cared for all the homes seemed to be. In all their years living in Vancouver, they had never found a reason to visit the southeast section of the city, so they were pleased to find out how attractive the area was.

***

They arrived at Eden Gardens for lunch, on Thursday, just past noon. After parking, they took a short stroll before entering the restaurant. They walked past the restaurant building to the entry pavilion, through the new entry hall, swiping their member cards at the entry kiosk, and went out onto the plaza. The sight of Fraserview Lake just beyond the entry plaza was stunning, as usual; the fragrant flowers, magenta fading to light mauve and ivory, sat above the field of green pads, but the air wasn't exactly warm.

They turned left and walked past a couple of smaller gardens, over to the Rose Garden, which was bordered by a low boxwood hedge and white gravel paths. They meandered past the many rose varieties interspersed with tall conical yews. As they ambled up and down the paths, they caught glimpses of the nearby formal gardens and the grass collections to the south and farther on, the low hill providing a lookout to some of the formal parterres nearby. The couple knew by heart all the name plaques that described the various rose types, but as the season was getting late, the bloom was coming off some of the plants. From this area, they could also look back at the warm looking dining room that they would soon be in.

"Bernice, I think it's trying to rain. Maybe we should head back, dear." Spots were showing up on the paving stones and the gravel, the paths slowly darkening as the drops became more frequent.

The couple turned and were happy to retrace their steps, first to the entry pavilion, and then back up the gentle rise to the restaurant. They warmed up in the lobby and gave their coats to the hostess. Bernice was in a pink floral printed dress with a white cable-knitted sweater, and William had on his grey flannels topped with a green plaid shirt. They sat at a table by the window, thankful to be warm and inside. The restaurant occupied what used to be the clubhouse and restaurant of the former golf club; the purchasing group making full use of existing infrastructure, not wanting to spend any more than necessary on the re-make. The dining area overlooked a couple of ordered garden areas to the east of the building and had a good view of the new entry pavilion.

Bernice and William appreciated their view of the formal Italianate Garden. It was framed by twisted wisteria, which seemed to be devouring the wood posts and beams just outside the window.

Sanjay, their server, came over, greeting them and handing out the menus. Neither of the couple were big eaters anymore, so after some extensive review of the offerings, they each ordered an Arugula and Frisée salad. Then, after Sanjay had pointed it out, they added a soup which was rarely on the menu: Lobster Bisque.

"This will be a treat." William said optimistically. "I don't remember ever having this soup before, do you?"

"I don't either, dear. This should be excellent."

After a brief wait, the salads were delivered, and they both started in on them.

"The arugula is particularly peppery today, and all the better for it, don't you think?" offered William.

"I agree," said Bernice, and then busied herself with the rest of the salad. No other conversation was exchanged. They had just finished the last of their salads when Sanjay brought the soup. After a few words, they both launched into the main course.

"The bisque is on the sweet side, but I like it. Has a bit of earthiness to it, I think." Bernice prided herself on her mind being open to change. The reality was quite the opposite, but no one would dare contradict her, least of all William. He nodded agreeably. After a mouthful or two he started chewing on a piece of lobster that did not quite match the other pieces in the broth, and it most definitely did not taste like lobster. He called the server over to their table.

"Sanjay, there's something not right with the soup today. Do you mind getting someone to taste it? There seems to be more than lobster in here." William liked Sanjay. He seemed to be a good immigrant. In reality, William didn't know anything about him, but that did not change his opinion. Sanjay went back into the kitchen to find Miguel, the sous chef.

Miguel was a stocky cook, on the older side. Miguel had emigrated to Canada in the 1990s and had bounced around before ending up in the food industry in Vancouver. He had a personal history that was unusual and being in a restaurant would help him confront this head on, or so the psychologist had said. It had worked out for Miguel so far.

"What's the problem this time?" The patrons at this restaurant were known for being picky, even crazy, in Miguel's opinion.

"They're complaining about the soup. They think there's something extra in it or something." Sanjay was used to complaints and luckily, mostly they weren't his problem. All he had to do was be diplomatic and smooth things over with the customers.

Dorks, thought Miguel. He had prepared the stock yesterday evening, processing the mixture, then straining it, and leaving it on the stove overnight. This morning he added the lobster chunks and heavy cream, letting it simmer, undisturbed, until service. He had ladled out the servings from near the top of the pot, and considered it one of his better soups in recent history, a big step up from the usual clam chowder that was the standard on the menu. Give them something better and it figures that they'd complain. Maybe his talents were being wasted here.

"Ok, I'll check it for the bozos." He didn't have to treat the customers with respect, because they were usually kept out of the kitchen, even though it was the right of a customer to ask to see the kitchen of any restaurant they dined in. Fortunately for the cooks, most customers didn't know this.

Miguel went over to the stock pot where the soup was simmering gently and dipped a ladle in, moving it around deeper. It bumped into something hard on the bottom that really shouldn't have been there, maybe a lobster shell that had slipped in with the lobster meat. He bumped against it again, and then took some tongs, grabbing it and slowly raised it out of the pot. He immediately knew what he was looking at. An arm bone. A human arm bone.

Nausea was immediate as he whispered *mierda* to himself. His face lost all colour, and he slumped over the counter. This couldn't be happening. Sanjay didn't look too sharpish either. He had an inkling of the shitstorm that was about to be unleashed. Miguel looked around, but no one else was paying attention.

Sanjay left to find Derek, the executive chef, who was in his office finishing a financial review, and told him an abbreviated version of what he knew. The chef knew immediately that this would not turn out well. He got on his cell and called the manager for the Gardens. Then he figured he better get out to the dining room and make good with the two seniors eating the offending soup.

He walked up to their table. "My apologies, Bernice and William. We seem to have had a slight problem with the bisque today. Let me remove that soup. Would you like a different soup, or something else to complete your meal? Of course, your meal today will be complimentary."

"We aren't going to get ill, are we?" Bernice was

concerned, but that was small potatoes next to getting a free meal. She was secretly pumped and couldn't wait until she told her friends. One thing she wouldn't be talking about, though, was why they were getting a free meal.

"No, you should be fine. It was just some other meat that unfortunately slipped into the soup." He removed the soups after the couple had declined the offer of a replacement and returned to the kitchen. Under no circumstances could these people or the public at large learn about what was really in the soup. Both he and the restaurant would be royally screwed if that were to happen. Of course, after the nerdy manager arrived, he had different ideas, and immediately left to go call the police. Derek raced after him to try to change his mind.

He walked into the office just as Dominic was going to dial the number. "Don't call the police, at least until we've talked this over. Do you know what this will do to the restaurant? Think about it. Right now, the patrons are leaving without a clue what happened."

"It's you who's not thinking clearly here." Dominic said. "You realize that arm belonged to someone, and maybe they want it back. At the very least, Miguel and Sanjay both know what happened. You don't seriously think this will be kept quiet, do you? This could end up being a murder investigation, you know." The manager may have been nerdy, but he had a good grasp of the issue.

"I am pretty sure that whatever happens, if we sit on this, it will not turn out well for any of us. The cops aren't stupid, you know." Dominic wasn't sure about that last statement but thought he would go with it for now.

He dialled 911, which was the only number he knew, even though strictly speaking, it wasn't an emergency. When he got relayed through to the Vancouver Police Department station, he was a bit excited and quickly spat out what he knew, which wasn't much.

On the other end, Norma van Kleet took a few notes down and hung up, then she set the wheels in motion so that a patrol car would respond. She called Robert Lui's line, Robert being one of several detectives tasked for this area of the city. Meanwhile, Bernice and William had wisely decided not to try anything else and had left the restaurant. They went out to the parking lot, stood there shaking their heads for a moment, then got into their old fin-tailed Cadillac to head home. They had had more than enough excitement for one day.

Sanjay went up to Derek. "Do you think you could help finish things off here? Miguel looks like he's down for the count after what he found. We need to get the rest of these customers out the door."

Derek thought about it but knew he didn't have much choice. "Yeah, okay. Let me know what orders need to be finished." Derek was pretty sure the word 'Executive' was in front of his title. How did he end up doing this crap? Maybe he'd need to have a talk with Dominic.

Sanjay went back out to the dining area, trying to look calm. He was calculating who needed to get the last parts of their orders, because he knew the restaurant would likely be shut down once the police arrived. The fewer customers left in the dining room when the police showed up, the better.

***

Down on Cambie Street, Robert Lui had just walked back from having an Americano at one of the coffee shops south of the police offices. No one was going to die from lack of caffeine in this city, he thought, least of all him. He had caught sight of Roller-Girl in the light rain, a person who liked to get dressed up in a pink outfit and drift around the Cambie Broadway intersection on old time roller skates, directing traffic using spiralling figure eight patterns. How Roller-Girl hadn't been run over was a mystery, but it was all very entertaining.

Other than a new missing person reported from the Downtown Eastside, there wasn't much to worry about at work. Missing people from this neighbourhood tended to show up eventually, at least in the last couple of years. He started thinking about dinner. Maybe I'll take the kids to that newer Taiwanese restaurant over on Victoria Street, where noodles were the specialty. These noodles were some of the best in town; cut, pushed, and dragged noodles with lots of hot sauce and green vegetables over spicy pork creations. They also apparently did a mean version of ginger fried beef. He was a noodle hound, and the rest of his family were no slouches either.

He thought about calling his parents to join, but after some consideration, thought it might be better if he checked the restaurant out first, his father's standards being on the high side. Robert didn't need the disapproving stare that might be the wrap-up to an evening if the restaurant wasn't all it should be. Added to this was his father's dislike of Robert's chosen profession. Robert was hazy about the details, but since Ethan's cooking in the old days had involved people on both sides of the law, he suspected that it was the sometimes violent outcomes that dictated his wish for Robert to avoid this profession. As he walked back to his office, he was barely paying attention to the sidewalk in front of him; noodles dangled in front of his brain.

Robert's life was about to get much busier. When he arrived back at the office, Norma, one of several civilian administrative assistants, called him over.

"I just got a call from Eden Gardens. They seem to be in a bit of a commotion over there, something about the soup of the day in the restaurant having more ingredients than it should, like an arm bone. They think it's human. I told patrol about it so they should have a car on the way. The Gardens is where the old Fraserview golf course used to be."

Good grief was all Robert could think. This sounded complicated on several levels. "Eden Gardens? I know where it is. I was just reading about it a couple of days ago. This is the second time that place has come up this week. I'll take Camille with me. If the lunch crowd is involved at the restaurant, it could get messy. I don't think the Parks Board are going be thrilled about what their menu options are today. Wait till the news gets hold of this."

"I don't think the city owns it anymore. I think it's private now." Norma seemed to be unusually well informed.

~ 4 ~

Robert went to the bullpen area where Camille Laurent spent her days and beckoned her. They took the elevator down to the parking area where a trusty old Crown Victoria squad car was parked. Driving over on East 41st Avenue, Robert briefed Camille on what he knew, which wasn't much.

"We may need to be careful on this one, gardeners and all." Robert said, then added, "This could be interesting."

Camille, who had previously worked with the *Service de Police de la Ville de Montreal*, had won this position as an aide to Robert by being precocious. She had curly blond hair framing an oval face with widely spaced blue eyes. She was good-looking, all angular cheekbones like some runway diva, which of course gave her no end of trouble within the department. Anyone would have assumed she hailed from Norway or some Baltic country, not Quebec.

Though Robert was a recent arrival back to the department, he tried to protect her as much as he could. His immediate superior, Steve Christie, was one of the worst offenders, with his crude remarks out of Camille's earshot. This troubled Robert. If he was honest with himself, he would have admitted that he was attracted to Camille, but Robert knew better. A workplace romance was not the smartest idea, and with someone you were working a case with? Double trouble. He kept his distance, but it was early days yet. He was just getting to know her. There was no way that he was going to let Steve harass Camille, and he was confident that Camille had a distinct distaste for Steve.

They drove south down Elliott Street, going a bit too far, then turned east, finally arriving at the entry to Eden and the restaurant, parking the car right in the no-parking zone in front of the entry doors. Ever since the erstwhile Mayor of Vancouver had started his anti-car campaign, Robert liked to drop his car wherever it made the most problems. They saw that the patrol car had arrived already and was parked in a similar manner. A little farther into the foyer, the two patrol officers were talking to someone, and it didn't appear to be going well.

Robert and Camille walked up to them and addressed the administrator. "Hi, where is the kitchen?"

"Why, are you hungry? People usually go to the dining room first. We don't often get the police in here. Who are you?"

Talk about a smart ass thought, Robert. "I'm a detective with the VPD. We don't wear uniforms." He showed him his ID. "We were told there was an issue in the kitchen, so we're here to take a look."

"I'm sorry, there is no issue that I know about, and no, we don't serve donuts here." Then he smiled at Camille. Okay, this guy was starting to really get on his nerves.

"I'd like to talk with the manager then." Robert said calmly, then added, "Smart ass." He could tell the other officers had not taken well to the donut joke. There was a bit of flint glowing in their eyes.

The administrator took a step back at this, realizing maybe his cleverness had gone unappreciated. "Okay, I'll go get him. By the way, you can't leave your cars there."

Robert didn't bother to respond, but waited with the other VPD members in the foyer. Maybe he would leave his car there for a few days just for spite. The group of officers looked back out the entry doors at the manicured beds of flowers, then, at Robert's signal, they all turned and headed for what appeared to be the restaurant entry. Robert had decided not to wait.

The girl at the end of the long entry foyer was a little confused as to what to do, so she went to the default question.

"Would you like a table?" She politely asked, not being fully aware of the latest excitement.

"I think we'll pass today but thank you for asking. We're here because someone called us. Is there a manager that can talk with us?" Robert was being extremely polite after dealing with the jackass at the entry. The hostess left her post and went down a short hall. She re-appeared quickly and beckoned them with her hand. Just behind her was Dominic LaPointe. Before they all got out of sight down the corridor, the few patrons in the dining room who were still finishing their lunch had spotted them. Excited talk immediately broke out from table to table.

"Follow me please," Dominic said, as he entered the

kitchen. Dominic had a pale face, horn-rimmed glasses, short black hair, and looked exactly like an accountant or banker in his dark suit and patterned blue tie, but a very nervous one. The kitchen was compact, and as the noon service was almost over, there were only a couple of people in the work area.

"The cooks found something unusual in the soup pot. You can look for yourselves." Robert and Camille walked over to the stock pot and selected a large spoon to poke around. They found the offending bone quickly and used some tongs to pull it out. A couple of fingers were still attached, along with some flesh. The other fingers were probably still in the pot. Robert didn't know what to say, as this was a little outside his experience. He wasn't queasy about it though, having seen lots of crime scenes in his career. He suspected the staff wouldn't be so unaffected. The two cooks did not look like they were having their best day.

"For starters, we'll be closing your kitchen and the restaurant for a while. Our officers here will take statements from everyone present, including the cooks and serving staff. Was there anyone else present on the staff side that left already?" Robert was trying to be thorough, although he really didn't think anyone on staff would be so stupid to have done this.

Dominic answered for the rest. "Everyone is still here. We have to prepare for the dinner service, so people wouldn't leave on break until everything was ready. How long will we be closed? I have to notify the people who reserved with us this evening." This was not good. He would have to come up with a nondescript reason for the closure and hope the real reason did not get out.

"Camille, could you help the officers with the statements please? Might as well do the questioning in the dining room once the last diners have left. I don't see any other place to do it." Robert continued while he did some thinking. "And call forensics first and ask them how this should be handled. I'm not sure what evidence can be got out of a stock pot, but if they want the soup, then they better get over here. Better check also to see if they have any video surveillance footage of the building."

"The only video we have for this building is from a camera in the foyer." Dominic said. "This whole operation runs on a very tight budget and there hasn't been a need for much security on any of the buildings yet. The new entry pavilion sucked all the money dry and to date, we've had no problems." Dominic frowned. "I guess maybe that's changed now."

"We'll need that camera feed, please." Robert wasn't through. "I'll also need your hours of operation, and who arrives when. If none of the people here did this, then we are looking at a break and enter, or at least an enter. This may be a crime scene. I didn't notice any card readers or things like that on the entry doors, am I correct?"

"Yes, we operate on locks with keys."

"We could use a list of those staff with keys then." This was going to be like working a case thirty years ago, as far as security was concerned. "Here is my card. If you remember anything that might be important, please call."

Robert stood in the hall leading to the dining room,

looking at the tables inside and the exterior terraces beyond. There were several wild light fixtures hanging from the ceiling that didn't look inexpensive. A place for the gardeners of Vancouver to dine, he thought. Why attack this establishment, of all places? He changed his mind and decided to leave the initial questioning to the police officers who were attending, beckoned to Camille and they said goodbye to Dominic. Robert doubted if there was anything to be learned from the remaining customers.

Robert received a call on his cell from someone at forensics. "We'll come out there to grab the soup pot and anything else we might fancy." Why did Robert get the feeling that the forensics people were completely untroubled by the situation?

"I feel like leaving my car in front of the restaurant for a day or two, but I don't think I want a ride in the rear of a cruiser to get back to the office." Robert said to Camille.

"I'm with you. Not keen on getting in one of those." All manner of foulness could be present in a patrol car even after the daily cleaning.

***

When Camille and Robert got back to their office on Cambie Street, Robert called a meeting. As he walked past Norma, she tilted her head in an inquisitive fashion and smiled at him.

"I'll fill you in later," he said.

Included in the meeting were Robert's immediate superior, Steve Christie, and a young uniformed officer who had grown up mostly in Burnaby, Tony Bortolo, who was helping Camille out. Robert had brought his boss up to date on the phone while Camille drove back to the station, so Steve knew the basics of the situation. The four met in Robert's small office, which made things a bit squishy.

"If we have an arm, then there must be a body somewhere. What do you think?" Steve asked. Steve had beady eyes which were too close together behind wire-rimmed glasses. His hair was thinning and of a nondescript colour. A threadbare tan suit completed the look that said, 'I don't spend too much on my appearance.'

He seems in sharp form, Robert thought sarcastically. "We left the bones and everything else for the forensic people to do their thing, if there is anything they can do with boiled bones. In addition, the kitchen at the restaurant is closed down while our team does a complete search." Robert was running through the process. "I think we should do a check on all the employees present and past at the restaurant; at least start there and we can expand the search if nothing turns up. Include the managers and everyone connected with the restaurant. I am not sure why someone would do this, other than to destroy the restaurant's reputation. Anyone got ideas?" Robert thought a bit more. "We should pursue the body angle as well. I hope other parts don't start showing up in places they don't belong." Robert added.

"Just keep me informed." Steve said as he stood up and left the room, having lost interest already.

Always a pleasure, Robert thought. Steve must have more important things to attend to. What these might be was a mystery to Robert.

As the end of the day approached, he started thinking about dinner again, apparently not put off by the culinary events of the afternoon. He called home and Robin answered. "Hey, it's Dad. I'm thinking about that new restaurant on Victoria. Interested? Can you ask Sophie?"

The Lui family lived in a rented townhouse on the east side of town, past Fraser Street. They were trying to save to buy a house or something of their own, but every year the goal seemed just out of reach. Robert and his wife, Susan, used to talk about dinner plans almost every day. Food was very important to their family, and they spent an inordinate amount of time thinking about, planning, and cooking dinners. Others thought them a little crazy, but the results spoke for themselves. Then disaster struck.

Susan didn't last a year after she was diagnosed with pancreatic cancer. The effect on the family was wrenching, and Robert was thrust into the role of being two parents while still trying to do successfully what was, at times, a very stressful job. His children needed his attention more than ever. His job didn't change, other than recently when he switched out of the special task force. The hours became more predictable, but only slightly. Whatever works, Robert thought. It had been a little over two years ago since Susan had passed. September each year was especially trying because of that. Robert was trying his best to be the father that his kids could depend on, without showing the stress that he was going through. He missed her terribly. Some people could hide their grief by working twice as hard at their job. That was not an option for Robert; Robin and Sophie needed him more than ever, being teenagers, although they would probably deny it.

Forty-five minutes later, they were ordering dinner in the restaurant.

"Can we have the noodles and prawns?" Sophie asked. His daughter was fifteen and was starting to take after her dad, culinary-wise. His son, Robin, at twelve, tended to the dumpling side of the menu, so he ordered the steamed pork and chive dumplings and asked if they could have spicy wontons. Robert was surprised they could get off their phones long enough to choose. A couple of other vegetable dishes rounded out the dinner. The restaurant made its own noodles on site. The chef doing this was on display and visible from the dining room. It looked complicated, and despite watching intently, no one could figure out how this guy produced them, or how he could make so many varieties. There was no denying the results, however.

As usual, the decor was not top-notch, but it rarely was in these types of restaurants. It was all about the cuisine. The Lui family always ordered more than they could possibly eat, so that there were leftovers to be hauled back home. These rarely lasted twenty-four hours before disappearing. Robert couldn't cook every day, but damned if his kids were going to have a poor diet because of the family's situation. Susan and Robert had made a point of teaching them the basics of building a good dinner, along with some of the skills needed, including how to handle a knife.

"How is the job going, Pops?" Robin asked after the server left. "Any robberies or murders to solve?"

Robert had to be careful when he talked to his children. As with most teens, they liked to show off at school, and stories about police cases were good currency in the race to be popular. "Not really. I think we have a missing person, but I'm sure we'll find him." He failed to mention that they might find him in more than one piece, but this was speculation at the moment.

"How are the new people you are working with?" Sophie asked.

"The ones under me are all fine, and I think we have a good team. It's the ones above me that I have to watch, as usual. We have a case now that is a little odd, but you know the drill. I can't say much yet." From there, they started talking about school and the small tragedies involved in school life. The two young teens were transitioning to high school life where, of course, more drama was added to every incident. If the kids were having problems, Robert, unfortunately, wasn't likely to hear about them, at least not directly. In the end, the food turned out to be everything he hoped for and more. The Lui family would definitely be back, with Robert's parents next time.

As they left the restaurant, Robert glanced at the noodle chef and couldn't help thinking about his new case. Something bizarre was going on, that was certain, and he realized he was pleased with the novelty of the circumstances. Where the evidence led, he couldn't guess, but he knew it wouldn't be boring.

~ 5 ~

Bernard Lily was a young reporter who had been trying desperately to make a name for himself. He had a feeling that the anonymous tip that he had received this morning was going to make him famous; maybe not Bob Woodward/*Washington Post* famous, but pretty darn close. Bernard worked for *VanDay*, which was shorthand for *Vancouver Newsday*, one of the several free tabloid papers that littered the transit stops. The newspaper was trying something out, that is, actually using a real reporter to find some local news. This was to complement the regular way of setting up the paper, which was to use other people's reporting or news feeds to get their content. Of course, *VanDay* wasn't going to shell out for a reporter who demanded real money, so they hired a young hotdog just out of journalism school at subsistence wages and figured that he would fend for himself. If he actually got some stories, then great.

Bernard had already picked up the technique of listening in on the VPD dispatch calls that sent cars out on their missions, so when a patrol car was sent over to Eden, his interest was piqued. The tipster had written that something newsworthy was happening there, though readers sometimes had an odd idea about what was newsworthy.

Since he was hired as a contributing writer, he of course had no office, and worked out of his rental apartment. He lived in one of the new buildings along the south side of False Creek to the west of the Olympic Village, where he could barely afford the rent. He also didn't own a car, so he went out the lobby door and grabbed the first co-op car he found to zip over to Oak Street, to VanDusen Gardens. After he arrived and entered the restaurant, he quickly discovered that nothing had happened there. He was hungry, so he checked over the menu. The prices were on the high side for him, so he declined the offer of a seat by the hostess. She then told him about the café in the visitor's centre where prices were more modest. He wandered down to the centre and ordered up a sandwich and coffee.

While eating, he re-checked the note he had received on his cell and realized he was at the wrong botanical garden. After finishing his lunch, he re-claimed his car and drove east to Eden Gardens. He parked and was about to walk over to the new entry pavilion, when he decided instead to go into the restaurant, just in case.

The hostess was finishing up organizing things for the closing down when Bernard came through the door. "Hi," he said, flashing his biggest smile. "There weren't some cops here a little while ago, were there?"

The hostess hadn't yet received the full briefing from Dominic, so she did the wrong thing and told the truth.

"Yes, a bunch were here earlier, but I don't know what they were doing. They went to talk with the manager."

"Is the manager here?"

"I'll check—and who are you?"

Dominic came out from the side office with a smile, holding onto Bernard's business card. He didn't get this job by being poor at public relations, but this was awfully quick to have the press here so soon after the lunch event. "Can I help you? We just had a food writer in here a couple of months ago, so we really don't need a second opinion."

Good forehand, thought Bernard, but he could return a volley himself. "I understand there was a police incident here a short time ago. Care to comment on what happened?"

Dominic was suddenly unsure how much this young guy knew. "We really don't have any comment at this time." Not a great comeback, but the best he could do.

Bernard had an inspiration. "Could I book a table for dinner?"

"Sorry, we're closed to the public tonight, special event." Dominic was still 'cooking.'

"Ok, thanks." Bernard turned and left. He didn't return to his car but went over to the entry pavilion. He went inside and eventually found out that four officers had been on site, but that the staff didn't know why, except it had something to do with the kitchen. He assumed that something was up but headed back into town. Once at his apartment, he called the restaurant to try to book a table for that evening.

"I am terribly sorry, but the restaurant is temporarily closed. We had a problem in our kitchen."

"That's fine, I'll try again another day." His instinct was correct, something was going on, and if the restaurant couldn't get its story together, then he would get to the bottom of it. It was obviously something more serious than a faulty deep-fryer or bad hamburger if the police were involved. He started writing. He could get this into Saturday's edition if he buckled down.

* * *

It wasn't until late the next afternoon, Friday, that preliminary investigative results from the arm were passed on to Camille. She was told that any DNA results would take a little longer. Camille went into Robert's office, which was across from her bullpen workstation. Robert was sitting at his desk, staring into space. She handed him the file, sat down, and took out her notes from the interviews that had taken place.

Robert perused the sparse file. He turned his eyes to Camille and immediately lost his train of thought. The more he stared at her, the more discombobulated he became. He wondered if she thought about him in a similar fashion. On the other hand, if she wasn't interested, then his thoughts could only be perceived as lecherous, no better than Steve.

Camille would never let on, but she was interested in Robert. He was athletically built, the results of extensive training that he put himself through while he was a member of the gang Taskforce. Short black hair that was just showing the beginnings of grey was combed precisely into place. His coal-black eyes and small nose topped off a wide mouth that was usually smiling. Even now, he looked up from the grim file and smiled.

"So, the arm was sawed off just above the elbow. A hacksaw or something similar was used, a rough blade, not a precision blade. That must have hurt."

Camille grimaced after Robert said this, then he added. "Because the arm has been boiled, there is not a lot of further information that can be teased out about it, but they'll get DNA out of the bones. Also, there didn't seem to be anything else in the soup pot that didn't belong. Did you read this yet?"

Camille shook her head. "I have been checking on the wait and kitchen staff. They come from all over; Italy, India, and Uruguay are a few of the countries they hail from. They all seem to have been good employees with at least two years at the restaurant."

"Ok, check a little deeper on them, please. I wouldn't think they would be behind this but look anyway. Maybe we should look at any missing persons reports that have been filed recently. I haven't heard of any missing arm reports, so we'll stick with persons. One got filed Wednesday. Downtown Eastside." Robert added, "We'll check the DNA results against our data base when we get them. Does anyone know how this got reported?"

"Apparently, two customers noticed something different about the soup." Camille was reading from her notes. "They were comp'd the meal and then they left soon after.

I assume they didn't get ill, but I'll check the hospital just in case. The couple have been there before to eat."

Robert thought about this, staring out his window. "Let's meet at eight Monday. I think this can wait until then. No need to come in this weekend. See what you can find out about the employees." After this, he ambled out and signalled Norma to have a word with her. He liked to keep her in the loop on some things, because she was a smoother in the office. Norma could iron out kinks from above and from below, keeping Robert's work life easier because of it. Robert was unaware, but Norma also had a bit of a thing for Robert.

***

It was Sunday, and Bernard was humming to himself as he wrote up the latest information on the Restaurant of Earthly Delights Caper, as he was calling it. His story in the Saturday edition was thin and did not point to any particular problem with the restaurant. Maybe caper wasn't the correct word after what he had found out from the phone call later on Saturday, but it would do for now.

Feathers were going to be ruffled once this hit the streets. Since the tip was anonymous, and he couldn't corroborate the story, he decided he should give the restaurant a chance to give their side of the story before he sent the story to his editor. He'd then have to wait until Monday morning before he could finish this off. No one was answering the phone there today. If the restaurant wouldn't or couldn't comment, then he would run with the story. He knew his editor would not get in the way, because the story was too bizarre not to publish.

***

Monday morning brought the usual showers and thick clouds that liked to call Vancouver home in the autumn months. The case meeting started at 8:00 am sharp in Robert's office without Steve present. Tony and Camille came in and sat down with their notebooks. Steve's absence confirmed to Robert that he had already lost interest in the case, leaving it to Robert to clean up. "I've been doing some thinking," Robert said as he bent back in his chair, one hand on his desk so he wouldn't fall over.

"That sounds dangerous. Better not let Steve find out," Camille offered.

"Hilarious, Camille. I think we should chase down this missing person angle as soon as we can." By we, he meant Camille. "Could you find out who called the report in and go interview the person?"

"Sure thing. We'll try to fit it into our busy agenda. I'll take Tony and head down to the Carnegie Centre after our meeting."

"I haven't heard back from forensics yet. Anything turn up from the restaurant?"

Tony looked up. "Tons of fingerprints, but all are linked to the employees. And there don't appear to be any signs of forced entry."

"So, someone had keys."

"We think so. Or it was an inside job. Security is pretty minimal around the whole site, just locks on doors and gates. No one wants to steal trees or shrubs, apparently."

Camille offered. "The playback from the one camera they had in the lobby didn't show anything. There are other ways to access the kitchen without going through the lobby, such as the service entry."

"Anything from the interviews on site?"

"Not yet, but we are going to see the kitchen staff this afternoon for some more in-depth questioning. The manager is asking when they can re-open the kitchen. I checked the Vancouver General Hospital, no admittances for food poisoning, so I am guessing the soup was well made."

"Lobster Bisque, not an everyday soup." Tony grimaced and then pulled out a copy of Saturday's *VanDay* and threw it on the table. "Seems like someone has got a sniff of what happened."

"What do you mean? How could the story get out already?" Robert asked.

"Not sure, but there aren't a lot of details, just a short paragraph about trouble at the Gardens. I think the guy is trolling for information."

"Ok, depending on what you find out from the interviews, we could let them have the kitchen back for tomorrow." Robert was feeling generous. "Let's meet back here around 4:30 today."

After the meeting, he looked at older files from a pile on his desk. A couple of hours later, he flipped through some requisition reports and his mind wandered to thinking about lunch. And naturally, his favourite food group was part of the fantasy. Sounded like a trip to Bountiful

Noodles up on West Broadway was in order. Maybe the paperwork would do itself while he was out.

***

Tony drove Camille over to the East Hastings area in a cruiser. He parked on Main Street close to the Carnegie Centre, right in front of the former Vancouver Police Department station. It was a large building, and according to the posted signs, was slated for a renovation into office space.

"All the scrubbing in the world is not going to get rid of the ghosts haunting that building." Tony said. "The guests back then weren't exactly treated with kid-gloves."

They got out and stared at the building, thanking their good luck at not having to work out of it, before walking down Main and across Hastings into the lobby of the Centre. As they asked for Lynette, they could see that the place was busy.

"We'd like to talk with the man who told you about the missing person last week, if we could. Assuming the person is still missing, correct?" Camille asked.

"Yes. You're in luck, I think. I saw Gorbi in here earlier and I didn't see him leave. I also tried to get a picture of Stan, that's the name of the missing person, but no luck."

"Is there an office or room we can use to talk to Gorbi?"

Tony couldn't help himself. "This guy's last name isn't Gorbachev, is it?" He was smirking. Camille rolled her eyes. Lynette shook her head slowly, looking at Tony with a raised eyebrow.

Eventually, after Lynette found Gorbi, the three of them packed into a small office and started the questions and answers. The police soon found out where Stan had last been seen and when. They also found out that Stan lived in the same single room occupancy hotel as Gorbi. Camille and Tony both knew what they had to do, so they asked Gorbi to come with them. Gorbi didn't look too comfortable with the people in the Centre eying Tony's uniform in close quarters with Gorbi Preshenko. They would only assume that Gorbi had been up to no good.

They all walked out of the Centre, crossed Main Street, and headed two blocks east, to the single room occupancy hotel that Gorbi called home. With the reluctant cooperation of the manager, they checked Stan's room. There was no sign of him, much to the manager's relief, who had been worried about finding a body, but Stan's possessions still littered the room.

The police thanked the manager before taking Gorbi over to the alley where he said Stan usually did his drugs. As they entered, a couple of the local citizens spotted them and promptly left the alley heading in the other direction. Camille wrinkled her nose at the urine stench mixed with the odour of diesel fuel coming from the walls and lane pavement as they walked west. There was an indent in the wall along the north side which the people had just vacated.

"This is where I last saw him that night." Gorbi said. Both Camille and Tony looked up, and sure enough, there were a few cameras mounted up high on the building walls. A couple of used needles littered the pavement along with the usual garbage.

"OK, thanks Gorbi. We'll take it from here." Camille and

Tony split up as they walked back the way they had come to the Hastings Street side to check each shop. They hoped the cameras were in working order, the owners agreeable, and that the overwrite period was more than twenty-four hours, otherwise they would be out of luck.

Tony was the one who scored. A restaurant proprietor reluctantly showed him some video which was of the night that Stan disappeared. Tony had the feeling that the guy was not comfortable having a cop in his restaurant. Doubtless, he was pulling some fiddle with supplies or the accounting and didn't want anybody looking at what happened in the back lane. Their overwrite period was a week, so it potentially would have what they were looking for. Tony demanded and got the video disk, after it seemed for a moment like the owner would not comply. He explained he was only interested in a missing person, nothing more. He went back outside, collected Camille who had come up empty, and they drove back to the Cambie office. When they got there, Tony gave the DVD into Norma's care. They drove over to Eden Gardens to interview the restaurant staff for a second time.

When Robert walked onto his floor after an extremely satisfying lunch, Norma called him over and gave him the DVD. He felt a tad sleepy after all that food, but Robert looked at the disk and figured that he'd need a computer with a video player. His latest laptop didn't have this option. His head started hurting every time he started thinking about technology changes. What a pain in the ass this was.

"I'm going to need an older laptop—one with a disk player. Could you rustle one up for me?"

"No problem," said Norma. She got him what he needed so he could while away his time looking at back-alley footage in his office.

* * *

Robert started on the Tuesday video. At first, he wasn't sure what he was looking at. It appeared that people from inside the restaurant were bringing packages out into the lane and handing them to drivers who idled slowly down the lane. Seemed a bit fishy to Robert as it didn't really look like late-night takeout service, however this wasn't what he was after. Tuesday evening was the last night Gorbi had seen Stan, so in theory, whatever had happened to Stan should be on this disk. The resolution was certainly not Hollywood level, with the movement choppy, and the night light didn't help. At 12:25 am he saw a man that must have been Stan stumble into the picture, sit down and proceed to do his thing. Robert scanned forward bit by bit, and sure enough, a panel van drove under the camera and past it a bit, stopping by the prone body of Stan. It was 1:33 am on the time tracker. Someone got out and lifted Stan into the back of the van. Inside of a minute, the van was gone, leaving behind the paraphernalia of an addict's life.

So, this was how people disappeared. Hard to believe how simple it was. He backed up the disk and played it a few more times. The licence plate was covered in something so that it couldn't be read. All he could see was the back of whoever had picked up Stan, and he was hooded, assuming it was a he. It was hard to tell the person's height, but he definitely was not short. Not much to go on, but that's why he had assistants, to do the hard work required for results.

***

After he finished, he packed up and went back to his office, smiling at Norma along the way.

He stopped at her desk. "Found what I was looking for on the disk, although we are not much farther ahead. Thanks."

She nodded in appreciation, a glimmer of a grin breaking out.

They would be lost without her, Robert thought. After sitting in his office for a minute, he decided to go for a walk and think about the case, even though there was a slight mist coming down. He pulled on his Gore-Tex coat, cap, and headed out of the building north across busy traffic lanes and down a lengthy street, to the seawall of False Creek. He came here to think when the station seemed too demanding or noisy. Parts of the seawall could be crowded, but this was the one stretch that had the least number of residences near it, so people were fewer and farther between. The rain also helped to reduce traffic. As he walked by the fleet cars, some of which belonged to the police force, parked in the otherwise empty lots, he knew it would be only a matter of time until these last land parcels would be developed like the rest of the lots along this stretch of the Creek. He looked north at the glass walled condo towers across the Creek and the hazy North Shore mountains beyond.

He turned east toward the Olympic Village. A jogger puffed his way past him, heading in the same direction. Maybe I need to get more exercise, he thought. Actually, there was no maybe about it—he knew he needed it. His fitness, won at a fair cost, was rapidly waning. Wasn't walking exercise? He had lapsed on his training regimen when he had switched out of the Taskforce. He would have to do something about it. No sense in losing too much of the edge that took so much effort to hone. He kept going, head down.

Not much about this case was making any sense to Robert. Why would someone go to all the trouble of sticking a human arm in a soup? What could they hope to gain? And at Eden Gardens? That place was about as removed from modern day Vancouver society as you could get. It really did seem as though it belonged to a kinder, gentler time. Robert had a bad feeling that the missing Stan guy might be connected, as the arm had to come from someone. He didn't really believe in coincidences, and this would be a doozy if it was.

None the wiser, after another few hundred metres he turned and headed back to his office. Birds flying low over the pathway were squawking incessantly, apparently unfazed by the bad weather. On the way back, he called Camille on her cell. There was no answer. Then he remembered that she was probably in the middle of interviews out at the Gardens.

~ 6 ~

Just before four thirty, Robert heard a commotion outside his office. Camille had made it back. She bounded into his room with a flushed face. "You are not going to believe this one, Robert," she said. "We were interviewing the sous chef, who it turns out is Uruguayan. Can you think of something famous that happened a long time ago in the Andes? Involving a plane crash?" she added, when Robert appeared not to be getting it.

"You mean the crash landing with those survivors eating each other?" He was not understanding the connection.

"Yes!" She practically yelled. "He was on that plane. He was one of them."

Robert sat down on his not so comfortable work chair. He was finding this hard to swallow, let alone understand. "Let me get this straight. The chef who works in the Restaurant of Earthly Delights is a former cannibal?" It probably wasn't the best way to put it, but it summarized things nicely, he thought.

"I guess you could say that." She took a seat and consulted her notebook.

"How did he end up here in Vancouver? Didn't that happen a long time ago?" Robert was starting to think again. "More importantly, how did he end up working in a restaurant?"

"He apparently emigrated to Canada fifteen years ago and became a citizen five years ago. At some point he moved to Vancouver, but it's a little hazy on when this was. He bounced around from job to job but seems to have found his niche in cooking. He says it was a way to confront his history head on, and it seemed to have worked for him, until now, that is."

"And who told him that this was a good idea? Robert asked.

"A psychologist, I think."

Robert looked up at the ceiling, shaking his head, but said nothing. At this point, Tony walked into the office, grinning. He leaned against the door frame.

"Camille tell you?" Tony asked. "Can you believe it?"

"You're right, this is going to make some good stories. Did you get anything out of any of the other employees?" Robert asked.

"No, and I don't think anyone else there knew about Miguel's history either." Tony replied, taking a seat.

"Seems to me that the Gardens haven't really embraced the idea of vetting their employees." Robert concluded. "Did you bring the guy in with you?"

"Yup. Got him here for questioning. We told him it's part of the ongoing investigation into the lunch incident last week. He maintains that he only found the bones in the pot, he has no idea how they got there." Camille added. "I'm also guessing that his career in foods is probably over if this gets out."

Camille had a bit to learn, Robert thought. "Not if Camille, when. This kind of stuff always gets out somehow."

"Did Miguel tell you all this?" Robert asked.

"No. He told us about coming to Canada, and where he came from, but I did some background research this weekend. Then I confronted him with it this afternoon, but I wanted to be sure before telling you guys," Camille added.

Robert then told the group what he had learned from the disk that Tony had brought back. "I have a funky feeling here. These things are connected. I can feel it. We need to do more investigative work now, just like the title of our department says."

Camille hated this part of the meeting. "We'll be looking for needles in haystacks. Don't worry, I know, it's all part of the job."

Was this a hint of mutiny from the troops? "First thing is to see whether we can connect the missing man, Stan, to the arm in the pot. Someone will have to get back to the east side to see if we can possibly get any DNA from Stan to match to. You guys were in his room, correct? Second thing to do is to see what we can find out about the van in the video. I know it's almost impossible, but let's give it a try." By 'let us,' Robert meant Camille and Tony. He had some thinking to do. "We'll interview this Miguel guy again tomorrow am. Better let him know he'll be enjoying our hospitality tonight." Robert concluded.

"We were in Stan's room, so we'll get it checked out." Camille said, as she got up and left the room.

Robert couldn't think of anything else that was pressing, so he decided to leave for the day, saving his case thinking for home. He went downstairs into the parkade and got into his small Honda, which he called The Silver Streak on account of how old and slow it was. He scrounged around in the glove compartment until he found what he was looking for and popped in an old Ian Tyson CD to make the commute a little easier.

His affinity for country music developed when he was younger after he met a couple of fellow officers in training from upcountry in Merritt. It was all they would listen to, so after a while, Robert was hooked. Like any genre, there was a lot of awful music, but the good songs were very good. The tie between the music and the land it came from was the clincher for Robert. Probably his favourite artist was Hank Williams, one of several prominent musicians who had died way too early in their career.

For once, he had not talked with the kids during the afternoon, so dinner was going to be a mystery that he would have to solve alone. He was trying to remember what was in the fridge that could be cobbled together. Robert eventually pulled up into the carport off the lane and walked through the garden to the back door. The garden backed onto the dining and family area, and was one of the truly great things about the townhouse they lived in. It was nice to be able to look at a green sanctuary during the winter months and live in it during the summer months. Sometimes Sophie took some initiative for dinner if she could put her phone aside for a second, and luckily, it looked like today was one of those days.

Gai lan was sitting on the counter next to leftover barbecued pork taken out of the fridge. And then he spied the rice cooker, ready to perform its magic. Chinese tonight, he thought, good choice. He grabbed a glass of white wine and went looking for the kids before starting the preparations.

"You guys upstairs?" He yelled.

Two voices called back, so he went into the living area and rested for a moment on the couch, drinking his wine, remembering Susan. Before Susan's death, most times he would share what was going on at the station with her, and she'd tell him about the challenges from her work. Susan had been a planner working for the City of Surrey. She had held a similar position at the City of Vancouver, but like several senior planners, she had decided that there was more opportunity in a younger city. That Surrey was booming and was expected to overtake Vancouver as the largest city in BC one day soon only added to the allure of the job. They often chatted over dinner preparation.

He realized that the food wouldn't cook itself, so he went back into the kitchen and poured another glass of his favourite wine. With no one to talk to, he started in on the rice preparation prior to figuring out how best to cook the *gai lan*. Then he started muttering to himself. "I get the feeling this is going to get more complicated. I really doubt that this chef would be doing all this, but maybe he came unhinged. Maybe something set him off. God knows, what he went through in his youth would probably never leave him."

When no one answered, he continued, "And of course, don't tell the kids."

"Don't tell us what, Pops?" Robin bounced down the stairs and into the room.

"Work. Nothing you need to know, at least not yet." Robert replied, realizing that he had been using his outside voice instead of his inside voice. Was he cracking up? Dinner was ready inside a half-hour and this time, there were no leftovers.

***

Robert had been in his office since before eight and was looking through some case files when Tony blew through his office door. "Wait until you read this!" He was breathless. The door banged against the wall and bounced back into Tony's chest.

"Calm down, what is it?"

"Latest version of *VanDay*. I pick it up on the train on my way into work. The whole story is in there, about the arm in the soup!" Tony seemed giddy.

"Great, this means a media circus at a minimum. And the Eden people aren't going to be thrilled about it, to say the least. Can you go get Camille if she's here? We have some planning to do."

Within five minutes, the three of them were in Robert's office with the door closed, and Robert, having read the article, handed the paper to Camille.

Robert started. "We are going to circle the wagons here. The first people to aggravate us will be everyone in this precinct. The next ones will be the media, asking for comments. Then there is Steve. I know he will be after me shortly. We'll treat the office and the media similarly, and I'll deal with Steve. No comment, an on-going investigation for the media. Can one of you track down who wrote this? I'm sure he won't give us his source, the wanker, but we may find out something that helps us." Robert thought some more. "Keep on those other leads from yesterday. If you need more help, get it. I need more coffee, anybody joining me?"

Neither answered, so Robert kept moving, out of his office and past Norma, on his way for coffee. She called out, "Steve is looking for you."

"Fantastic. Tell him I'll come by as soon as possible." He then left the precinct to go to his favourite coffee establishment. Robert long ago stopped drinking coffee made in the office. He was pretty sure that was how cancer, or worse, started. He wouldn't feed that stuff to a rabbit.

Robert walked up Cambie and sniffed the air before entering Café Paulo. "Hey Gilberto! Set me up, a double long please. Thanks."

"How are you a do-in Roberto?"

"Just fine Gilberto, great day out there. Smells like rain though." They couldn't resist talking about the weather, like everyone else in Vancouver. Gilberto was from Sao Paulo in Brazil, but everyone thought he was Italian, even after the clue in the café's name. Vancouver really was becoming a melting pot, when it came to cultures, Robert thought, and Gilberto did make the best espresso or Americano in town. However, for drip coffee, Robert usually went elsewhere. It was fine by him, he was a coffee snob, pure and simple.

He thought about how he was going to handle Steve. Rope-a-dope, he figured. That's what usually worked. Just take the questions, and feign ignorance, but not too stupid, he didn't want to get fired. He also understood that their team was likely to get larger due to the attention. The police media liaison guys always liked to boast about how many officers they had working a case. Steve would add a few officers to the team with no thought as to how that would affect it. That was Robert's problem.

He ambled back to the office, thinking the whole way. As he walked past reception, he asked Norma if Steve was in his office. "He's still waiting to see you, I think," she answered, smiling. "Is it true about the arm thing?"

Robert looked at her, smiled, and put his finger in front of his lips. "Shush. I'll talk to you later."

Feeling sufficiently alert from his caffeine shots and ready for mental combat, he entered Steve's office, which was located toward the north end of the floor. He sat down across from Steve in one of the guest chairs that looked like they came from some senior's rest home. Steve's desk was huge, had curlicued legs, and was made of some kind of old wood; mahogany, if Robert had to guess. What was inside the drawers was a mystery. There certainly wasn't much on the top. It was hard to fathom exactly what look Steve was going for. Sort of Value Village meets Fathers of Confederation was Robert's best guess.

Steve was twirling a pen in his fingers, one of those circus acts that engineers seemed to be good at. Robert couldn't figure out how it was done, or where Steve had learned this.

"I am already getting calls from all over, including the Deputy Chief. What are you doing about this soup mess? And before you answer, I am assigning three more officers to your team. As you might guess, the higher ups are getting excited." Steve seemed to be working himself into a state. "I am getting the impression that you are not taking this seriously enough. How'd you like a transfer back to that gang unit? I can make it happen right away if you like."

Robert was trying to figure out where he had misstepped. Probably wasn't getting results fast enough even though it had been only a few days since the incident. "There's not much difference between those gangs, as you call them, and the high society types we may be dealing with on this case. In the end, they all want the same things: money, power, and respect. Except the respect for gang members comes from fear, not love."

Steve looked perplexed. Robert realized he had made a mistake; he had raised a complex issue with Steve—not a wise move. The threat about a transfer was also not good. He had only been back with the Investigative Branch for a couple of months. If he was shifted out again so quickly, he could pretty much kiss off his career at the VPD. Instead of grovelling, however, he went with neutral.

"We are exploring a couple of leads right now. We're waiting on forensics for some DNA, then we'll see if we have anything in our files for a match on the arm bone. We have the sous chef in custody for another interview today. He has an interesting history that we want to check on."

One would think that the word 'interesting' might generate some curiosity from Steve, but apparently not. He kept twirling his stupid pen. "Ok, keep me in the loop. And please prep a short statement for our media officer to read out. The press is nipping at my heels. Run it by me first."

Robert got up. "Anything else? Or can I get on this?"

Steve waved his arm. It looked like he was already pondering other matters, but Robert knew this was a mirage, thinking not being Steve's strong suit.

Robert went into his office and called for Camille. When she came to his doorway, he beckoned her in. "We should talk with this Miguel and figure out whether we need to keep him or not. Can you get him into a room and let me know when we're ready? Thanks." Robert believed in being polite, at least to some people. Others just didn't deserve good manners. "We're also getting three more officers attached to the team, so I think we'll move them onto the mystery van search, and the Stan search as well."

Camille left to set up the interview, while Robert pondered the ramifications of all the publicity. Then he started working on the press statement. While he was writing, he looked out his window northeast toward the Olympic athlete's village area built for the 2010 games, and pondered the extra taxes all Vancouver citizens were paying to cover the fallout from the city's meddling in that development.

Camille called him on his desk phone and said she

was ready, so he went downstairs to one of the interview rooms near the cell area in the basement.

* * *

Meanwhile, on the west side of Vancouver, in Southlands, Sam Greene was drinking morning coffee in the kitchen, scrolling through his laptop when his cell rang. All he heard was some music which he couldn't identify. Then a voice came on. "Recognize that, Sam?"

"Vaguely. Who is this?"

"It's Dick." Dick was one of Sam's competitors in the development game, or an ally, depending upon the situation. "It's 'She Drives Me Crazy' by the *Fine Young Cannibals*!"

"Why are you playing that to me?"

"Haven't you heard what your little restaurant is serving up these days?"

"What restaurant? I don't own a restaurant."

"I heard recently that you are the owner behind Eden Gardens, no? The restaurant over there has been serving 'arm soup' apparently. It's all over the news this morning." Dick paused. "You don't know about this? And why wasn't I invited? You know it's my favourite. Someone found an arm in a soup pot and you're clueless?"

Sam had enough of this, so he hung up on Dick, and then called Dominic at the Gardens.

Dominic and Derek were going over the preparations underway for the re-opening of the restaurant that evening. They had received permission from the police to use the kitchen the night before, so all the little things that needed doing before opening were set in motion.

They wouldn't be able to make the lunch service, but dinner could be done, and if there were fewer people than normal, so much the better. One problem was the absence of their sous chef, but Derek would just have to do some real work for once in Miguel's place.

"Dominic, this is Sam Greene. What is this I hear about a problem with the restaurant?"

Craps, thought Dominic. This was exactly what he had been trying to avoid. "Yeah, we had a small problem last week and had to close for a few days. But things are good, and we are going to re-open tonight." Dominic apparently was not someone who kept up to date on the news.

"Are you crazy?" Sam yelled. "I hear you've been selling arm soup. Don't you listen to the news? No way you are re-opening. We have to figure out what to do here."

Oh God, Dominic thought. Here goes my career, "We were trying to keep this quiet, but I guess that didn't work."

"No kidding, Einstein." Sam wasn't holding back. "How did this happen?"

"We still don't know. The police are looking into it. And they have our sous chef in custody for questioning."

"Why is that?"

Dominic was going to have to fess up now. "Apparently he is Uruguayan and was one of those guys on that crashed plane in the Andes a long time ago."

"You mean the guys eating each other to survive?" Sam could not believe what he was hearing.

"Yes."

"Jeez Louise. Don't you guys check people when you hire them?"

"Not that far back, we don't." Dominic said defensively.

"I think we need a meeting tomorrow." Sam said. "Bring your chef. The restaurant stays closed." He had only hung up for a moment when his phone rang again.

* * *

Robert swiped his access card on the door pad and walked into the interview room where Camille was sitting across a table from Miguel. Miguel was a stocky man with a slightly puzzled look on his face. Robert let Camille take the lead.

"How long have you worked at the restaurant Miguel?"

"Three years."

"Are you happy there?"

"Yes, until now."

"Where did the arm come from, Miguel?" Robert's questioning was directed at establishing a motive, and secondly, trying to find the source of the arm. Miguel was not much help, so either he wasn't cooperating, or he really didn't have a clue about the incident.

"I don't know. It wasn't in the soup the night before when we closed up."

"Are the soups usually made the night before service?"

"The more complicated ones are, like the Lobster Bisque we served that day."

"What time do you close up at night usually?" Camille asked.

"About nine, and then another hour or so to clean and prepare for the next day.

"How many other chefs are there in the restaurant?"

"Just me, and Derek, the guy who is my boss. I have a couple of people under me to do all the prep work needed to set up for service."

"Do you have any enemies, Miguel? Someone who has it in for you? Maybe someone who worked at Eden Gardens?"

"No, *per favore*." Miguel responded. "I just do my job and stay out of trouble." His eyes were darting around as he responded.

This was going nowhere, so Robert ended their meeting. The length of employment was a good lead though, as it gave a possible time frame to work through as they tried to narrow the suspect field. It also pointed to a midnight affair, someone accessing the kitchen after everyone was gone.

After the interview, Robert and Camille went back to Robert's office. They called Tony in.

"Based on what Miguel told us, and what the server said, what was his name?" Robert asked.

"Sanjay," responded Tony.

"Sanjay. What Sanjay said was that Miguel looked like he had seen a ghost when he pulled the bone out of the soup. If I read your notes correctly, I think his surprise was probably real. Which means we should be casting our net wider. And we need to find a why for all this. From our interview, I really don't think this guy did it, but we'll keep our options open. I also think he was lying to us, just a feeling right now, but he didn't look comfortable when I asked him about disputes with other employees. I think we can release Miguel, but on a short leash. Address, phone number, and make him check in every couple of days until we know more. Sounds to me like someone was trying to set this guy up. Any news on Stan?"

"I sent two new team members back to the rooming hotel. With any luck, we could get some DNA from Stan's room to compare with the arm bone." Camille said. "The other officer is working on the van angle."

"That sounds good. Tony, I think we need to check out all the employees who work for Eden Gardens, not just the restaurant staff, and start reviewing the board members, but quietly. Do some research. Don't want to ruffle feathers just yet. We may need a few more people to help out, but let's see how the new team members work out first. Not sure if we want to explore the Garden's volunteer list yet, as I'm guessing that list will be extensive." Robert paused, "Now, if you will excuse me, I have a press release to finish."

***

Instead of working on his writing skills he headed down to the seawall to clear his head. By the time Robert got there he had scrolled through the usual motives for getting into trouble; money, love or hate, revenge, and stupidity. Money wasn't a motive, at least on the face of things. Stupidity didn't seem apt here also. Revenge of some sort seemed like it might fit. The obvious target seemed to be Miguel, but Robert also felt, it was a little too obvious. Then there was the arm in the soup, which pointed to a killer on the loose, perhaps. Maybe they should widen their search, and start looking through the rest of the Gardens, just to be thorough. At a hundred and forty acres, this would be a tall task, and he left that idea alone for now.

He kept walking east until he was almost at the western buildings of former Olympic Village, the expensive condos. The gulls and the crows above his head were having a screech contest. He looked north and caught the splash of paddles as some dragon boats made their way up the Creek on a training run. Robert looked up at the low towers he was nearing and knew that he could never afford to live down here. Living anywhere in the city was a struggle financially, but it wasn't like his family were the only ones going through it. Most working people were in the same circumstances - it was just the way things were, and frankly always had been in Vancouver the last forty years. Robert wasn't going to get into a knot about it. Others in town seemed to believe it their right to rent or own something right where they worked. If you wanted that, there were many small towns in Canada where one could do that. Living in big cities required accommodation in your desires, at least that's what he felt.

He headed back to Cambie Street with the wind and rain at his back. It was getting cold, not the dry, smiley, kicking at fresh snow kind, but the kind that latched onto your spine as rain dribbled down your collar. The kind that Vancouver winters specialized in, making you ache, and wishing for Arizona or somewhere farther south.

After returning, he finished the press item, which as usual, said little, and walked it over to Steve's office. Steve wasn't there, so Robert left it on his desk. He hoped it would mollify the media people and divert some of Steve's attention away from himself. As he walked by Norma's desk, he debated telling her about the release on Steve's desk, but said to himself, screw it, if he couldn't find it, too bad.

~ 7 ~

Wednesday morning Camille called Bernard's cell, wanting to meet with him, and asked him to come to the station. Bernard said he would be there in a half-hour and started over to the precinct. Bernard lived not far from the route Robert liked to walk when he was thinking through his cases.

Once Bernard got there, Camille escorted him into a meeting room and started the questions. She wasn't so stupid as to ask him about the name of his source, but it turned out that there was no name, anyway.

"The whole thing was very cloak and dagger." Bernard led off.

"What did you discuss?"

"Pretty much what I put in the article."

"Did you get the feeling that the caller was on the inside, as an employee, for instance?" Camille asked.

"I couldn't really say. He seemed pretty pleased to be telling me the story, and he mentioned a Sam Greene. I later found out that Sam is the owner of Eden Gardens. He didn't spend very long on the phone." Then Bernard gave a short laugh. "They don't prepare you for this in school."

"You realize this could be a murder investigation, correct?"

"I guess..." Bernard had not got past the excitement of the story to think this far ahead yet. Camille wasn't surprised when he started to fidget. People usually exhibited something when you mentioned murder.

"Can I check your cell?"

"No, I don't think you have that right."

"Ok, your choice. We'll get a court order to get your phone records. You can leave, but we may be in touch. Let us know if you hear from this guy again, okay?" She added, "And leave your contact details on this piece of paper. Cell, e-mail, address, workplace information."

"I am a free-lancer. I work out of my apartment."

"Lucky you. Fill in all the information. We'll want to know before you leave the Lower Mainland for any reason. Here is my card." Camille ended the interview and waited for Bernard to fill out the information. She was a little ticked at the snot-nosed attitude.

* * *

Bernice was in her drawing room. It was late morning, and she was sipping a cup of Earl Grey tea when the phone rang. It was her friend, Mildred, calling to discuss the latest news. "Hi Bernice, have you heard about what happened at the Eden Gardens?" Mildred was a member as well, so she was always excited when the Gardens made the papers, no matter how small the story was.

"No, what?"

"They found that one of their soups contained a human arm, and the restaurant has been closed!"

"What?" Bernice squeaked thinly.

"Check the paper, Bernice. They found a human bone in their soup. Last Thursday. Can you imagine such a thing? I'm not eating there again!"

"The paper?" Bernice was feeling dizzy.

"Are you okay, Bernice?"

"I think I have to go, Mildred. I'll call you back." Bernice couldn't believe what she was hearing.

Mildred was confused by Bernice's reaction, but immediately called a few other friends to spread the word. Meanwhile, Bernice went to look for William, who was probably working on his stamps in the study.

"William! Where are you? Have you heard the news?"

"In here, darling."

"Do you remember the lunch we had at Eden Gardens last week?"

"The free lunch? Of course. It wasn't bad, really."

"Yes, it was bad, William." Bernice was almost screeching now. "There was a human bone in the soup. I just found out from Mildred." Her eyes were wide open, and she was rubbing her hands together furiously.

Suddenly, William was feeling ill. "Are you sure about this?"

She paused. "Well, I guess so. Maybe we should check the paper." Bernice proceeded back out into the kitchen to get the *Vancouver Sun*, which was sitting there unopened. She brought the paper back into the study unsteadily. After William looked through the front section, he found a short piece near the back in an area devoted to local news items and read the piece.

"Good grief, it looks like you are correct." They both sat, looking at each other. After a couple of minutes, William called the restaurant. Of course, there was no answer because the restaurant was closed.

***

Camille was at her desk when the officers who had been out searching Stan's room returned. They came by and leaned against her partition. Camille suggested moving to a room to hear their report. This story was weird enough that even the other officers in the squad room were trying to listen to get any information they could. Once in the room with the door closed, they sat around the table and the two officers laid out what they had found.

"It's creepy in that hotel. We eventually found the manager and he let us in to Stan's room. We picked up a couple of personal items that should be good for DNA testing, a toothbrush and a comb," one officer added.

"The manager said that Stan has not been seen since over a week ago. He didn't have a real fix on the last date he saw him; there are too many people coming and going," said the other officer. "It's true, it is creepy in there. I hope I didn't pick up any bugs," she grimaced, then added, "It's unbelievable that people have to live like that. It's no wonder that some of them prefer to sleep outside on the street."

Camille responded, "You guys are new to the force, right?" They both nodded. "That is how it is for some of the less fortunate people. Thanks for the efforts. Leave the bags with me and I'll get them to forensics. You can go back to the van search, please." Camille finished up and they all left the room, followed by the eyes of their fellow officers in the squad room.

Late on Wednesday, Camille and Tony went back to Eden to meet with the grounds crew. Again, they parked in the no-parking zone in front of the restaurant They considered it their personal spot now, especially when they found out that the Garden's management didn't like them doing it. Kind of made it more special. It was a tiny part of their rebellion against city hall's anti-car campaign, all fomented by a certain Robert Lui.

An admin assistant led them back outside, over to the new entry pavilion, and into a large meeting room, where they waited for the employees. The room had a glass wall facing the expansive plaza that was the starting point for visitor excursions into the Gardens. It wasn't a surprise that they were kept waiting more than ten minutes before Marty Peachtree led his crew of eight in.

Marty stood ramrod straight. His hair was tight to the scalp, basically a buzz cut, and his face was hard, all angles with a couple of scars across his cheek. His eyes were grey and unsmiling. His crew of gardeners were more casual, but unsure of what was happening. They were all wearing their work clothes, some a little dirtier than others after a day in the Gardens.

"Please take a seat, all of you." Camille started, then introduced herself and Tony, "We'd like you to tell us how your operation works, if you wouldn't mind."

Marty explained that all the temporary summer help was gone and that the remaining grounds crew and gardeners were sufficient to get the Gardens through the winter, along with repairing the machinery that required attention. He told them he assigned each gardener a particular area to look after. Camille mulled this over. In other words, the list of workers was longer than appeared.

"How many service areas and buildings do you have?"

"The main service buildings are along a road a couple of hundred yards east of here. There are some other minor facilities out at the northeast corner. And there are several service gates around the perimeter, all locked usually."

"How many people do you have on full time, year-round?"

"I am the foreman, and we usually have ten plus me full time. One of our regulars just went on long-term disability, so we need to find a replacement." The words came spitting out like he was answering a drill sergeant. Camille was wondering if that was what he had been in a former life.

"And in the summer?"

"We usually add up to twenty students or casual labour. They work from April to October generally."

"Are there any security systems in place? Or night watchmen, that sort of thing?"

"There is a company used by the Gardens, but there are no night patrols or anything like that. Everything is locks and keys as far as security goes." Marty concluded.

"So, what does the company actually do?"

Marty shrugged. "Not much that I can see."

"Has any of your employees got into disputes with the kitchen staff at the restaurant?"

"Not to my knowledge. But I know that sometimes, our people may go over there for a staff lunch."

Camille thought about this but declined to pursue it further. Checking all the prior employees was going to be a real job, she thought. Marty did not seem inclined to say anything more, so after a couple of questions to the groundskeepers that elicited one-word responses, Camille decided that she had had enough.

After Camille and Tony returned to the precinct, they both went and knocked on Robert's door. It was after six, and the evening shift in the squad room was on but Robert was still in his office, catching up on some of his other cases.

"Come in. How did it go?"

"We got to interview the gardeners, and this Marty chap, who is in charge of the gardeners, runs them like a dictatorship. He calls himself a foreman. Kind of like a one star general, without the star. Someone who's been in charge of people before. Get this, his last name is Peachtree. Seems like an apt job for him. I think he may be ex-military. We can check that pretty quickly." Camille led off. "The others didn't have a lot to say. I would guess that if we got them separated from Marty, we might find out more than we did today."

"So apparently you didn't learn much?"

"That's about the size of it. Although Marty did say that, on occasion, some of the gardening staff might eat a meal in the kitchen of the restaurant. I think we should go back during the day and wander around the Gardens, maybe bump into the others kind of by accident and see what else we can learn. They all seem a little afraid of Marty, so as long as he is present, they're not going to open up. There is another thing. In April, Marty brings up to twenty more part-time helpers for the spring, summer, and fall season. So, we have a few more people to research. I'm guessing a fair number of those would be students, so not sure how a motive would fit in there. I think we should go back a few years to get a complete list of those no longer working at the Gardens. Maybe several years after what Miguel told us, to be thorough. Don't forget that Eden's security runs on keys, so I am betting that there have been multiple copies made over the years."

Camille then ran through what she had learned from the Stan search, highlighting the DNA possibilities. She then followed up with the summary of her meeting with the reporter.

Robert was staring at Camille while he was thinking. "We're getting somewhere, and nowhere. You guys have any thoughts?"

"I can't think of much to say until we get the phone records for that reporter's cell. Even then, there may not be much to go on. I have to write up a request for a court order. Can I run it by you when I am ready?" Tony asked.

"Sure."

"And until forensics gets back, we don't have a lot else to go on." Camille added.

"Okay. We should try to work out a plan to visit the Gardens with a couple of people to hit on those workers.

It would be good to get the lay of the place. Either of you been inside there before?" Robert asked.

Both Camille and Tony shook their heads.

"I guess there's not much left to do today. Get a list of all the employees, past and present. Go back three years because that is how long Miguel said he had been working at the restaurant. I bet Steve will come looking for me tomorrow. Let's get out of here." Robert was ready to vacate the premises and head home.

* * *

The rain was holding off for now, but it was windy, and very dark as he slowly made his way home in the heavy traffic. As Robert was firing up an older Don Williams CD in his car, a car in front of him signalled to turn left, then promptly veered right. Robert was getting used to this kind of driving. Or was it that other drivers, like him, had grown so tired of all the cars that they didn't much care anymore? Not his problem, however. That's what the traffic cops were for. It was a good thing Mr. William's music was a mellowing influence so that his blood pressure didn't rise too much. As he turned into the lane leading to his carport, he pushed the traffic to the back of his thoughts, and started thinking about his kids, and what he was going to come up with for dinner.

Before he went inside, he sat in his car and reviewed the motives for what was happening. On the face of it, the arm soup thing was not a huge deal, the restaurant excluded, but that the arm came from someone made it a big deal. If it came from some poor soul from the east side, it made it contemptible. He knew that Camille and Tony were working hard on the case, and that maybe after a few more results came in on their enquiries, some clarity might come. Even re-examining his motive list didn't provide any light. We're going to need to dig a little deeper, he thought. There was always stuff under the surface, it was just a matter of finding it. Perhaps the target here was one or more of the customers in the restaurant. The more he thought along this line, the more unlikely it seemed. No one could predict who would order what on any given day. Nevertheless, he would ask Camille to get a list of the patrons from the day in question. Most people paid with cards these days, so the list wouldn't likely be missing too many names.

~ 8 ~

The next couple of days didn't produce much progress. Robert was working on reports and all the casework that constituted modern police processes. The search for the van from the alley behind Hastings Street was going nowhere without a plate number. The vehicle appeared to be so old that there weren't any recent records matching it as far as sales or re-sales. The DNA results had come back as a positive match for Stan, but that didn't surprise Robert. He was expecting this result, but now the police had a body to find. Tony was dispatched to go over to the Carnegie Centre to let Lynette know, so she could inform any of Stan's friends of his death if they came by, including Gorbi.

One of the things Robert and the team had to figure out was whether kidnapping Stan was targeted or random. They had little to go on in this respect, but Robert believed it was probably chance. There was no connection between Stan and anyone at Eden that the police could find so far. The full list of employees came back, and the team divided it up to do their research. Stan also did not seem to show up on the police records for any transgressions.

From all appearances, it didn't look like he would be showing up alive anywhere in the future either, unfortunately for Stan.

A few days later, Camille and Tony went back to the Gardens, this time as visitors. They chose not to bring more officers with them, as there were only nine groundskeepers to talk to. To keep their profile a little lower, they parked in the regular visitor area just to the west of the main older building. Tony was able to ditch his uniform for a day, for which he was grateful, and together their goal was to wander the grounds, keeping an eye out for their targets. The restaurant remained closed. There were rumours that a renovation was in the works.

Camille and Tony looked north after they got through the entry area and stepped out onto the plaza in front of Fraserview Lake, which fronted a picturesque view of an English-style countryside; romantic, pastoral, and totally fabricated. They headed north up the Silver Walk, past trees found commonly in eastern America such as maple, walnut, and beech. They then headed northeast onto the Whistler Stroll, where cedars, firs, larch, and some spruce trees called home. These paths were very close to the gardener's service area. There was no sign of any workers, so they kept walking northeast past a grove of what looked like oak trees to Tony. A few geese waddled around, likely escapees from Fraserview Lake just to the south. Camille and Tony were keeping a weather eye out for Marty—if he saw them, they were sunk. As they walked into the next grove, they finally spied one of the gardeners amongst the maple and linden trees. The maple's brilliant show of scarlet reds and saffron yellows made Camille immediately think of the Laurentians in the fall and she felt a tug from her former life in Quebec. Camille beckoned the gardener over. "Nate, right?"

"That's correct. You guys were here last week? Police?"

"Yup. Just wanted to ask you a couple of things, if you don't mind." No point in telling him why they wanted to ask some more questions. After a few queries, it appeared that he hadn't seen anything out of the ordinary recently.

Camille and Tony walked quietly for a moment, then looked back south at the sandstone outcrops interspersed with tall grasses, all framing the north edge of Fraserview Lake. They turned and continued northeast upwards into formal areas where the hedges and flower beds were more exotic. After a few more minutes, they saw another of the workers and closed in on him. He had a Gator ATV nearby and appeared to be cutting up some deadfall. "Rollie, correct?"

"That's right, you were with the police?" He was standing there, fiddling with his saw. He didn't look comfortable.

"Still are. Just want to ask you a couple of questions, trying to see if you remember anything weird or out of the ordinary, the last couple of weeks."

"The only thing I can remember is the wheelbarrow that was outside of the barn on the day that the soup thing took place. We always lock up all the tools and equipment every night, and this was sitting outside when I arrived in the morning. I didn't tell Marty because he doesn't take well to stuff like that. He runs a tight ship."

"Anything else? Were all the doors locked?"

"I checked and they were. I didn't see anything else out of place. The weird thing is that at the volunteers' area farther east, there are wheelbarrows left out all the time."

"Thanks for your time. You have a beautiful garden." Camille added, "Must be satisfying working here."

"Yes, we are lucky to have this job. A lot of people apply for this, only a few get hired. Of course, you have to know your plants and trees, but you also need to get along with others. Some people just don't seem to be able to do that." He seemed relieved that the questioning was over. Except that it wasn't.

Camille had a thought. "Did any of your staff get into an argument with Miguel, the sous chef in the restaurant?"

Rollie was silent, evidently casting his mind back. "There might have been an incident or two over the years."

"With who?"

"Probably people who are no longer here. I don't remember specifically."

Camille studied Rollie, searching his eyes, deciding that maybe he wasn't telling her everything he knew, but she declined to pursue it.

The two officers continued in the same direction and were eventually able to talk to the other workers, but Rollie was the only one with anything to tell them. Camille and Tony turned east and ambled along the path through the wide-open expanse of one of the former fairways. They could see hints of other fairways that made up the golf course pre-dating the Gardens. The entry to one broad meadow was framed by a couple of stern statues backed by old masonry niches. It was as though a warning was being issued to whomever had the temerity to enter.

They eventually turned back to the entry area, in no hurry to leave the calming environment they found themselves in. It was when they were abreast of a small pond called appropriately, The Beaver Pond, that a cart came flying up behind them and skidded to a slightly skewed stop on the path. Marty was aboard and his face was an unpleasant shade of crimson. He dismounted and walked up to them in an aggressive manner.

"Have you two been talking to my workers?"

"Yes, we had a few questions to ask them." Tony said.

"I didn't authorize that. You have no right to ask them questions without my presence." Marty was spitting as he was talking. Camille had seen this act before on other cases and was no longer bothered by it.

"Actually, we have every right to ask them whatever we choose. Maybe you should head over to your barn and calm down a bit." Camille knew this was likely to stoke the furnace, but she couldn't help herself.

Marty stood there, seething, with his fists clenched by his sides. Camille and Tony could see Marty visibly try to get himself under control. Finally, his military training kicked in and he got back on his cart. "You're going to hear about this," was all he said, then he turned around quickly, leaving a mark on the pebbled path as he headed back off the way he had come.

"Not very Eden-like. Maybe he thinks he's a lawyer." Camille commented as they slowly resumed their walk back to the entry. "I'm guessing that those workers are going to catch hell for talking to us. Too bad."

Back at the station, they told Robert what they found out, and Marty's reaction.

"I think we had better search the service buildings. If Marty doesn't like it, we'll get a warrant." Robert said. I wonder what Marty has to hide, thought Robert. As the head gardener, he had control of a lot of things at Eden Gardens. Maybe we should be looking at this guy a little closer. It wouldn't be the first time a former soldier had slid off the rails into something bad. Robert wondered if the remainder of Stan would be found somewhere in the Gardens. Perhaps a search might be in order.

~ 9 ~

Wednesday started with sun in the sky, a welcome sight for late October in Vancouver. Eden Gardens opened promptly at 10:00 am and an older couple were the first to gain entry. The lady was sporting a tall purple velvet hat that wrapped around her head with wide, matching straps tied under her chin in a gaudy bow. Quite the look, the hostess thought. Attendance was always slow in the winter months, so the hostess at the ticket kiosk was hoping for an uptick in visitors because of the weather. It was a long day for her when the weather was bad and people were scarce. Fortunately for her, it was about to turn into a very interesting day.

After the first couple went through, a few others made their way out but headed north. There was no one else in the foyer, so the hostess watched as the couple made their way east to Fraserview Lake where the waterlilies called home. Farther out in the lake a fountain display was ratcheting up that would put most of the waterworks in Las Vegas to shame, that is—when it was working properly. Per Sam's usual methods, the cheapest components and designers were used to construct the water display, with the result that half the time it was out of service.

The couple paused by the lake's south edge, right next to the ginkgo trees. The next thing the hostess knew, the woman was screaming, with her hands at her mouth. The hostess could hear the screams thinly through the plate glass as the man was leading her away from the water and back to the entry doors. "There is a hand sticking out of the water," the man said as they came inside. They were shaking as they went over to a bench and sat down.

The hostess looked outside but couldn't see anything. Nevertheless, she dialled the manager's number and told him what was happening. "Don't let anybody else out there." Dominic said. "I'll be there in a minute. Get Marty over here as well."

A few minutes later, once Marty and Dominic had taken a look and assessed the situation, they figured correctly that the police had better be called. Dominic went to his office to call Robert directly, but after asking the hostess to attend to the couple until he could return. Robert answered, then asked for a patrol car to be sent over to the Gardens to put up some tape and to make sure no one left the premises. He called in Camille and Tony.

"Sounds as though Stan has been sighted. Just a guess, but I'm putting money on it. Any takers?" The other two shook their heads. Robert then told them about the hand being spotted in the pond. Robert called the dive team and warned them that their services might be required. After calling the coroner, they all went down to the Crown

Victoria in the garage and piled in for the trip over to the Gardens.

When they arrived at the restaurant building, Robert was disappointed to see the patrol car parked in the prime spot out front, so he parked in behind it. The staff seemed to be getting used to seeing the police, but they weren't any happier about it. This probably had something to do with the advertising value of parking a police car in plain view of visitors to the Gardens. All three walked over to the entry pavilion and out onto the concrete deck that stretched from the entry to the pond's edge, then they turned north. Marty was standing on the other side of the ginkgo trees, staring at the waterlilies. "There's the hand alright," Marty offered.

"Do you have anything we can snag it with?" Robert asked. The hand wasn't all that far from the water's edge, but it looked badly distended.

"I have a pole we can push it with, if you want."

"Ok, let's give it a push and see if there is more to this."

After a couple of tentative probes, Robert called in the dive team. He talked with them and made sure that they knew that diving wasn't really involved here, more like wading. He then asked for a few more officers to control the area and the crime scene team. Nothing else was visible in the pond except lily pads from side to side, and the remainder of the body was not being cooperative. They all went back into the entry pavilion and after a brief discussion with the couple that spotted the hand, the police got their particulars and let them leave if they wished. Robert went up to Dominic and let him know that Eden Gardens was to be closed until further notice.

"Marty, can you get a couple of the volunteers and get into carts to go find the rest of the visitors?" Dominic asked. "We'll get you a definite number and call you, so you don't leave anyone out there. Try heading north first, that's where they were headed. I don't think there are very many to find."

After the dive team had come and done their work, it was evident why only the hand had appeared. A concrete block was attached to one ankle of the victim. The bloated and decomposing body had filled with gas and tried to rise to the surface of the pond. There was no doubt about the body's identity. It was missing one of its arms, having been cut off just above the elbow.

Once the pavilion was cleared of the guests, the police questioned the staff one at a time. None of them recalled seeing anything out of the ordinary and were not helpful. Robert figured now would be the time to search the grounds keeper's areas to the northeast and he let Marty know. Marty couldn't say much against the idea, now that a body had been found on his grounds, but he wasn't happy about it.

After Robert saw his officers off to do their duties, the coroner and photographer from the crime scene group arrived. Robert headed back to Cambie Street to wait for anything resulting from the search, leaving Camille and Tony to find their own way back in a patrol car.

***

As Robert drove slowly in the heavy traffic back down Cambie Street toward the precinct, he thought about the peculiarities of the case. In all his years, he had never heard of food being manipulated this way, and in this unusual location. Sure, there were reports of rodent infestations and other hygiene problems associated with kitchens all over Vancouver, but this was on another level. There had to be a reason for it, especially if the Uruguayan chef was not responsible. Since few people knew about the chef's past, it had to be someone who knew his background and wanted to pin this on him. Which pointed to someone in Miguel's past, most likely. If the chef wasn't the target of this elaborate scheme, then who was?

After Robert returned to his office, he realized he was visiting the same thoughts over and over. He correctly decided that he needed some caffeine to rectify his thinking problem and headed over to Café Paulo for a fix and maybe a bite to eat.

"Hey Roberto, goes good?"

"I am pretty sure it is going good Gilberto."

"Hear bout that soup thing?"

"Yup, pretty strange."

"Makes ya want to eat at home. Right?"

"Home cooking is usually best Gilberto, except of course with this establishment. You know that!"

Gilberto slid the double shot across the marble counter, smiling at the compliment. Robert took it and went over to stand by the window counter while he sipped the steaming hot espresso. He was staring at the traffic when his cell rang.

"We're just about done here." Said Camille. "We think we have some evidence from one of the storage buildings, but we'll have to wait on forensics. We'll head back to the office as soon as we can."

Robert finished his coffee and went back to the counter to purchase some sweet pastries to take back with him to his office, where he settled in to wait for his team. He called home while he was waiting, to find out what his kids wanted for dinner. After a bit of back and forth, they agreed that a Bolognese sauce with pasta would best deal with the cold of the autumn day. It would also be easier to fill up the bottomless stomachs of the two teenagers.

It was around four before Tony and Camille got back. It was already getting dark. They slowly entered Robert's office, obviously tired out from their day at the Gardens. As before, the eyes of their fellow officers were on them as they made their way through the squad room. News had travelled fast about the found body.

"So, what did you find in the barns?" Robert asked.

Camille started off. "We may have found where Stan lost his arm. There was a reciprocating saw in one of the storage rooms with some stuff on the blade. Stuff is not a very technical term, but we're not sure what it is yet. There was a wheelbarrow in there as well, so we took that, although not sure what we'll find on it. I'd guess it was used to haul Stan over to the pond. Not much else to relate about the room. It has an older chest freezer in it that is in working order, so we are getting that brought in as well. We're doing the usual dusting for prints and getting photos of the whole barn. We'll get them in here as soon as they are printed. The weird thing is that there didn't seem to be any blood around, so that is why I got the freezer. If there is blood, I'm sure the forensic people will find it. Like someone said, there are only padlocks on the doors, so anyone with the correct key would have no problem getting access."

"Have some sweets, you two. You look like you need something to perk you up." Robert liked to make sure his team wasn't hungry when they were trying to think, even it was late in the day. "I think it is time to get a display board going on the wall in here, so we can keep track of what this is becoming." Neither Tony nor Camille could offer any further insight.

After they had polished off their pastries, licking their fingers afterwards, they all agreed to meet up when the report on Stan's body came back from the coroner. This was likely to take a day or two. Unfortunately, Stan wasn't the only customer for their services. People were still dying regularly from the drugs being ingested all over the city, and every one of them needed official causes of death to put a sad exclamation point to the stories of their lives. Robert couldn't think of what else to say, so he called it a day.

***

Robert trudged down to his car in the police garage and drove home, where hopefully brighter things lay waiting. He walked into the townhouse and immediately went over to the fridge for some wine. If things kept going as they were, he'd need alcohol counselling sometime in his future. Not that he was worried about his drinking yet—there were lots worse than him on the force. He also wasn't sure if his transfer to the Investigative Branch would have made any difference to his alcohol intake or not. There was plenty of stress on the gang side of police work as well.

"I'm home," he yelled out. He pulled out onions, ground beef, celery, and carrots along with a tin of tomatoes and spices, and after some furious chopping, got the Bolognese sauce bubbling on top of the stove. Several minutes later, after the addition of some wine and milk, the odour became luxurious, like hot comfort. He poured himself a more than half full glass of wine, then yelled up to the kids, "Another hour before it's ready." The recipe said three to four hours, but the kids would be eating their homework if he waited that long. He hoped that whatever they snacked on after they got home from school would hold them until then.

Robert set the table for dinner, pulled out a pot for the pasta, then went into the family area and sprawled onto the couch with his wine. He flipped on the TV news to see what the darling local media were making of the discovery of the body at Eden Gardens. Predictably, both announcers were excited. It seemed news programs could no longer rely on one host but needed two at a time due to the exhausting demands of the job. The missing arm angle was getting all the attention, but that this took place at Eden was also big news. Robert guessed that the *VanDay* reporter would get job offers soon, perhaps by one of the daily newspapers.

After Robert had watched for a while, it became evident that they couldn't come up with much more to the story. Robert knew he would be writing another press release tomorrow morning. It wouldn't take long to write because he wasn't going to say anything. He also figured he would hear from Steve. Steve wasn't big on publicity, unless it was good and about Steve. He tried to look out the window facing their garden, but it was almost completely black—the short days of October forcing everyone to withdraw inwards.

An hour later, after Robert had added some nutmeg and parmesan cheese, the sauce was ready. At dinner, the table seemed subdued. Usually, the kids were yakking about something from school or from their other activities, but they were strangely quiet. Robert told them a few things about the Eden case, nothing more than what the public would eventually know. Even this didn't elicit much in the way of curiosity. The few questions that Robert asked were met with short answers. Robert put this down to the fact that their kids were teenagers, and it was probably going to be the state of the union for a couple of years.

After the dinner was over and the children had gone back up to their respective rooms, Robert went into the living room and flopped on the sofa. Dishes could wait. What's going on with those two, Robert wondered. I get it if one or the other doesn't feel like saying much, but it is a little unusual for both of them to act like that.

"Probably school, or Facebook, or whatever they are using these days." Susan answered.

Robert wondered if it was unusual to be conversing

with your dead wife. He bet that the police psychologist would think so, but there was no way he was going to see that wacko again. Robert was perfectly fine getting a little advice from Susan now and again.

* * *

The next day, Bernard was writing up the latest instalment in the Eden caper, as he was now calling it. His editor had been on his back, asking for more stories after the success of the first two. Bernard had made his way out to the Gardens again later on Wednesday after hearing activity on the police band. Unfortunately, this time, other news organizations had also shown up. He couldn't get very close to what was being cordoned off, but he eventually got to talk with the couple who had made the discovery just before they left. Other than a hand waving at them from a pond, he had little to write about, so he started making it up. This had to be the guy with the missing arm, so he wrote it up in a way that wasn't exactly factual. He was already receiving some interesting e-mails from one of his social media sites about working for other news organizations. If he played it right, maybe he could get a real job out of all this. Bernard made a call to the Vancouver Police Department to get their view of things and was given Robert's number, but Robert declined to offer any comment.

* * *

At the police station, Robert got his small group together. Tony was looking spiffy in a newish blue suit. He was going undercover for the second time in a week, on another case, and seemed happy about it. Tony's glistening black hair was pomaded into place and even his nose, which you could open a can with, was shiny.

Camille reported back on what she had learned about the reporter. "I asked Tony to get hold of his phone records, and as Bernard told us, there wasn't a lot of news there. The call by the mystery man was made from a public phone downtown. Even if you could find one, who uses those anymore?" Camille continued, "A reference to Sam Greene is pretty much all we have to go on at this point."

"Tread carefully." Robert started. "Tony, you can start doing some light digging into Sam Greene, see what you come up with. Don't palm this off on anyone else and check in with Camille while you go about it. We don't want any feathers ruffled just yet."

"Yes, boss." Tony answered. Robert was pretty sure that Tony's dream was to become a detective, like Robert.

Robert's phone rang. It was Steve asking him to come to his office. "Looks like I have to report. Wish me luck." Robert left his office, walked a little way down the corridor, winked at Norma, then entered Steve's office. Robert held his tongue, waiting for the first salvo from Steve.

"Take a seat Robert."

This was not a good sign. It meant a good old tongue lashing was heading Robert's way.

"Is this case getting too big for you?" Steve started in.

Robert preferred to stay silent for a moment, waiting for more.

"I heard you visited our psychologist a while back."

Again, Robert refrained from answering, but he was angry at this comment. How did Steve get access to that information?

"Want some advice? If you want to solve a case, come to me. Don't ask your dead wife how to do it."

Robert was astounded. Not only had the fact of his visit been revealed, but also the contents of the discussions. It was all he could do to stay quiet.

After a couple of moments where Robert could almost see the wheels moving slowly in Steve's mind, he spoke again. "We need some solutions here. The Deputy Chief is on my back, so I am putting six more officers onto your little case. Get me some answers before this gets worse. You can go."

Robert got out of the office as quickly as he could, heading back to his office. He wondered if the psychologist had revealed the information about Robert's visit, but realized that the more likely explanation was that Steve somehow accessed the information on file. He closed his door, tried not to think about Steve's comments, and wondered what he would do with six more people. But he couldn't ignore what Steve had just said to him. He was seething.

~ 10 ~

After the excitement of the previous week, Marty and his crew were nervous when they showed up for work each day, the Gardens having re-opened two days after Stan had been found. No one was keen on finding another body in the weeds. As the gardeners went about their daily tasks, they were both looking and not looking, if that made any sense. None of them knew what was behind the goings-on—at least that is what they told each other. The smarter ones knew that each of them was under consideration by the police. The not so smart ones didn't think about it overly, they just went about their business in the Gardens.

It was Nate who made the discovery, mid-morning on a Thursday. Nate's area of responsibility was the German Garden on the east side of Eden and the section to the south of this, including a commemorative garden dedicated by a previous prime minister.

In July of 2008, not long after Eden Gardens had begun its transformation under its new owners, the Canadian Prime Minister of the day visited British Columbia. This Prime Minister wasn't above sticking it to institutions he felt might have been friendly to the previous administration, so when an invitation came his way from Eden Gardens, as well as VanDusen Gardens to come and visit, his inner circle went with Eden. The previous national administration had helped VanDusen get off the ground, so Eden it was, this time. Of course, when important visitors arrive, their hosts love planting things to commemorate the occasion. This time around, the receiving army overdid it. Not satisfied with planting twenty-five Japanese Maple trees moved over from the downtown Bayshore Hotel, they also planted a Tulip tree in honour of the Prime Minister.

After the ceremonial planting for the press, the tree was properly planted, and grew well. Although not native to the West Coast, it survived in a coastal climate. The species was known for the beauty of its wood used in furniture making. It was also a good-looking tree, not gnarly or twisted like some species. It was notable in the eastern United States for a historical reason, which the Prime Minister's group may not have known about. Its nickname was the Freedom Tree. The British would burn it wherever they found it in the run-up to the War of Independence, angering the Americans a little more each time.

Nate pulled up in front of this tree and got out of his Gator. "Looks like some furniture may be on order shortly," he said to himself.

The tree was laying horizontally beside the stump it had been decapitated from. A note was nailed to the stump. It said, "Happy Thursday Sam". That was it, nothing else.

Nate did not touch the note, in case it was evidence, but got on his radio.

"Marty? Over."

"Marty here, is this Nate? Over." Marty loved that military lingo.

"You better get on over here. I'm just south of the German Folly, in the Commemorative Garden, over."

"What's happened?"

"Just get over here. Over." Two overs in a row. Nate switched off his radio, satisfied that he had baited Marty enough. Marty was still cranked up about them talking to the police, so he had to know how far to go.

Marty came flying down the path in his Gator and skidded to a stop beside Nate. He slowly got out, his eyes on the dead tree just off the path. Then he noticed the note pinned to the stump.

"Looks like someone is trying to send a message to our leader. Maybe not a friend of the Conservative Party, either." Marty was referring to the plaque in front of the ex-tree that told the story of its planting. "Get some tape and cordon off the area if you can. Cover up the stump as well. Did you notice anything else?"

Nate shook his head.

"I'll go see Dominic." With that snappy set of orders, Marty swung back onto his ride and sped off, heading west. Nate shook his head and got onto his Gator to go fetch some tape.

Marty drove up to the entry pavilion and parked to the north of the building. He went in the service entrance and found Dominic in his office.

"Hey, our *Liriodendron tulipifera* got chopped down last night." No pleasantries: Marty just launched right in, standing ramrod straight.

"English please. What are you talking about?"

"You know, the Tulip tree out by the German area that was planted for that Prime Minister in the early 2000s. It's been lopped off, by a chainsaw."

"What?"

"Wait, there's more. A note was pinned to the stump. It said and I quote, 'Happy Thursday Sam.'"

"Oh boy. I don't think I like where this is heading," was all Dominic could come up with, after a pause.

"I don't think you should call the police on this one."

"Why not?"

"No one has been hurt here, and I don't like them nosing around, asking questions."

"Property has been damaged, and in a malicious way. I think we have to call them. Something like this is going to be noticed pretty quickly by the regular patrons."

"I suppose," responded Marty.

"Got any alternatives? Like maybe erect a cardboard model of the tree and hope the guests don't notice?" Dominic shook his head.

"Ok, go ahead and call. I'm roping the area off for now." With that, Marty did an about face and marched out. He didn't look happy as he left.

* * *

At the Cambie station, Robert took the call from Dominic. After Robert digested the contents of Dominic's call, he grabbed his coat, left his office, and signalled Camille to follow him.

"Sounds like we have a psycho on our hands. Our perpetrator has turned to property destruction today. Cut a prized tree down last night at Eden." Robert explained. "This guy seems to be a jack of all trades, doesn't he?" He told her about the note as they descended into the parkade to get their ride.

"Sounds like our guy alright. You'd think a saw would make some noise." Camille said.

"Yeah, we'll see where it happened, and if there are houses close by, we'll do a canvass. I think it is located close to the eastern edge of the Gardens."

"I had a meeting with Steve a couple of days ago. I don't know how that guy thinks, which makes me wary when I have to converse with him. I am pretty sure he doesn't think like you or me. To serve and protect, all that stuff; I don't think he went to that seminar when he was in training, if he was ever in training. In addition, it seems like he got into my personal file for information he shouldn't have."

"Glad I don't have to deal with him then." Camille said.

"Sometimes I wonder whose side he is on."

"Ha-ha. I come from Montreal. You don't have the luxury of thinking like that there. More than a few of their cops are on the take. You can be sure whose side they are on—their own."

They arrived and parked the Crown Victoria in their favourite place. Dominic was waiting for them in a guest cart.

The three of them drove south to the scene of the crime. They pulled up not far from the German Folly, and the first thing Robert noticed was how large the tree was, considering when it had been planted. The second thing was that nothing else had been hit or taken out when the tree was felled. Just behind the tree was a group of camellias untouched by the destruction. The Japanese Maples were also undamaged.

"Someone must have known what they were doing here," Robert said. "Someone who's handled a chainsaw before, I would guess."

Camille took a few photos before going over and removing the note carefully and slipping it into an evidence bag. Robert stood there, looking southeast. They weren't that far from a service gate that opened onto Kerr Street. Immediately to the east on the far side of Kerr looked to be a park, with some houses a little farther north.

"Thanks Dominic, we'll make our way back if you want to leave." This was Robert's way of telling Dominic to get the hell out of there so they could do their work. Dominic took the hint, wheeled the cart around, and headed back to the pavilion. Robert and Camille checked the immediate area for footprints and any other evidence before walking over to the locked service gate and peering out north at the houses on the other side of the street. Some were new, some older, all were large, and quite a number seemed to be well looked after, their lawns in meticulous condition.

"Get Tony to do a canvass of these places, see if anyone heard or saw anything last night. Pretty hard to hide the noise of a chainsaw, I would think. And get him to photograph the boot prints we found. I imagine whoever found the tree would have left their prints, so it will be confusing at best." He paused, then asked, "Hungry?"

"Yes, I guess so," Camille answered.

"There's a good Chinese café just up Kerr Street. Let's go."

While they were munching on some *siu mai* twenty minutes later, Robert called Dominic and said they were almost done with the crime scene, and he could do whatever he needed to do with it after Tony was finished.

"It's one weird case, isn't it?" Robert asked.

"Unusual."

"Want chicken feet? It's a tasty dish and they have big feet here for some reason."

"Ugh."

"That a no? More for me, I guess." Robert collared the next server walking by and ordered a plate. Robert also asked for some pea tips in garlic sauce, so they could say that they were eating healthy, if anyone asked.

"Is this how you ate growing up? Camille asked.

"Pretty much. Food is so important for Chinese families, and my dad was a chef. He spent a lot of effort on meals at home, which is how I picked it up. How about you? You grew up in Quebec, right?"

"My mother was an excellent cook. We never wanted for good meals. She made a *tourtière* that would knock your shoes off."

"Socks."

"What?"

"Socks, knock your socks off."

"Don't be a gomer." Camille smiled. It was then that Robert figured they better get out of there before he said anything inappropriate. When they got back to the station, they added the tree photos to the growing evidence board. Camille asked Tony to take a drive to canvas some east siders, then the pair of them went to Robert's office to ponder where the case was taking them.

"Who follows up an apparent murder with cutting a tree down?" Camille seemed genuinely puzzled.

"Like I said earlier, a psychotic individual. Which may make this really hard to solve. No logic to what this individual does, assuming it is one person. We don't even know that as yet."

"The common link seems to be Sam Greene."

Robert nodded his head. "Well, at least that's something for us to hang onto. When Tony returns, I'll ask him how the Sam research is progressing."

~ 11 ~

It was Saturday afternoon, and Sam Greene was taking his dog for a walk. The Greene family dog was a purebred Standard Poodle. Sam loved the dog: in fact, he loved the dog more than any human. It really wasn't a family dog. It was his dog, and he named it Lucky, as it was so fortunate as to be owned by Sam. He had bought it from a breeder up the valley past Langley five years earlier and had paid an exorbitant price for it. He continued to shell out money for training, vets, kennel stays, and dog spas. When Sam had driven out to the valley to pick out the dog, his wife, Lydia, tagged along, thinking she might have a say in what kind of dog they would get. Unfortunately, that was never an option. Sam had done his research and wasn't going to be listening to any other opinions. She supposed it was just fortunate that he hadn't wanted a Doberman, Pit Bull, or whatever the drug lords' latest favourite pet was.

For his walk, Lucky was resplendent with perfectly coiffed hair and a jewelled collar attached to a hand-tooled leather leash. Sam was heading west to Pacific Spirit Park. As he was about to cross the last street before the park began, a brown panel van zoomed past him, just missing Lucky. He didn't see who was driving but let off a loud curse at the rear of the van. Sam regularly walked his dog in the park, which was a series of trails through an urban forest adjacent to the University of British Columbia. This was not a small forest, and a couple of people had just plain disappeared over the years, never to be found again. This didn't dissuade anyone from using the trails but walking or running alone was not encouraged by the police. Sam would let his dog run off-leash when they were on the trails, in contravention of the Vancouver by-law requiring dogs to be leashed. Sam was far from the only one transgressing in this fashion in these woods.

The trail floor was soft, covered in pine needles and moss, the occasional muddy depression waiting to spring its messy trap for the unwary. Shafts of sun sliced through the mist that crawled around the trunks of the larch, red cedar, and fir trees. Sam bent over and released Lucky, who bounded ahead up the trail.

He then reached into his jacket for his cellphone, wanting to check up on Eden Gardens. "This is Sam. Is Dominic around?"

"No, it's Saturday, his day off."

"Who is this, then?"

"A volunteer, manning the desk today. Who are you?"

"Dominic's boss. Has anything else gone wrong the last couple of days? No more bodies, I hope?"

"No, it's pretty quiet here, hardly any visitors the last couple of days."

"That isn't good for the bottom line."

The volunteer could not argue with this logic, so wisely stayed silent, not being used to dealing with Sam.

"Okay, I'll talk to Dominic next week." Sam ended the call.

He had walked deep into the woods, and he hadn't heard his dog for a while. He whistled. Silence. He whistled again. Still nothing. This wasn't like Lucky. Sam increased his stride, looking from side to side. The undergrowth was thick, so he couldn't see far off the trail. He kept whistling until he saw another walker up ahead. "Have you seen a light brown Standard Poodle?" Sam asked when they met up.

"Sorry, no, but I caught a glimpse of a coyote about twenty minutes ago."

Sam stared at the man. "Well, it's the coyote who should be worried, not my dog." However, the farther Sam walked, with still no signs of the dog, the more concerned he got. Maybe Lucky wasn't so lucky anymore. After he had looked for another hour, it was getting dark, so he gave up and headed home, trying to figure out what to do next. He sure didn't want to do what most people did when they lost a pet. Dammed if he was going to go around pinning up lost dog posters on telephone poles. Reward Offered! On the other hand, he couldn't come up with an alternative.

Sam returned home and called out as he took his jacket off, "Lydia, did Lucky come home?"

Lydia was in the kitchen, making some tea. She yelled back, "Just a moment, I'll check." Then, without missing a beat, "No. What do you think? Lucky opens the door and lets himself in?" She shook her head and poured herself a cup.

Sam came into the kitchen. "No need to get snarky. Lucky is missing. He disappeared on the trails."

Lydia smiled. "That's a shame." She dropped some bread into their toaster.

"You don't like Lucky, do you?"

"I hate that dog. You spend more on that dog than me. Good riddance." Her eyes were flickering with intensity.

Now, it was Sam's eyes that were blazing, "Well, if you don't want a tougher dog in this house, maybe you'll think about helping me find Lucky."

To Lydia, this sounded exactly like the threat it was, so she relented. "Why don't you call the SPCA? Aren't cats and dogs their specialty?" She then returned her attention to the toast, ignoring Sam.

* * *

It was Monday, and Eden Gardens had been open for a couple of days after the disruptions of the previous week. By noon, there still weren't more than twenty customers wandering amongst the flower beds and meadows. The weather was overcast, but not raining, at least not yet. A middle-aged couple up from Oregon had made their way to the southern end of the Gardens. One couldn't go much further south at this point without coming up against a busy bordering street called Marine Drive, but one of the attractions in this area was the maze. This was a blatant copy of the maze at VanDusen, but Sam was shameless in his efforts to one up VanDusen. This maze was larger and more complicated, therefore, in Sam's mind, better. The jury was still out on whether having visitors getting lost inside was a good thing.

The couple were just to the north of the maze's entrance on the side of a low rise in the meadow, having descended from a stone garden at the top, so they could see the layout from above. They then snapped a few pictures with their phones for later texting to their friends and children. The maze looked complicated to them, and they were hesitant about their ability to find their way out if they entered it. As well, they both couldn't help thinking of the movie *The Shining* where the end of Jack Nicholson's character had made people consider mazes in an entirely different and not good way. But now they were here, they were going to enter; nothing ventured, nothing gained.

They walked down to the entry on the north side and started in. This was going to be fun, they thought, like being kids again. They hadn't gone too far in, taking a couple of dead-end routes, when they heard buzzing. It sounded like flies, which was strange, they thought. It didn't seem warm enough for flies to be around. As they walked forward, they could see some flies coming out from under the hedging and then returning the other way. Perhaps a dog had left its business in there, and the staff hadn't cleaned it up, but they were unsure if dogs were even allowed onto the grounds. They walked down to the end of the path and did a U-turn into the next corridor. Then they saw the pile on the path. They hesitantly moved closer; it looked like an animal, and it seemed to be moving. This illusion turned out to be the mass of flies hovering and crawling over the carcass. They ventured closer and, after figuring out that it looked like the remains of a dog, they turned and fled.

The couple hadn't gone far into the maze, so they were able to exit quickly. What wouldn't be quick was getting anyone's attention. They were a long distance from the entry pavilion. They sat down, both feeling ill. They looked around but didn't see anyone else. The husband then examined the guide pamphlet they had been given and found a number that he dialled. The membership office answered. As soon as he told his story, he was told to stay put and someone would be along to fetch them in an electric cart.

***

Dominic was shell-shocked. Had someone cast a voodoo spell upon the Gardens? This was the fourth disturbing event to happen in the last three weeks. He didn't know if he could handle much more of this. He called Marty over to the pavilion and into his office. Dominic was on the verge of telling Marty to clean up the mess, but Marty beat him to it by suggesting that maybe the police should be called first. After a moment, Dominic agreed.

"Ok, I'll call them again. I've got Robert Lui's card here somewhere." Let the police handle this, Dominic thought. The publicity couldn't get much worse, could it? Dominic had been hoping for an uptick in attendance since the body had been discovered in the lake, after re-opening happened. Maybe all this fame or infamy might have an upside? Dominic liked to be optimistic when he could be.

"I'll get out there and cordon the area off." Marty offered. "Do we need to close again?"

"No, forget it. Just rope it off, keep people away, and we'll wait to see what the police tell us to do."

***

Robert answered the call from Dominic, "What now?"

"Apparently a dead dog has been discovered in the middle of the maze that we have on site."

"Different. Last week a tree, now a dog. I'll get a patrol car over there. Can you open up a service gate for them at the south end of Kerr Street near Marine, if that is closest to the maze? Camille and I will drive out there too, to the main entrance. Please keep people away from the maze until we get there." Robert wasn't taking any chances, considering the recent events at Eden. He then informed Camille that it was time for their weekly visit to Eden, telling her what he knew as they went to get their car. He left Tony behind for this visit. After all, it wasn't a human this time.

They arrived at the entry pavilion and spoke with the couple who had made the discovery. Robert let them go after getting their contact information. They planned to stay in Vancouver for a couple of more days before heading back to Oregon. They couldn't tell him much.

Robert then got Marty to ferry them out to the southern edge in a Gator, where they met the uniformed officers securing the area. Asking Marty to wait outside, they all entered the maze. When they got to the dog, the first thing Robert noticed was the lack of any identifiable reason for its demise. It was as though it had just lain down and decided to pass away. There was a big landscaper's tarp close to their feet, apparently the method of transportation for the dog. On closer inspection, there appeared to be blood on the side of the dog's coat, which was where the flies were landing. It looked to be some kind of poodle was about all Robert could figure out, and not a very lucky one either, although it had on a very elegant collar.

Normally they wouldn't treat this like a human death, but with all the shenanigans going on at the Gardens, Robert figured they better treat this dog differently. He asked Camille to call in a crime scene team to document the site, then had a look around outside the maze. "Looks like we're going to need a dogtopsy done to determine cause of death."

Camille looked at Robert while raising her eyes. "I'll let the coroner know, but I don't know what they'll say. Shouldn't a veterinarian handle this?"

"They'll be happy for something different, I'd say." Robert responded.

* * *

As the crime scene people arrived through the service gate off Kerr Street, Robert and Camille decided to walk slowly back across the Great Meadow. While leaving the maze, Robert suggested to Marty that the staff should inspect the whole Gardens. They noticed Marty was still hanging around as they departed but didn't think anything of it. Robert supposed Marty was going to keep an eye on everything until the police left. That was the way Marty was wired, a control freak to the core.

As Camille and Robert ambled back east, Robert remembered something from his past. "I was here over ten years ago in the summer, on this lawn."

"What for?" Camille asked.

"It was a summer solstice celebration, June 21. The Society for Creative Anachronism was holding a little get-together at the Gardens."

"The what?"

"Exactly. A bunch of people dedicated in part to reliving the past, as in Medieval Europe. You know; sword fights, archery, maids a singing, everybody dressed in costume. I'm still not sure what the Creative part in their title refers to. I swear, here in the middle of this meadow, you could not hear any car traffic, and basically, it was as if you had time travelled back to a much earlier age. It was both magical, and a bit weird, at the same time."

"I've heard about those Civil War people in the States, the ones who re-enact battles once a year."

"Similar idea, maybe. This place is made for that kind of thing. It's like the original Garden of Eden in here, once you get away from the edges. Vancouver is fortunate to have this place." Robert glanced to his left and was looking upon a small group of golfers, thin and whispery. There were three ladies, each pulling a small bag on wheels. Their hair was pulled tight in curled buns or ponytails, and all wore dark skirts descending to mid-calf above white ankle-socks. He looked back at Camille, wondering if she was seeing the same thing. When he glanced back, only the wide lawn remained.

"Did you see those golfers over there?" He pointed to the middle of the meadow.

Camille stared at him after scanning the area he had pointed to. She shook her head. "What drugs are you doing? And can I get some?"

* * *

After the police techs had taken their photos and arranged to get the dog out of the maze, Marty went up to one of them and asked what kind of dog it was. The tech made the error of allowing Marty to see the dog, figuring that it wasn't the same as a human body. Marty immediately knew that it looked like Sam's dog, recognizing the collar, but this didn't make sense. How could it end up in the maze? He moved back and let the officers pack up to leave, again through the service gate. The fewer people who saw the police at the Gardens, the better.

Marty headed back to the entry pavilion in his Gator, parked at the side, and went in the service door straight to Dominic's office. Dominic was sitting at his desk contemplating what Robert had advised him to do after he and Camille had returned to the pavilion. Think about hiring some night security for your operation, he had suggested. Dominic had to admit that all the malfeasance had happened at night, and this was not such a bad idea. It just cost money, unfortunately.

"You know who's dog I think that is?" Marty asked.

"No idea."

"I think it is Sam's. Sam was out here a few months back with his dog. I'm pretty sure it is the same dog. I recognized its collar. Maybe you should call and let him know."

"Jeez." Dominic didn't ask why it was up to him to do this unpleasant task. He knew—it was all part of the job. Didn't make it any easier though. "Okay. If you are sure, I'll call him shortly. The police suggested getting some security company in to do night patrols. What do you think?"

"I don't know. It's a lot of territory to cover. Might cost a bit. Maybe you should talk to the company that we use already."

"Okay, that's what I'm thinking. Or maybe instead we buy a few cameras and do something along those lines? Plant them out there on some paths and maybe along the fences. Everyone seems to have one in their car these days, so they can't cost too much, can they?"

"I'll do some research for you." With that, Marty left the office.

Dominic contemplated how he was going to make the phone call to Sam. No point in delaying it, he thought, so he dialled Sam's cell number. "Hi Sam, it's Dominic. Got some bad news again."

"Really? Seems that's what you are specializing in these days."

Sam was setting a record for getting on Dominic's nerves, so he let him have it bluntly. "Your dog is dead. It was discovered in the middle of the maze this morning. Seems like someone has it in for you bad."

"What?" Sam yelled.

"Yeah. Someone must have put the dog there last night. Don't know yet how it died, though. The police were here and have taken it."

"What the?" Sam was spluttering now, losing his grip, Dominic thought.

"What kind of operation are you running out there? I'm going to look for a new manager." Then Sam hung up.

Dominic wasn't too worried. Good luck finding a manager willing to work for the peanuts the Gardens offered. If Sam found someone, maybe it would be just as well. Working for this rat was no picnic. Once Sam calmed down, he'd probably regret what he said to Dominic, or so he hoped.

***

When Robert and Camille arrived back at headquarters, they held a meeting with the extended team in Robert's office. The team didn't yet include the extras that Steve had ordered up, but Robert figured they'd be meeting elsewhere soon in a larger room. Robert's office was where Tony had installed the display board with all the graphic information known so far. The six of them did not fit the office that was sized for two or three people, so three officers were standing. The forensics information on Stan had come back. Robert read this slowly, not quite understanding it at first.

"Looks like our victim died from a drug overdose. He apparently had more than enough fentanyl in his system to kill him twice over. Then he managed to lose his arm. Seems like someone had it in for this chap."

"They may not be linked, though," Camille offered. "From what we learned from his friend downtown, Stan was quite the drugster. So, it may not be a stretch that he had all that inside him."

"Agreed, but it seems a strange coincidence. You know I don't like coincidences. On another topic, we need a bigger room. Tony, can you secure a case room for us, and make sure it can be locked? I don't want the rest of the squad room yakking about this until we know what's going on. Our team is about to double in size."

Robert continued, "There is more to the report. The stuff on the saw, as Camille so technically put it, was a mixture of bone and flesh fragments, all matching the victim. There was no sign of blood in the barn or storage room, so the theory is that the victim was frozen in the chest freezer before losing his arm. Either that, or he had been dead for a time. Forensics examined the freezer, and there were minute traces of clothing matched to Stan's clothes. Maybe the body was dumped one night and then the perpetrator came back the next night to add his ingredient to the soup. The arm was sawed off at the humerus just above the elbow."

"I'm betting Stan didn't find it very humorous." Camille offered.

Robert waited a bit, smiling at Camille. "That was pretty bad, Camille. Someday you're going to be running this group, I just know it."

Tony just looked at the two of them before adding, "What about the wheelbarrow?"

"It was apparently washed down, but it is a good bet that it was used to get Stan over to the lake where he was dumped. It had some scratches that could have come from the concrete block that Stan was wearing as an ankle accessory. As the bad guy couldn't exactly throw Stan out into the middle of the lake where it would be deeper, he had to settle for the shore, which is why Stan was found. He wasn't in deep waters. Also, the morning that the wheelbarrow was found outside the barn, by who?" Robert checked his notes. "Rollie. This gives us a clear idea of the day it was done. It seems all pretty quick. But then, I don't suppose the perpetrator would want the body hanging around for several days in the freezer. Chances are that it might be discovered."

Camille offered, "I think we might have a problem here."

"What?"

"We've found that Stan potentially died a couple of different ways. How are we going to prove what really killed him? Maybe he was dead in that alley over by East Hastings Street before losing his arm. A good lawyer is going to shoot big holes in this case."

"Indignity to a corpse, then," Robert countered. "And dogicide one for good measure."

"Dogicide one?"

"Premeditated dog killing!" Robert smiled. "We're going to get this guy for something. If not those, then tree-slaughter."

"We still don't know how the dog died yet." Camille pointed out.

After the team left Robert's office, he had to figure out whether he needed coffee to think, or a walk down along the Creek. He went with neither option and gave Dominic a call. Robert wanted to make sure nothing else had been found on the grounds. He looked out the window at the rain starting to come down in a fine mist, fogging up the glass because of the gentle southeast breeze. "Dominic, Robert here from the VPD. Did you find anything else on the grounds? I asked Marty to have a look around the entire area."

"No, it doesn't look like anything else has come up so far. You're going to find out sooner or later, so I'll tell you now, the dog that was found was Sam Greene's dog. It went missing on the weekend."

Robert wasn't stunned by this announcement, but he was slightly surprised, until he started thinking again. "Ok, thanks for the information. If you find anything else, let me know. Wait a second please, what kind of dog was it?"

"I think it was a Standard Poodle, a purebred from what I know."

"Thanks. Sounds a little unusual for these days. Aren't those dogs a bit squirrelly?"

"Yeah, I think so."

"Okay, thanks for the information." Robert ended the call.

He sat there for a few moments, looking through the mist outside. So, Mr. Greene is definitely the target, not the Uruguayan chef. Why would he be riling someone up enough to commit crimes? And why now, not earlier? There was obviously a lot that the police didn't know yet. He called in Camille.

"What's up?"

"I think we now have the direct connection between Sam Greene and all the goings-on at Eden, if that tree decapitation wasn't enough. Dominic just told me that the dog found in the maze belonged to Sam."

"That is interesting." Camille said slowly.

"Darn right it is. I think we need to ask Sam to come pay us a visit, or we go visit him. This is where it gets a little tricky, Camille. I want you to dig deeper on this Sam Greene, recent and older history. Tell Tony that you are leading this now. He can help but listen to me carefully; find out everything you can about his developments over the years. Better check on his personal life as well. And you need to be discreet while you go about it. These types of people can be more dangerous than gang members if they find someone digging in their past." Then he thought of something else. "Can you also find a Nicholas Ng and talk to him?"

"Why?"

"He is a developer in town and got into a fight with Sam a few weeks back over at VanDusen Gardens. I'd like to know what led to the fight, if possible."

As far as Robert was concerned, this sealed the deal. Whoever was behind all the blood and mayhem had a problem with Mr. Greene, and Robert had to find out what that problem was. "We also need to continue to check the employee list from VanDusen more carefully, present and past. This is going to take a lot of research. I think we'll need to look at the officers Steve is sending our way and find out who has the research skills we need."

After all the day's excitement, Robert had had enough and took the stairs down to his Honda. He didn't feel much like listening to country music today. He needed something a lot harder, so he searched around until he found a Wintersleep CD. He inserted it, then cranked up the volume until the windows were quivering with the sounds of blood music. His thoughts immediately went back to his wife and all that she had been through. The music somehow soothed him, despite the volume. He pulled out of the police garage, checked for traffic, then headed home where he intended not to think about the case at all, if he could manage that.

~ 12 ~

In the end, Sam Greene declined to come down to Cambie Street, so Robert and Camille made the trek out to Sam's residence in Southlands, just to the west of Crown Street. Sam wasn't being charged with anything, so a visit to his home wasn't out of order. They debated taking a squad car instead of the Ford to make a point but decided that the Crown Victoria stood out enough. The neighbours would know what was going on and the gossip would start.

It was a couple of days after the discovery of the body, the tree, and the dog, and the news people had taken notice. Robert was always amazed at how quickly the story got out, and how inaccurately it related what was really happening. The body, the tree, and the dog. It sounded like a kid's book from his childhood. What was the title? Maybe the body part wasn't really for kids, but....

The police car pulled up in front of Sam's mansion. They sat in the car for a moment, looking at the house. The style was modern, as far as Robert could tell. A lot of flat roofs, large panes of glass, tan brick, black window frames, and lush landscaping. The lot seemed to be at least a double wide lot. Residential land in Vancouver was based on a standard thirty-three-foot-wide lot, and most people knew it. Always fun visiting the milieu of the other half, he thought. Sam seemed to have done well for himself. The houses on each side of Sam's were more traditional, but also very well looked after. The area reeked of money.

There was no one else on the street. The area was deserted. Robert realized that the decision about which car to take was useless thinking. Probably nobody walked anywhere around here unless they had a dog to take care of and he assumed that chore was often palmed off on other people. He also guessed that more than a few of the neighbours were away on vacation.

The few cars parked on the street were high-end models: Range Rovers, Audis, the occasional Alpha Romeo, and a Mercedes sports utility vehicle farther down the road. Why someone would park these cars on a street was beyond Robert's comprehension. He was sure all the homes had nice garages off the lanes that ran down the middle of every block. The driving skill around Vancouver had dropped so much that leaving expensive cars on the street seemed like asking for trouble. Robert also assumed that they didn't have many block parties around this neighbourhood. He looked west and noticed that the street terminated at a tall green wall of forest. Must be the University Endowment Lands, he thought.

They walked up three front steps and pressed the bell. After a full minute, just as Robert was ready to try again, an older man answered the door. Everything about him exuded wealth. His head looked like a lion's, with a dark mane that could only be dyed. Sam's eyes were set wide apart, with wrinkles running back behind his hair. He was smiling the smile of a know-it-all, and his ochre tan spoke of holidays in sun-drenched locales. He wore corded olive pants with a flashy cream coloured patterned shirt, and a sweater slung over his shoulders knotted below his throat like a cape. Beware people in capes, Robert thought. Pricey looking loafers with no socks rounded out the look. He looked to be on the shiny side of sixty, but Robert knew Sam was past seventy years old. Robert couldn't help thinking of a famous rock star's hair. Sam's was long, bushy, and thicker than it should have been for someone of his age.

"Mr. Greene?"

"Please come in. You must be from the police." The charm was starting already. "My wife is out, so it's just us. You can follow me into the living room."

He led the way as they moved across the granite stone entry floor and into a large living area. The spacious room was decorated with several separate seating areas on expensive looking oriental carpets. Unlike the house, the furniture was traditional. There was a faint odour of tobacco smoke; unmistakable, all the more so since it had become so rare in the city, at least indoors.

"Would you like some coffee or tea?" Sam asked, extending his hands palms up. "It's no trouble."

"Thanks, no." Robert spoke for both. "No children or servants around?" Robert already knew the answer to this question, but asked it anyway, like a good lawyer would.

"I don't have any children, and the help only come in

occasionally when needed. Please have a seat over here by the window."

The sofa that Sam indicated faced a beautiful part of the garden outside. A bluestone walk enclosed a water feature while on the outer edges a border of dark green kinnikinnick with red berries surrounded the path. It was a partially sunny day, and the sun reflected off the water feature into Robert and Camille's faces. They knew why Sam had placed them on this sofa.

"When did your dog go missing?" Robert went to the heart of the matter, trying to ignore the dancing sunlight in his eyes.

Sam looked slightly pained, but responded, "The weekend, Saturday afternoon."

"Where were you when he went missing?"

"Pacific Spirit Park. I walk the trails with Lucky for exercise."

"Pacific Spirit Park?"

"You know, the park at the end of our street." Sam pointed west.

"I thought it was called the University Endowment Lands."

"Not for some time. How long have you lived in Vancouver, anyway?"

Robert immediately started to get angry, both with Sam, and the fact that people kept changing names of places. It was the kind of minor annoyance that drove Robert crazy. He forced himself to ignore the jibe and continued.

"Lucky is the dog? Sorry, was the dog?"

"Yes."

"I assume he wandered off?"

"I always take him off-leash when I am on the trails."

"You realize it's a little dangerous in there?" Robert asked, hoping to provoke something. "People have gone missing permanently on those paths."

"So, I've heard, but I can take care of myself."

"Yeah, they all say that until something bad happens. Your dog seemed to have been hit by something. We assume it was a vehicle of some kind."

Sam squinted at them. "I don't understand." His hands were rubbing each other nervously.

Camille spoke at last, also having trouble with the sunlight, "Have you noticed anything unusual around your home or neighbourhood lately?"

"No."

"Would you say the dog is yours or your wife's?"

"It's my dog. My wife didn't like it at all." That was unequivocal.

"Enemies?" This from Robert.

"What?"

Robert loved it when people started playing silly buggers. It usually meant they had something to hide. "Do you have any enemies?" This came out loudly.

"I won't say everybody loves me, but no, no enemies that I can think of." The hand rubbing continued unabated.

"That would be unusual for a developer in this city. From what I know, it is a very competitive business."

Sam declined to comment on this thought, so Robert

continued. "Do you know any of the kitchen staff at the Restaurant of Earthly Delights?"

"No. Why would I?" Sam responded with a hint of indignation.

"Someone is after you, or at the least trying to make you look bad, so you are going to have to bear with us as we make our enquiries." Robert had had enough and stood up. Camille followed suit.

"We'll be in touch." Robert said as he started back to the entry hall.

"So, you don't know who did this?" Sam complained to their backs.

"Not yet, but I'm sure we'll get to the bottom of it soon. Thanks for your time." Camille and Robert left Sam standing in the hall, a puzzled expression on his face. Robert figured it would be only a matter of time before he heard from Steve about this interview. Mr. Greene looked angry when the officers left.

Robert and Camille slowly walked out the front door and down the steps to the curb.

"Let's take a stroll around here, see what the neighbourhood is like. Leave the car a bit longer so more people might notice it." Robert said. Together, they strolled around the block once. When they arrived back at the car and got into it, Robert saw Mr. Greene in the window watching them. He didn't look happy.

* * *

A couple of days later, the inevitable happened. Robert was summoned for another sit down with Steve. Even though Robert had a fair idea what was going to be said, he held his tongue, waiting for steam to be let off on the other side of the desk. Steve was looking natty in a new beige suit that looked like it came right off the rack of one of the cheapest clothiers in the city.

"I have given you how many, nine extra officers for this problem? I'm not seeing results." Steve was spluttering. "And now I've found out that you have been out to Southlands insulting one of the major developers in this city! My superiors are not pleased with how this is all going, Robert. And if they are not happy, I am the one who gets the crap."

Robert was impressed that Steve knew how many people he had put on the case but decided to keep things general. "We think all the events are connected, and the team is conducting the research we need to build up the case. Once we have the suspect, we don't want him walking away because our case isn't as tight as it should be, correct?"

Steve reluctantly agreed. Nothing more embarrassing than to have a case fall apart because of shoddy police work. "I guess."

"It's going to take a little longer to come up with a suspect, but this Mr. Greene is no prince, and the list of people who have it in for him might be pretty long. We'll come up with someone soon." Robert didn't normally like to put himself behind the eight ball like that, but he had to respond with something. He was already kicking himself.

"Keep me informed," was Steve's snappy comeback.

Robert hated it when he painted himself into a corner.

Always better to hold your tongue. He kept telling himself this, and then would do the opposite. Maybe my brain isn't wired correctly, or maybe it's just a human condition. I'll have to meditate on that one some day soon, he thought, maybe when the case is finished.

* * *

Bernard Lily, the reporter, had been out to the Gardens again late Monday. He knew the police had been out there again but didn't know why. He sprung for the price of admission to see if he could talk to any of the groundskeepers on the sly. After about twenty minutes, he came across one of them working off the path, so Bernard approached him. It turned out to be Nate, and he wasn't shy about talking, even after the chewing out by Marty a few days earlier. He told Bernard about the dog discovered in the maze. After all, a couple of visitors had found it, so it was no big secret as far as Nate was concerned. Nate didn't know about the connection to Sam Greene, so that nugget didn't make it into the story. Bernard thanked him, then asked Nate to call him if anything else happened or came to mind. Satisfied that he had enough for another pot boiler, Bernard got into his co-op car and drove back to False Creek to write up the latest instalment in the Eden Gardens saga. By the end of the week, the dog stories were circulating in the media, and in the gossip salons all over the city.

~ 13 ~

Eighteen Months Earlier

On the east side of Vancouver, a young couple had become latest victims of West Coast development results. Several years ago, they had scraped together every last dollar they could find to get a down payment for a condominium in a project being developed by a company called Windfall Ventures. It would be a windfall alright, but not for the people lining up to put their hard-earned cash down.

The couple had qualified for the maximum mortgage possible given their earnings and were ecstatic to finally get into the Vancouver housing market as owners. The thrill lasted a couple of months until they realized how screwed up their lifestyle had become. Most of their money was going to the mortgage, and their 'urban hipster' lifestyle was fast becoming a 'stay at home eating macaroni' lifestyle. Meanwhile, disaster crept up on them.

About three years into their thirty-year mortgage, the wife was standing at the living room window looking out at the traffic driving by on Main Street on a Saturday morning. Something near the window caught her eye. "What is this black stuff?"

"What are you looking at?" Her partner slowly got up and shuffled over to the window, where she was pointing at something black and evil on the side of the window frame. "That looks like mould to me."

Thus started the downward spiral for the couple. A few other owners in their building spotted the same problem. After some condo board meetings and an investigation by a consulting company specializing in this sort of tragedy, the board had no choice but to enact a special levy so that the entire face of the building could be ripped apart and re-installed. The problem was rainwater finding its way into the walls and sitting there until mould formed. It had happened in a couple of locations in the building, but the only solution was to re-build all the exterior walls. This was the repair every time a problem of this type was discovered, no matter how isolated the leaks appeared to be. Some consulting firms made their living off this and limited intervention wasn't in their vocabulary, probably as a result of a few talks with lawyers.

The young couple had no family to fall back on for an extra loan to cover this unforeseen problem. They also couldn't sell their unit because who was going to buy a leaky condo? Windfall Ventures had long since ceased to exist, as had the holding company that owned it. After the bank foreclosed on them, their only option was bankruptcy.

Present Day

At Cambie Street, a couple of weeks passed with no identifiable progress made by Robert's team. Dead lead after dead lead was examined and found wanting. Robert had caught up on some of his other cases but was perplexed at the lack of progress on the Eden Gardens case. Finally, Camille told Robert that she had enough to tell a tale. There was more to do, but a picture was emerging. After lunch, she gave Tony a look that beckoned him and they went into Robert's office.

Camille started off, smiling. "We've had two of the extra officers on the team helping us, Michael and Janice. They seem to be diligent and know what they're doing, unlike some of the other officers on loan. It's like a miracle. If it were closer to Christmas, I'd call it a Christmas miracle."

"Fantastic, I love miracles." Robert said. "What do you two have?"

"We have a lot to tell. Sam Greene is a big wheel in the development community, with a long history of projects all over the city. The projects seem to be mostly residential, with some retail stores thrown in. He has a sister who is active in the horticultural area. That's how he started his connection with VanDusen Gardens. The Gardens were probably looking for some fund-raising moxie to help them out and asked him to join the board of directors. From there, it only took a year before they realized what they had acquired, and he subsequently got voted off the board. They are always looking for funding, and a successful developer probably looked like gold to them."

"It all sounds like a fairy tale so far. What's going wrong?"

"What's going wrong is that Sam seems to be on the bad side of the development spectrum. Most of his projects have run into trouble at some point after they were completed. From what we have found, a good number have had leaks and other problems. More than a few buyers of his condos have had to declare bankruptcy because they couldn't come up with the extra money needed to fix the problems in their buildings. In other words, the developer is long gone, and the buyers are on their own."

"That's not good for us. Instead of narrowing the field of suspects, the opposite has happened. Crikey."

Camille wondered where Robert got these expressions from. It wasn't like he was born in England, as far as she knew. She shook her head. "I don't think a lot of the victims know that Sam is behind their problems, but I am guessing a few have figured it out. So, we have a plausible motive, but no real idea of who the culprit might be. Mr. Greene has been pretty good at obscuring his involvement in these projects through the use of several levels of companies that sort of own each other. It's enough to give you a headache following it all through. Each project has taken a lot of research to sort through all the intermediary companies that he obviously set up to deflect liability."

Camille continued. "Developing property in Vancouver is apparently not for the faint of heart. It takes finances, time, knowledge, and, in Sam's case, tons of guile. There are good developers and bad developers. Sam apparently belongs to the latter group."

"We've learned that he seems to have a formula, which is actually followed by more than a few developers—he just takes it farther than many would in order to line his pockets a bit more. He starts by hiring the cheapest architects he can find, and then grinds their fees down to a level where, by extension, they have to hire the cheapest engineering sub-consultants they can find. Sam also makes sure the architects directly hire as many of the sub-consultants as possible, thereby keeping more legal liability away from himself. He then repeats this process with the general contractor, hiring the cheapest one, and by extension, the cheapest sub-contractors. Once the project is ready to build, he gets the team together and asks them to find several hundred thousand dollars in savings, telling them he will cancel the project without these savings. Of course, with that threat, the savings are always found, and the project continues, by now so bereft of anything resembling quality that it would make you weep. It isn't that all these other people are trying to do a lousy job, on the contrary, but poor quality is one of the inevitable results of not spending the necessary amount of money." Camille wrapped this portion up with, "We have talked with a few architects and other consultants. They requested anonymity as they told us this."

She wasn't finished. "But wait, there's more. The one company that Sam does pay properly is the marketing group. How otherwise is he going to sell this shit? For a little extra zip to the deal, he will sometimes forget to pay the last consultant invoices. It seems as though he isn't worried about not finding someone to design the next project; there is always another firm desperate enough to do it on his terms. By the time the owners are taking possession of their bright sparkly new condo units, they are probably already leaking. The effects of the leaks just won't be apparent until a few years later, long after Sam had dissolved the company that he had formed to develop the project in the first place and the warranty period has elapsed."

Robert was shaking his head, but apparently Camille still wasn't done. "We also talked with another type of consultant, one that provides expertise on how water is kept out of buildings. This type of consultant didn't even exist a couple of decades ago. He told us something everyone kind of knows already, that Vancouver is situated on the edge of a coastal rainforest, where trees are born, grow, then die and break down, starting the process over again. The constant rain generates rot on a herculean scale. When the bright sparks in Ottawa, a world away from the rain forest, decided it would be great to seal up all buildings across the country so that energy would be saved, they didn't anticipate the catastrophe that it would precipitate in the Lower Mainland. When this was combined with a provincial mantra to use wood first as a construction material, because, after all, isn't that what British Columbia has the most of? Disaster struck."

"Older buildings built before the mandated changes, which came about in the late eighties by the way, leaked just like the new buildings, but they dried out, not being sealed up like leftovers in a fridge. The newer buildings kept the water inside their walls once it entered, and it always entered somehow. Rot and mould were the inevitable outcomes. Sam probably didn't even understand the problem and could not have cared less about it anyway. He builds his buildings with wood because it is the cheapest way to build."

She concluded with, "If, on occasion, some enterprising soul somehow managed to find out that Sam was actually the guy behind the company that didn't exist anymore, he just told them to take a hike and contact his lawyer."

Tony added, "We are learning way more about developers in Vancouver than we would ever want to. Sure makes you think twice about buying a new condo. I think I'll continue renting my place." Camille nodded in agreement.

"I don't think all the developers are like Sam, but someone has a bee in their bonnet, so we need to dig a little deeper. Anything learned from the employee list at the Gardens?" Robert asked.

"Not yet, but we think we have a comprehensive list of current and former employees from the last eight years. We are going through them starting with the most recent to see if anyone has a grudge. It is going to be hard, though. It's not like Sam has direct contact with any of the employees, at least that we can find so far."

Robert nodded and started thinking about rewarding his crew. "Let's go. I'm buying coffee. That was good work, Camille, very comprehensive." The three of them walked outside and up to Café Paulo, where they sat at his favourite table by the window facing Cambie Street.

Robert returned to the counter and ordered coffees from Gilberto. After a fair exchange of gossip with the proprietor, he brought them over to the table. All three sat back, thinking while they sipped their drinks.

"We have some pissed off condo buyers who might want a piece of Sam, if they even knew he was the one behind their woes. But we also have some events at Eden Gardens that look like inside work," Robert mused. "Nothing was broken to get into the barn or restaurant. It speaks to someone who has keys and knows their way around. So, for now, put the smartest people on the employees list. The rest of them can do research on the condo owners. That should keep them busy for a while."

Camille said, "One thing that is not apparent is where Sam got his land from. What I am learning is that land seems to be key to a developer's success." She was picking things up fast, Robert thought. His wife, Susan, had told him basically the same thing.

"Good point. Maybe you two could dig a little deeper on the land end of things. Figure exactly which projects Sam Greene had a hand in and then look through land titles. But be careful, like I said before. I don't want Mr. Greene to know what we are doing." Robert concluded. "Sweets anyone? No? Let's get back then." He piled up their cups and brought them back to the counter, waving goodbye to Gilberto.

Robert thought that he might have to call a planner at the city for assistance. His wife had worked there long enough that Robert was familiar with a couple of names he could contact. It looked like they had to go further back in history to see what Mr. Greene had been up to in the City of Vancouver.

* * *

The coroner's review of Lucky's death came up with a verdict of blunt force trauma. The best explanation was that he had been hit by a vehicle; so maybe an accident, or maybe purposely, it was impossible to tell, but after the discovery of where Lucky ended up, the accident verdict probably didn't make sense.

With that news and Camille and Tony's report about Sam's development career, Robert decided it was time to make a second visit out to see Sam Greene. He took Camille along again, as it was always good to have a witness if things went off the rails. To change things up, they drove in Robert's car, not the Crown Victoria. This wasn't strictly countenanced by the police department, but Robert liked to keep people off balance whenever he could.

This time Sam's wife, Lydia, answered the door. There were obvious trophy aspects to Lydia. The large breasts and ample ass were not all that surprising. She had long streaked blond hair and looked to be at least twenty-five years younger than Mr. Greene. Robert didn't consider Lydia especially beautiful. She had more of a country girl face, with clear skin and blue eyes. She was decked out in designer jeans and a crimson blouse bright enough to make your eyes water. Silver bangles of a quantity to sink a small barge were hanging off her right arm. Her appearance seemed to be the beneficiary of a lot of money, not surprisingly.

"Please come in," Lydia offered. She seemed nervous, but that was to be expected when cops showed up in your house. Again, they were led into the living room. Sam Greene was sitting there, wearing a very snazzy suit—it looked Italian, if Robert knew anything about suits. He was still missing his socks. Robert assumed it was a fashion thing that he had no hope of understanding. After they took their seats, on a different couch this time, they started the questions.

"We were wondering if you remembered anything else about the days leading up to your dog's disappearance?" Robert began.

"I thought you were coming to tell us you had solved the murder of my dog." This helpful opening from Sam.

"We wouldn't have wasted our time coming out here just to tell you that." What a wanker, Robert thought. "We're still investigating, but it may or may not be a killing here. The likely cause of death was being hit by a vehicle."

"What about the van?" Lydia asked.

"What van?" Sam looked at Lydia.

"The van that I'd see up the street from the living room window. It always seemed to be around on weekends. It was really old and beat-up, unlike most of the vehicles in our neighbourhood. It also didn't have any insignias or company logos that I could see. But I never saw who was driving it. It would stay awhile and then leave."

Sam was looking at Lydia like this was all news to him.

"Can you give us a description? A make or colour?

Licence plate number, perhaps?" This from Camille. This sounded like the break they had been waiting for.

"Not really. It was tan coloured and had a lot of dents. It didn't belong here. I do remember that it didn't have any names on it or anything like that."

"Okay. We may have a photo of a van for you to look at, if you wouldn't mind coming down to the station." Camille asked politely. "Have you seen it since the dog disappeared?"

"No." Lydia was fidgeting nervously.

"She's not going to any station." Another helpful offering from Sam.

"If we want her down to the station, that is where she will come." Robert's eyes were drilling holes into Sam's head. Robert then decided that it wasn't the moment to get heavier, although he really wanted to. "I'm feeling extra nice today, so we'll bring the photo back out here. We'll call before we come."

"Fine." Sam answered, Lydia having lost her ability to speak, apparently.

Robert and Camille left before they lost their tempers any further. As they got into their car, Camille mentioned Lydia's nervousness. "I wonder if she is the smoker in the house?"

"Yah, probably. I can't imagine any of the help smoking in there. They'd be out on their ears if they did. Maybe she smokes and Sam disapproves." It was something additional to mull over.

"This van could be the link. It would be nice if we had a picture of the plates. This whole investigation would be wrapped up." Robert was thinking aloud. He started the engine and after a few backfires, the Honda slowly made its way up the street. Maybe it was time to get the Silver Streak serviced.

When they got back to Cambie Street, Robert went into his office and got on the phone with his kids. Robin answered. "You know why I'm calling." Robert said.

"How about barbecued chicken tonight? I don't think we have any chicken in the fridge, though."

"Yup, no problem. Do we have enough vegetables?" There was a high-end grocery store a couple of blocks from the police station.

"I think so. We've got potatoes."

"I'll grab a bird and see you at home soon." Why was it that most kids equated vegetables with potatoes? Technically, they were vegetables, but that really wasn't what Robert had in mind when he asked the question. Robert went for a walk to procure the chicken, added some green beans, and then drove home.

"Hey kids," Robert yelled at the upstairs when he arrived. "If you do the potatoes, I'll get the chicken going."

"Okay, be down in a bit," Sophie yelled back.

After Robert prepared all the tools he would need, he cut the back out of the bird, oiled it, and added salt and pepper, laying it out flat on a large plate ready to do its duty. He then went outside, lit the charcoal in his barbecue, and while it stoked up, he prepared hickory chips in a foil packet. Once the fire was going, he dropped the chicken on the grill to the side where the fire wasn't, put the wood chip package over the fire and closed the lid.

Then he went back inside to drink some wine and supervise the potato production. A little over an hour and a couple of glasses of wine later, the food was ready for the feast.

Nobody was complaining about the chicken, but the table conversation with the children was stilted again. Robert figured a discussion with the kids was in order soon, but not yet. He was still pre-occupied with the case and was thinking things through. After dinner was over and the kids had gone up to work on their homework (hopefully), Robert loaded the dishwasher and then sat on the sofa, contemplating life and thinking about Susan. I wonder what's wrong with those kids, he asked himself.

"Probably a problem at school." Susan answered. That could be, Robert thought. Other than home, it was the main thing they had in common.

* * *

The next day at work, Robert looked at his in-basket later in the morning and decided that he didn't like what he saw, so after an early lunch he walked back right past the police station and headed down to the Creek. The weather continued to be a pain, with a light drizzle coming down, the air heavy with humidity. Grouse Mountain on the North Shore didn't look like it would be making an appearance at all today. A silky grey mist shrouded half of the downtown towers.

All this was fine with Robert. He never had a problem with rain. Other people, especially those with the seasonal affliction who found the rain so depressing, probably shouldn't be living in Vancouver, he thought. If one became sick of the rain, a short trip either east or north of Vancouver in the winter months would bring you face to face with real cold and snow, a trip Robert never felt the need to make. He was just fine without the white stuff.

As scolding crows crossed back and forth above his head, Robert was narrowing his suspect list. He was pretty sure it would have to be someone from the groundskeeper staff, someone off the lists that Camille was compiling. Who else could gain access to the barn and service areas so easily? Although Miguel could be on the list because of his previous encounter with human bodies, a motive just didn't present itself for his actions. That encounter was so long ago that it was almost like another lifetime, something to forget, not to revive.

Robert was heading west today, toward the Granville Street Bridge, and past the False Creek low-rise condos and co-ops built in the 1970s. In Robert's eyes, the apparent disparity in density of development compared to the north side of the Creek presented itself as a target. Most people wouldn't even notice this, but he had been conditioned by his wife to at least consider such things. The zoning for the area was probably protected by the city, but Robert could easily imagine a developer making a case for some more housing to be planted there. Even the city planners were probably thinking along the same lines as they came up with ways to densify the city. Planners were always trying to get more people living downtown, and frankly, land was running out fast, even the poorer sites. Hard to develop sites or sites with well-known problems were slowly working their way to the top of the list of available land. It all only continued to drive the price higher for housing in Vancouver. Being built in the nineteen-seventies, he assumed that the homes he was looking at wouldn't have the mould problems that later developments had but didn't know this for sure.

As he ambled along the path, he realized the team needed to find someone hired in the last five years. The suspect knew Miguel's story and tried to take advantage of it. That the Gardens took on summer help each year would make the number of people to be checked on the long side. But wasn't that what police work was all about, the exhaustive and dogged pursuit of the facts? Not very glamorous, but that was why he had help. He turned around well short of the east tip of Granville Island and made his way slowly back to the office.

While returning, he remembered that he should call the planner he knew to see what information, if any, he could glean. Back in his office, he called Jean Kwok, who had worked with his wife.

"Hello Jean."

"How are you doing, Robert? How are the kids?"

"They are fine, Jean. Thanks for asking. And your family?" They made small talk for a few minutes before Robert came to the point of his call. "I'm trying to learn something about development in the city." Robert explained about what the police were doing and asked what Mr. Greene was like.

"Good for you, and good luck with your case. This will

take a while because it's sort of complicated. Mr. Greene is also one P.O.W."

"What?"

"You know, a piece of work."

"Why do you say that?"

"Because every time it came to the point of arranging a development agreement for a particular project, Sam would bring his lawyers to the meetings and make life hell for everyone working on the agreement. We would ask him to not bring his lawyers, that there was a time and place for that, but he would ignore us. He also didn't want to give much toward the community obligations that are part of all projects. We would have to explain that he wouldn't get any permits until this was ironed out. He would always go over our head and try to get someone higher up, even a councillor, to squash us so he could get his way. Each time was the same. It was as if he had never developed a project in Vancouver before and was somehow special. Neither I nor your wife could stomach dealing with him. He mostly wouldn't get his way, but the whole process was not good."

"That bad, eh?" Robert said.

"No, not entirely, but he seemed intent on being a bully. He seemed to relish it. Maybe it made him feel more influential than he really is. I don't know."

Robert thought for a while. "We're also finding out things about Mr. Greene that make him seem a bit slimy. Do you know his history by chance?"

"Not really. I know he was born and raised in Vancouver, but that's about it. There were a few rumours about how he accumulated his land, but they were just gossip as far as I could determine."

"Do you remember what kind of rumours?"

"Some say he fleeced somebody to get the land, but again, no one could pin anything on him."

Robert told Jean a bit of what they had learned about Sam's developments. "He seems to be a piece of society that Vancouver's housing market might be better off without. Bad enough that all the money flooding into Vancouver makes it harder and harder to afford anything, but to have someone building what amounts to garbage seems to be a sort of crime all by itself." Robert's mood was getting darker by the minute. "What drives people to be like this? Is it greed? Or a large sense of entitlement?"

"Not everyone is like that, Robert." Jean then added, "Your kids are in high school now, correct?"

"Yes. It's a bit of a struggle at times, but good."

"I think about you guys often."

"Thanks Jean, and thanks for your insight. It helps."

"There is something else you might like to know. A while back, maybe a year ago, we were getting calls from a person trying to find out if Mr. Greene was the developer of the Windfall project. Eventually I told him yes, to get him off our back. I haven't heard from him since."

"Did he give a name?"

"No."

"What is the Windfall project?"

"It is another one of those unfortunate leaky condo projects."

"Thanks Jean, for your help. If you by chance hear from this guy again, let me know, okay?"

"Will do Robert, bye."

Someone was trying to find out if Sam was behind a bad project. It could be their perpetrator, or not. They needed more.

***

That same afternoon, Camille phoned Lydia, "Hi, I have some pictures of a van that may be the one you saw on your street. Can I come and show them to you?"

The pictures were fuzzy and dark, but Camille was hopeful. She parked in front of the house and went up to ring the doorbell. Lydia answered. She was dressed up in fancy workout clothing. Camille exercised at the office gym but wondered what people living on the tony side did to keep in shape.

"Going to the gym?" Camille asked.

"No, I was doing some yoga. There is a program on TV that I follow sometimes."

Camille didn't know how to respond, so she said, "Well, it's always good to get some exercise, isn't it?"

"Please come in."

Camille entered and when they got to the kitchen table, and after deflecting the offer of coffee, she carefully laid out three photos taken from the lane cameras behind Hastings Street. Lydia spent a minute examining them before finally answering.

"I think it's the same van. I'm pretty sure. The dent at

the back looks the same as the one on the van that parked down the street."

Not exactly ironclad, Camille was thinking, but it was probably as good as it was going to get with this lady.

"Is this the guy who killed Sam's dog?"

"Not the family dog?"

"I couldn't stand that dog. Sam bought it without my input at all." Lydia's were glinting as she answered.

"Okay." Camille said slowly, "We don't know yet if the van person is the one responsible, but thanks for the help, I'll let myself out. You said you only saw the van on the weekends, correct?"

"Yes."

Camille gathered up the photos and got ready to leave. "You don't have any security cameras looking out on the street, do you?"

"No, we have one on our front porch and at the back where we park the cars. That's it. Some of our neighbours probably have cameras as well."

"Ok, thought I'd ask," said Camille before she walked out the front door. As she headed to her car, she looked at the other houses along the street.

After Camille returned to the precinct, she went into Robert's office. "Might be a good idea to do a canvass of the street that Sam lives on. See if anyone else remembers the van or has seen who was driving it. It seemed to be parked on the street only on the weekends, from what Lydia said. And maybe check for security footage if anyone has it."

"Make it so." Robert said. "Send those others out there,

all three of them. I've heard rumours that the last six cops added by Steve might get pulled off our team soon anyway, so leave them out of it. It should shake up the neighbourhood a little, having three cops go door to door." Robert wasn't overly optimistic about learning anything this way. It didn't appear there were many people around that neighbourhood. It was the time of year for visits to Mexico and Hawaii for that crowd.

~ 14 ~

By mid-November, the Eden Gardens affair had died back. There were no further stories in the papers, and as far as the public knew, the police didn't seem to have any suspects. Maybe they had fallen asleep or were out chasing drug lords.

Robert's team, however, had made some progress on possible suspects from the current and former employee list. They were a diverse group of people, mostly men, who still lived in Vancouver or the surrounding cities as far as the VPD knew. The team hadn't found the connection to Sam Greene. This was proving harder to determine. Robert was certain that they were looking for a man, not a woman. How Stan had been handled in the alley near the start of this investigation pretty much told the story. The tree falling was another arrow pointing at a male, either that, or a very strong female. But Robert also knew that wrong assumptions could lead them down a long dead-end path if the team wasn't diligent and thorough.

The other area his team had started examining was Mr. Greene's family. Half the time in cases such as these, it was some angry relative who was behind the crimes. In

Sam's case, this might run to a whole bunch of people unhappy with him. In Robert's eyes, Mr. Greene didn't seem to be the warm and fuzzy type, and if he treated his family the way he treated others, then bingo—maybe. Robert also hadn't forgotten the two divorces that Mr. Greene had gone through. Camille had managed to run down the locations of the two ex-wives. One was alive and the other one was dead, now residing in Mountain View Cemetery in the centre of Vancouver.

Why was it that after all the excitement and events of October, nothing further seemed to have happened? Could the perpetrator be away, out of the city? Would they return, only to unleash new crimes and mayhem? This was getting to be so outside the norm for criminal cases that maybe they were dealing with a mentally unstable person. I am losing my way with this case, he thought. The gangland stuff that I was used to working on is looking pretty good now. At least I would know who was doing what and why, even if proof was awfully hard to come up with.

One thing he was certain of, and that was his need for some coffee. He slipped on his jacket and as he went out into the office area, he nodded to Camille, who promptly joined him. This time they walked past Café Sao Paulo up to one of the chain shops for a drip coffee. Robert wanted something to linger over while he thought. After he had paid for the coffees and a pastry for each of them, they went to sit down.

"Any sharp ideas, Camille?" He was trying hard not to stare at Camille. He wasn't succeeding very well. What he really wanted with Camille had nothing to do with the case.

"I did some research into Sam's exes. His first wife died from a car accident in Vancouver, a hit and run. Unsolved to this day. I went over to the cemetery to check on her and she was there. The place is called Mountain View and they are not kidding; the views are stupendous, if you are alive, that is. Sam's second wife seems to have left town, now living in Calgary. Perhaps she fancied her life options in another city, or maybe she just liked being alive, period. I tried to contact her, with no success. I still think one of the staff is the more likely option. Even if it was some relative or an ex, that wouldn't explain how they could move around so easily at night and access certain areas. And if the sole surviving ex-wife isn't even around, then...."

"Yeah. Good coffee today." Robert's attention was drifting.

"What?"

"You know, some days the drip coffee isn't so good. It's a hit-or-miss thing I find. Today is a good day."

Camille rolled her eyes. Robert wondered if one day they might just roll right out onto the table.

"Grabbing a dog out in the Endowment Lands is not an easy trick, either. You'd have to do it quietly, and not be seen by other walkers or runners." Camille started back in.

"Agreed."

Good, Camille thought, back on track.

"The butter tart seems over sweet today. What do you think?"

"Sweet mother of pearl. Are you nuts?" Camille answered, "I like it."

"Good. Let's get back and convene a meeting with our small team. We need to summarize where we've been and where we are going. I can feel Steve getting itchy again." Robert the detective was back.

Once they returned to the office, they grabbed Tony, Lawrence, Winnie, and Erwin, who was the last of the threesome that Steve had kindly donated to Robert for the investigation. All of them entered the meeting room, sat down, and looked at the large white board with its pictures, drawings, and lines connecting some items. Tony was drumming his fingers on the table. The others were sitting still, barely moving a muscle.

"Steve is going on a holiday next week, so he wants a report before he leaves." Robert led off. "I'll write something up tomorrow for him. Where do we stand? Steve seems to have lightened up a bit the last couple of weeks. I suppose it helps that nothing further has happened."

Tony started, "We got the final report back on the dog. It had been hit by something, probably a vehicle. We are not sure how that could have happened out in the park where Sam walks. The toxicology report told us nothing."

"It speaks to some rage, I think. Someone who lost control a little. Agreed?" Said Robert.

"I agree," said Camille

"Which makes the hiatus in events all the more strange. I would think that someone who is this angry would keep going."

"Maybe they're gearing up for something bigger?" This from Lawrence.

"Unfortunately, you might have something there. Either that, or the steam has dissipated. Maybe they've given up." These new guys aren't so dumb after all, Robert thought, which was a bonus as far as he was concerned. "Any more progress on the suspect list?"

Camille took a deep breath and summarized. "We've got three lists going. The A list has about seventeen staff members on it, mostly former staff, but we still have Marty and Miguel on it. The B list has some relatives on it and exes, and the C list has a few condo owners who haven't made out too well after experiencing the 'Greene' effect. Tony and I are concentrating on the A list while the other three are looking into the others. We're still looking for a motive and a connection."

"No sign of the van, I assume?"

"No. But we have the word out. When I went out to visit Sam's wife, I found out that she hated his dog."

There was silence while this was digested. "Anybody have anything else?"

More silence. "Ok then, I'll write this up tomorrow for Steve's vacation reading."

The meeting ended and Robert headed back to his office to ponder his inability to make any headway on the case. Am I that slow? Am I missing something? The other people on the team must be getting frustrated as well, he thought. He just hoped that Lawrence wouldn't be correct. He started to tap out the report for Steve on his laptop but gave up and decided to head home.

***

As he was getting ready to leave, his cellphone rang.

Sophie was on the line, "Hey Dad, think we could have pizza tonight?"

"Good thinking, I'm just leaving. I'll stop by the usual place for some takeout, okay?"

"Great, I'll tell Robin."

Excellent, he thought, this was the kind of executive level thinking that he was trying to install in his kids. He called the pizza place that they normally used when he wasn't making it from scratch, and right after he hung up, his phone rang again.

"Robert Lui?"

"Yes. Who is this?"

"It's Maria Esmeraldo. My daughter Rose attends school with Sophie."

Since Robert had just been talking to Sophie, he knew it couldn't be an emergency. "Yes?"

"Rose just told me something that I think you should know. Sophie told Rose that some students at their school had been approaching her, as well as Robin, about joining a gang. They've been getting pressure."

"Jeez, no wonder they've been quiet the last few weeks. I'll talk to them." He paused for a few seconds. "And I won't mention Rose's name. Thanks Maria, I really appreciate your call." He hung up and sat there a few minutes considering how his life was not getting any simpler, then left the office.

Robert slid into his car, switched the radio from CBC

to the local country station, and swung out onto the lane leading to Yukon Street, then headed east on 2nd Avenue for home. After picking up the two pizzas, he drove up the lane behind their townhouse and parked next to the garden. He sat in the car considering how to approach this without making Sophie think her friend ratted her out. Telling Rose was Sophie's way of getting the word out, he figured. It isn't good, walking around with that kind of thing hanging over you. Robert decided to talk things out before they ate, so he called for them when he walked through the door.

"Hi Pops." Robin bounced into the room. Sophie wasn't far behind.

"Hey you two." He started in as he was taking his coat off. "I heard some unsettling news about your school at the station today. Apparently, some students are trying to do some recruiting for gangs. If you run up against it, just say no. I'm going to talk with the authorities there. There is an anti-gang group that goes around from school to school. They'll know how to handle it." He paused. "Have they tried it on you guys?"

Sophie looked at Robin before answering, "Actually, they have. They promised us stuff and threatened us as well."

Robert felt his jaw clench. "Doing it outside or inside the school is crossing a line. I will deal with this. I'm not going to ask you the names of the students threatening you, at least not yet, but it could very well come to that. I assume that you are not the only ones they are targeting, but we'll see." He waited, then, "Robin, anything to add?"

Robin looked relieved. "They said that they know our dad is a cop."

"And that didn't put them off, did it?"

"I don't think so."

"What they forget is that not only am I a cop, but I'm part of a large police force. They're going to regret playing this game." He added, "You guys know you can talk to me, right? I know talking to your parent when you're a teenager sucks, but sometimes I can actually help. Yes?"

"You're right, Dad," Sophie responded. She looked suddenly better.

"Ok, let's eat. Who wants what?"

Sophie got some plates out and the two children appeared to be happier as they chattered back and forth, starting in on the pizza. Robert was under no illusion that the next year or two was going to be easy, however. He had an appointment to make with the gang squad. Joining that Special Enforcement Unit might not have been my most brilliant idea to date, he thought. The gang's tentacles were everywhere. Well, I'm going to do something about it. Family was off-limits and those scum were going to have to understand that.

Later that evening, after everyone had retired to their bedrooms, Robert lay in bed, wide awake. If I am being brutally honest with myself, I haven't done any better than my kids. In fact, worse I would say, considering my so-called maturity. He considered what he had said earlier that evening. I haven't told them everything about the reasons behind leaving the task force. I haven't even told the task force what happened, and it looked as though it was coming home to roost at my doorstep. If he had handled his end a little better, the kids wouldn't have to go through this—maybe, he thought. He hated hypocrites, and it didn't feel very good realizing that he was joining that group. *I'll have a word with the task force leader tomorrow.* With that decided, he was finally able to fall into a troubled sleep.

* * *

The next day, after Robert arrived at Cambie Street, he had an early decision to make; coffee, or go find the task force leader. Duty won out, at least temporarily, even though he desperately needed some coffee after his restless night. After calling Thomas on his office phone, he walked out and dropped down a floor to the nerve centre of the task force.

He went up to the admin assistant. "Hey Gladys, looking very nice today." She was wearing tailored black slacks with a cream top and a simple gold chain necklace.

"Thanks Robert, to what do we owe this pleasure? How are you doing now that your life is so much simpler?"

"Hah, hah. Very good, Gladys. Don't you read the papers?"

"It all sounds a little like first grade stuff to me."

"We're hoping that's all it amounts to in the end. Still trying to figure it out. How goes the chase down here?"

"It still seems like the wild west out there. I'm not sure if we are winning or losing. Here to see Thomas?"

"Thanks, yes. I just talked to him."

"Go on in. Nice to see you again, Robert. You should

visit more often." Gladys smiled at him, attracted to his mixed racial looks like half the women in the office.

Robert knocked on the door to Thomas's office as he entered.

"Great to see you, Robert." Thomas hadn't been thrilled when Robert had decided to leave the squad, but he found that he couldn't get Robert to change his mind, even after working on him for a few days.

"Hey Tom. Here to see you about my leaving your group."

"No chitchat first?"

"You mean like how crappy the hockey team is doing? Or whether it's going to rain tomorrow? That kind of thing?" Tom had a framed picture on his wall, signed by Trevor Linden, one of the greats from the Canucks' past glory days, when winning hockey games was expected every time they played.

"Ya, no kidding. You seem to be in a mood. Better to talk about something meaningful."

Robert sat down in one of the guest chairs and remained silent for a minute, looking at the floor. "True confession time, Tom. I wasn't entirely candid about my reason for leaving the task force."

Thomas was looking at Robert with a stare that might melt metal.

"Someone threatened me, or more accurately, my kids. I wasn't sure that anyone could protect them properly. So, I made a change."

"That's not how we do things here Robert. You know this." Thomas's stare relaxed.

"You have children Tom. Do you think they could be protected?"

Thomas was silent for a moment, reflecting. "Why are you telling me this now?" But he thought he knew the answer to this already.

"They're coming at me again. I guess I knew this might happen, but I was hoping it wouldn't."

"Well, they don't have anything to lose, do they? They'll look for any crack, any sign of weakness to exploit. And frankly, sounds like you gave them that when you resigned."

"My kids are getting approached in school, both of them. The usual, promises and threats to get them to join a gang. They made it a point of telling my kids that they know who their dad is."

"Not entirely surprising. Sounds like they are being coached. What school are they going to? I can get Surinder to take a visit over there. Those kids who are doing this think they are tough. They'll find out what tough is." Surinder was the head of the anti-gang education unit, and a former gang member himself.

Robert had to agree with Thomas. He wouldn't want to get on the bad side of Surinder. Together, they formalized some details, then Robert got ready to leave. He felt the relief of unburdening one's conscience, but he knew some hard times lay ahead.

"You realize you are always welcome back here."

"Well, if I can't solve this one, not sure I'd be all that useful to you, would I?"

"Good luck on it anyway." Tom added as Robert left.

Robert smiled and headed out for a shot of his favourite beverage.

~ 15 ~

It was a Friday morning, late November, in the Greene household. Not for the first time, Sam and Lydia were starting their day with an argument.

"I was thinking that it might be time to redo the kitchen." Lydia fired the opening salvo.

Sam started laughing. "What is wrong with the one we have? You hardly do any cooking in it, anyway."

"The Jeffries down the street are re-doing theirs."

"Forget it. She can actually cook, whereas you...." The sentence frittered away.

"You know, you can be quite the asshole when you put your mind to it."

Sam ignored this. "I'm thinking of going up the valley to get another dog, maybe a Pit Bull this time."

"You spend more on your stupid dogs than on me, and I am not going to stand around in here with unexploded ordinance. I don't fancy losing an arm or getting my face bitten off. If you bring a Pit Bull in here, I'm leaving."

Sam considered this threat but declined to answer. Instead, he switched topics.

"There is a fundraiser tonight at the Gardens. Raising

some money to help the redo of the restaurant. We're re-branding it, new design, it'll be like a completely new restaurant. I'd like you there."

"I hate those things, all those gardeners yakking about plants and species. Could you come up with anything more boring? Who would attend it anyway, with all the bad things that have happened there?"

"It has sold out, so just show up. It starts at six. You'll have to drive yourself over there. I have meetings all afternoon on that new Falls project I am launching, and I'll head over to Eden after I'm done."

"It had better be a catered affair after what had happened in that kitchen, or I'll be walking out."

"It's catered, don't worry. You'll have a great time," he added insincerely.

Lydia had her doubts but nodded, tired of the arguing.

The fund-raising event had been Sam's idea, enthusiastically supported by some other board members. Nothing further had happened in Gardens since the unfortunate events of October, so people were more relaxed. Sam had put together a team specifically to manage the event, including promoting it to the members and public at large, so that he wouldn't have to do much work.

He had also put feelers out into the design community to come up with a design package for the redo of the restaurant. Several interiors firms had said they were kind of busy, maybe next time. Which was code for 'no way will we work for you, for what you pay'. But a couple of small firms and one-man outfits said they would do it; so, per Sam's traditional methods, he chose the cheapest company and got them working. He was also musing about a name change for the restaurant. Some of the newer board members had brought the idea up as a means to help complete the re-branding and shed the old image. One director had suggested 'Ginkgo Club'. Sam was having some trouble with that one. It sounded too highbrow to him, but he put it down for consideration.

Sam's team, which included a few board members, decided not to wait too long before hosting the dinner because the installation for the Seasonal Lights Festival was getting underway. The organization for the light display was no small thing. The whole city looked forward to fantasy light displays every Christmas season and since Eden was in direct competition with VanDusen, Sam made sure Eden's was bigger and better. However, the restaurant was a small but important source of revenue for the Gardens, so waiting until after Christmas to get going on the renovations was not an option. The committee decided to get the dinner over before the festival started. Holding two major events at the same time seemed overly complex to some of the board members.

* * *

Robert had been monitoring the Eden Gardens fundraiser publicity. As soon as it was announced, he thought it might be an idea to get someone to sit in on the event. Whether this was a good or bad idea, he had yet to decide. Who would go was the next question. He had to figure whether it was better to make a show of it, with himself or Camille going in order to send a message, or to send someone incognito, like Tony. When he brought it up at their weekly meeting, Tony was onboard, like an over friendly puppy.

"Yeah, I'll go. I got a girl I can take." Tony was so keen to get out of uniform, even if only for a night, it was comical.

"Great, but I haven't decided if it is a good or bad idea yet. Any thoughts, you two?"

"If you go, Robert, Mr. Greene might point you out and start in on why the police haven't solved anything yet. There is that to consider." Camille added, "I don't think he likes us very much."

"Tony has been to the Gardens a couple of times. He might be recognized, which would probably be even worse for us," Robert said. "I doubt if the groundskeepers will be there, but has the manager seen his face?"

"No." This from Tony. "I was there when we interviewed the kitchen staff, but the manager wasn't around. The only other times I was there was to interview the groundskeepers. No way they are going to be at a fundraiser. C'mon boss, I know I can do this."

Talk about keen, Robert thought. "Ok, let me ponder this, and I'll let you know. I think it's on a Friday night. Last Friday in November."

The meeting broke up after Camille reported on what the rest of the team was doing. Steve had taken back the six extra officers just as Robert had predicted, so there were only three people working the research angles in addition to the three in the meeting. They hadn't got anywhere with the aggrieved condo owner list. Apparently,

Sam wasn't the only developer in the city building questionable products. One thing the police were all learning was how cautious they would need to be if any of them ever managed to save up a down payment to buy a home instead of renting.

***

Robert speculated that Sam attending a public event at Eden Gardens just might provoke his enemy to try something or even perhaps make an appearance. This idea was plausible enough to Robert that the week before the fundraiser, he decided to have Tony attend, and they purchased a pair of tickets in his name. Waiting too long almost cost them the opportunity. The event was going to be sold out, with some two hundred seats being filled. When Robert told Tony, the smile on Tony's face said it all. Robert warned Tony that the guests attending were going to be on the elderly side, so Tony had better come up with some topics for conversation, or even better, keep his mouth shut.

"No problem boss, and my girlfriend has done some gardening, you know, growing tomatoes."

Robert started to wonder if this was such a good idea after all. Too late, however. Trying to stop Tony now would be like trying to stop a charging bull.

"Tony, just remember that this isn't an Italian Cultural Centre dinner. Some of the owners are from the west side, and things will be a little different. Just stay cool, keep your eyes open, and don't say much, okay?" Robert added, "And enjoy yourself."

"Don't worry, boss, we will."

This was exactly when Robert did start to worry.

~ 16 ~

The day of the fundraiser saw Sam downtown before lunch time, meeting with potential partners about a new east side residential condominium development he had named The Falls. The same group had lunch at a high-end downtown restaurant, with several martinis mixed in amongst the food. At the conclusion, Sam gave Dominic a call. "Everything going to plan?"

"I think so. Tables are set, the caterers are here, and the food and booze have arrived. We're just prepping things, doing the final touches."

"Good, I have another meeting this afternoon, then I'll head over." The dinner was slated to start at six. He texted a couple of people, one to finalize some other preparations, then he went along to his next and last meeting, feeling satisfied. His final meeting was for financing the upcoming project. He, like most developers, never used his own money for a project. Getting the right terms from these financiers was always a pain in the rear, but a necessary step for the ultimate success of the project.

When Sam's last meeting ended on a sour note, he slammed the door on his way out, deciding to head directly over to Eden Gardens. He might have to use alternate financing if he could not get the terms he wanted for his project, which wasn't good. Alternate money always equalled more expensive money.

* * *

Sam swung in off Elliott Street with a mild squeal of his tires, headed up Vivian and parked crookedly in his usual spot north of the entry pavilion's service area, then went in the back way. He walked slowly and carefully up the corridor into the hall where the tables were. Most fundraisers were held in hotels, with round tables of eight or ten seats each. This was different in that there were two long lines of tables, serpentine in pattern, constricted at the middle point where the walls were closer to each other, meaning that the pre-dinner socialization would be more important than normal. Once seated, the only people diners could talk to would be on either side of them and across the table. The pre-dinner drinks and social gabfest were an important part of generating money for the cause. Dominic saw Sam from across the foyer and came over to him. He could tell immediately that Sam was drunk, from his appearance and the odour emanating from his mouth. He also knew that Sam could rebound quickly, no doubt as a result of years of practice.

"How are you doing, Sam?"

"I could use a sit down, I think, before the dinner starts."

No kidding, Dominic thought. "Why don't you take a seat on the couch in my office?"

"Sounds good, I'll be right as rain in a few minutes." Sam then about turned and went back down the corridor to Dominic's office, where he crashed on the sofa. Dominic followed him after a few moments and closed the door. Sam hadn't even bothered to do that.

Dominic returned to the hall to ensure that the floral displays were set up properly. They were the main decorative attraction in the hall. There were small bouquets of chrysanthemums on the dining tables, purposefully left low so people could see each other as they conversed. Huge collections of white and pale-yellow calla-lilies sat in large Grecian urns by the entry and at the glass doors out to the plaza by the lake. A couple of large bouquets of crimson roses with ferns and white lilies of the valley sat in cut crystal vases on two tables against a wall, part of the silent auction that accompanied most fundraisers. The rest of the auction table was laden with various forms of booze, including magnums of wine, always a good way to raise money with any crowd. Several gigantic bouquets of white and mauve tulips graced each of the two bar areas. The scents wafting through the air were intoxicating and underscored the special nature of an event held at Eden Gardens.

Dominic continued with monitoring the preparations until he noticed it was getting close to five. He slid back down the corridor and knocked on his office door. A groggy sounding reply came, so he opened the door a crack.

"Dinner starts in one hour, Sam."

Sam managed to mumble, "Sounds good. I'll go get my suit. Be right back."

***

Just before six, guests started to arrive. Some board members, along with Sam, were greeting people inside the entry as they arrived. Lydia had not shown up yet, but Sam expected this antic. He was all smiles in the receiving lineup and looking more or less sober. About twenty after six, Lydia wandered in and joined Sam at the receiving line.

"Sorry dear. The traffic was bad on Marine Drive," she offered.

Sam ignored her and greeted more guests. The lobby was filling up and the noise level was rising. All the hard surfaces made the noise bounce all over, and it was getting tough to understand what people were saying, especially since a good portion of the people were hard of hearing. The bars were doing fabulously.

A much younger couple came in and up to the receiving group. With their black glistening hair and avant-garde clothing, they looked more like a club was their destination, not a staid dinner.

"Welcome. Are you two members of the Gardens?"

"Not yet, but we're thinking about it. My girlfriend here does a lot of gardening." Tony replied, smiling.

"Good, welcome, and please enjoy the evening."

Tony and Chiara sauntered down the table line and headed for the bar.

"Just one won't hurt, but I need to stay sharp tonight, Chiara. You can drink what you want."

"Don't worry, I intend to, Tony," she was smiling at the prospect of free booze.

Now all they had to do was to find someone remotely close to their age group to converse with at what seemed to be a seniors' convention.

Another young person entered the hall, dressed nicely but by himself, and looking out of place. It was Bernard Lily, the reporter, lately of *VanDay* but now working for the *Vancouver Province*, the morning tabloid in the city. He had convinced his new bosses to fund a ticket to the event so that he could keep tabs on possible hijinks if they happened. The editor was dubious, but eventually agreed to the request in the hopes that Bernard might repeat his first scoop. Though Bernard had visited the Gardens a few times, he had not bumped into Tony, so they were both ignorant of who the other was. Unlike Tony, here to observe, what Bernard had in mind was more in the way of direct action. He would buttonhole Sam Greene at some point later in the proceedings to see if he could get a comment out of him.

At the east end of the hall stood Bernice and William. They had not wanted to come to the fundraiser after the events of October, but a couple of their friends persuaded them otherwise. They reluctantly agreed after all, and were surprised to see how many people were attending. They talked quietly with their friends, discombobulated by all the curves in the table layout.

"I suppose this hall is all supposed to be very, what do

you call it? Green construction? But I think I still prefer the older buildings, don't you?" Bernice asked her friend.

"I couldn't agree more," replied Mildred. "And I don't know about these long tables. I've never seen anything like it, have you?"

"No, but I heard about a similar thing in Winnipeg, something about a long table across a bridge and everyone wearing white. I don't know why we are copying what they come up with in Winnipeg. Thank God we're not wearing white and thank God the tables aren't outside." Bernice was very precise in expressing her opinions.

William picked up the menu and order of service off the closest place setting. The menu had been discussed and reviewed ad nauseam by the organizing committee after October's events. William's first appraisal was of the wines listed on the back of the menu.

"There seems to be some very nice California cabernets as well as some chardonnays from Burgundy. Not inexpensive, however."

"Well dear, it is a fundraiser, after all." Bernice chided William.

"The starters are a hearty Luxembourg salad and a warm hors d'oeuvre. The main is a traditional roast beef with a potato gratin, roasted carrots, and cauliflower. A vegetarian option is apparently also available." William shook his head at that.

He continued. "Dessert is a choice between a molten chocolate pudding and a fruit flan. This all sounds great." He noticed that a couple of complimentary light wines were on every table, but he bet that the drinkers in the crowd would quickly switch to the more expensive wines. They'd be changing not only because their palettes were more refined, but, more importantly, so they could show off in front of their friends and enemies.

Mildred did not know that Bernice and William were the unlucky soup eaters that day in October, but she did know about the excitement of the event from the papers, so she offered this nugget, "So, no soup on offer tonight? I wonder if the people who ate that soup in the Restaurant of Earthly Delights are here?"

Maybe Bernice misheard what Mildred said. No one knows, but Bernice responded in a way she would later regret.

"How did you find out?"

"What?"

"Who told you it was us?" Bernice shrieked.

"What do you mean?" Mildred paused, then said. "I think you just told us!"

William offered this helpful comment, "Calm down, Bernice." Which, of course, had the opposite effect.

"Did you tell Mildred?" This was aimed at William rather loudly. "I don't understand."

"Of course not, dear." said William, who was also getting confused. "Would you like a cocktail?"

At last, something that Bernice did understand. "That would be delightful, dear."

William wandered off toward the bar while Mildred tried to change the subject. "Have you seen the flower displays on the auction table?"

"No. Should we go over there to see them?"

Mildred led Bernice over to the table, all the while contemplating what she had just learned. Of course, she could not wait to tell her other friends that William and Bernice were basically cannibals.

* * *

Most of the crowd was at first off kilter, but this soon got smoothed over with the liberal application of cocktails and wine. Each pair of tickets included a taxi chit for later in the evening, as most of the crowd had no idea about ride-hailing, which had only recently been approved to operate in the city. The organizing committee knew their crowd. As the gathering grew, people were milling about, greeting old friends. Most of the attendees were members of the Gardens and therefore knew each other. The greeting line had broken down, with the board members now dispersed throughout the room.

Sam saw Dick coming his way, glass in hand. It was too late to move, so he prepared himself for what was coming.

"Sam, how's it going? We haven't talked since the Fine Young Cannibals were playing music."

"Yeah Dick, thanks for that. And you?"

"Great Sam, as long as we're not having soup tonight."

"Ha-ha, good one Dick. You're a riot."

"I try Sam, I try. Any news on the dog killer?"

"Still nothing. I don't think the police know what they're doing."

"Well, they're not used to looking for pet killers, I guess. Maybe they need a dog detective. Next time I meet the mayor, I'll be sure to bring it up. Hear you also lost a tree. Tree detective, I'll let the mayor know about that as well." Evidently, Dick tired of the clever talk, as he moved along to harass someone else. Sam was fast tiring of it also and was relieved to see Dick's back.

Farther down the hall, Tony and Chiara were having a rousing non-botanical discussion with a calmed-down Bernice and William. Chiara's family was from Lecce on the heel of Italy's boot, where tomatoes ruled the local cuisine.

"What kind of tomatoes do you grow, dear?" Bernice asked.

"My family always grew the Roma, of course. It's the base for so many good meals. Beefsteaks, Sweet One Hundreds, and a newer variety, something called the Midnight Snack. It actually shows a black side facing the sun, very delicious. What do you grow?"

"We like the Sweet One Hundreds as well. Lemon Boys and Fantastics rounded out our garden this year."

This conversation was a delight to Bernice. She and William had not been interested in the scientific side of botany anyway and found those types of discussions boring in the extreme. All this was even finer with Tony. Being undercover meant having a good story, which Chiara was providing non-stop. Who would have thought it? Tony hadn't known much about Chiara's gardening side, but he knew that her family was from the south of Italy. Tony's was from the north, so he was pretty sure this would not work out in the end. They had only been dating for a couple of months. When Tony told her about the mission, she was all in. So far, they had been holding their own and trying hard not to drink too much—at least Tony was trying. The way Chiara was pouring it back was unsettling to Tony.

Sam was making small talk to a couple by the entry. His wife was down at the other end of the hall talking with one of the few people she knew at the event. They were both ignoring each other and going heavy on the cocktails. Eventually Jake, a board member who had agreed to emcee the festivities, asked people to take their seats. Name tags had been placed at each setting, so it took a while for everyone to find their place. The long tables didn't help things. There were more than a couple of oaths muttered under the breath as people shuffled about looking for their landing spots.

"Welcome to the evening, ladies and gentlemen. We'll start service shortly, but first I want to thank you for being generous enough to attend this event. As you know, funding for the various projects at the Gardens has always taken exceptional effort from all the members, for which we are eternally grateful." Jake then added, "While there are complimentary bottles of wine on your tables, we also have some most outstanding wines available for purchase, should you feel a need to upgrade with your dinner."

Chuckles were heard from all over the hall, so Jake knew he had hit the mark. Before the starters were served, he also pointed out the silent auction table to the crowd, then told them that Sam Greene would address them just before dessert was to be served.

Sam, meanwhile, ordered two Mondavi Cabernets for himself, Lydia, and those around him. At the rate he was going, it would be lucky if he would be able to stand after the main course, much less talk coherently.

Tony and Chiara were seated amongst strangers, but they weren't that far from where Sam and Lydia were located farther down the next long table, so Tony had a good view of his target. It didn't take long for a third, then a fourth Mondavi to come to their table, and Tony could see Sam coming unhinged as the dinner wore on. One thing clear was that Sam and his wife didn't waste much time talking with each other. There wasn't a lot of love or even civility going on. Tony was trying hard not to stare, but he had been drinking more than he had promised himself.

The couples on either side of Tony and Chiara also ordered their own wine. Very few were drinking the complimentary wines on the table. Tony and Chiara were only too happy to discover this and polished off a couple of bottles during the dinner. Tony was relaxed about his indiscretion, his earlier promise to himself forgotten. Everything seemed under control and for once no bosses were around. Chiara looked to be having a great time, which Tony was happy to see despite his earlier worries. He was aware enough to realize that they should cab it or use a ride-hailing service to get home.

* * *

Dominic and Derek were watching the entire event from the sidelines, making sure the staff were filling glasses, delivering plates on time, and clearing plates when the food was obliterated.

"Our royal leaders don't seem to be getting along very well," Dominic said to Derek.

"Have you noticed how much booze they've been pouring back?"

"Yes. They might be writing stories about this one, the way things are going." He had been busy making sure the wait staff had been selling as many bottles of wine as possible, upping the Garden's take on the evening.

Dominic added, "Think I better warn the cab companies. I'm guessing that not too many of these folks'll be using ride-hailing." It looked like there were going to be quite a few leftover cars in the lot to be picked up on Saturday.

Bernard got up and moved over to the area behind the director's table, coincidentally, the route to the washrooms. Bernard was no dummy. He had been watching Sam pig out on wine and figured he'd be needing to use the facilities sooner or later. He planned to buttonhole him and ask Sam a few hard questions.

As the dessert was being served, Jake came over to talk to Sam. It was evident to Jake that Sam shouldn't be making any speeches, so Jake offered to step in and finish the evening's proceedings. Sam accepted.

A couple of minutes later, Sam slowly got to his feet and wandered past Bernard down the corridor to the washroom. Bernard was studying the notice board in the hall. A few minutes later, Sam was making his way back. Bernard pounced.

"Mr. Greene?"

"Who are you?" Pleasantries immediately dispensed with.

"Bernard with the *Vancouver Province* newspaper."

"I know what the *Province* is, smart ass."

"I'd like to ask you a couple of questions, if I may?"

"Get lost."

"Why do you think someone killed and dumped a body in your Gardens, in fact, just outside that door over there?"

"I said scram. How did you get in here, anyway?"

"I bought a ticket, that's how."

Sam was losing control.

"Who would kill a dog and dump it in the maze? Are they targeting you?"

That was all it took. Sam hauled back and took at swing at Bernard. Fortunately for Bernard, Sam was so far gone that he telegraphed what was coming, and Bernard stepped aside. The punch grazed his ear. Sam lurched to the side, stumbled, and fell. Bernard felt his welcome had faded somehow, so he decided to exit the party. He turned around, and as he passed by his seat, grabbed his jacket, then headed back up and out of the entry pavilion.

Sam was seething mad. By the time he found his balance, got back up and looked around, the young man had vanished.

Tony had been watching the action from his seat and was relieved that it hadn't turned into something more. He had no wish to announce that he was with the police. Probably most of the room hadn't any idea what had happened, but those close by had seen the altercation and wondered what it was about. Lydia, however, had heard the two men talking, and had watched as Sam attempted to get into a fight. After the young man had vanished, Sam tried to gather himself and returned to his seat next to Lydia.

Whatever he muttered to Lydia was not repeatable. He looked the other way and started talking with the man to his right while grabbing for his scotch glass. Sam had switched beverages to something he felt was more substantial before the dessert was served.

Lydia had had about enough. She stood up. Sam turned back to her. "Maybe you need to go outside and grab a smoke, calm down a bit."

"Yeah, and maybe I'll keep going." With that, she grabbed her sweater and purse and headed for the doors. She exited the building, passing by a no-smoking sign and a couple of other people doing what she was heading to do. It was not really allowed; the Parks Board deciding that no one should be able to enjoy a cigarette anywhere near a park, which the Gardens technically was after all the sub-rules had been added to the original sales agreement. She had been craving it since she had started dinner and couldn't wait anymore. She also had to get away from Sam. Luckily it wasn't raining, and not too cold either for November. Sam was vaguely aware that she had left the table. After his altercation with the reporter, he continued with the scotch that he had ordered earlier. This was going to be the coup de grâce for him.

Lydia ignored the couple on the terrace and walked unsteadily past, heading east over a short wooden bridge near some ornamental grasses. The couple watched her briefly as she disappeared beyond where the light shone, then went back to their discussion.

Lydia pulled her sweater tighter around her chest. It was cooler than she expected. The moon was only at a quarter full, but with clouds scudding across its face, it wasn't shedding much light anywhere. The lights for the seasonal display were partially installed, but not ready for action, so they were off. The area she chose for a smoke was dim as a result. The only real light was from the foyer's glass wall of the entry pavilion and the few pot lights at the edge of the overhanging roof. This light washed across the concrete plaza toward the lake and the lily pads, but was swallowed whole by the darkness beyond.

Lydia dug into her purse and came up with cigarettes and a lighter. Shaking both from the cold and the nicotine deficit, she lit up, took a mighty drag on the cigarette, and immediately relaxed. She looked up at the second to last thing she would ever see, the moon. She sensed rather than heard a soft footstep before a pair of strong hands grabbed her neck.

The last thing Lydia saw was bright sparkling flashes just before she blacked out. Her purse slid off her shoulder, and the cigarette in her fingers fell onto the concrete path, flashing briefly before dulling as it rolled to the edge. Lydia was dragged backwards while the man finished the job, crushing her neck, making sure she was dead. He waited further until the couple on the terrace had finished their smokes and gone back in. He relieved Lydia of her sweater, blouse, and bra, and had a good look at her breasts before dragging Lydia to the edge of the lake and sliding her headfirst into the water. He tossed the sweater and the blouse into the water, then walked away with the bra in hand like he hadn't a care in the world. He headed north, deep into the Gardens. When he got close to the German displays, he turned east, went through the rhododendrons, over to the edge bounded by Kerr Street. He then jumped over the low fence, walked up to his vehicle on Kerr, and drove away, heading south.

Lydia's cigarette slowly burned down to the filter, the smoke tendrils lingering in the air before the remains extinguished itself at the edge of the path.

* * *

Inside the pavilion, dessert had been served and the evening was winding down. Drunken patrons filled the room. The few who didn't drink would be providing chauffeur services for their loved ones. The rest were at the mercy of the taxi industry. Dominic tried to anticipate the rate of people leaving and had a few cabs lined up. Many of the rides weren't very far, so the same cab could make several trips. Sam walked up to Dominic and demanded a cab right away.

Dominic didn't argue, but asked "What about Lydia?"

"Think she left already." The words came out slurred.

Dominic was just happy to get rid of Sam, so he didn't think much of the exchange. Shortly after Sam took his leave, Tony and Chiara also left in a cab.

After most of the guests had left and the staff were doing the cleanup, Dominic realized that a couple of coats were still in the cloakroom. He grabbed them, sticking them in his office. He'd deal with it tomorrow. He tallied up the receipts and made sure it was all locked away in his desk before closing for the evening. After wishing the cleaners a good night, he headed for his car and home.

~ 17 ~

Saturday dawned bright, with a sun rarely seen at the end of November in Vancouver. Over at Eden Gardens, the first volunteers had arrived at the entry pavilion and prepared for the Garden's opening. Most of the previous night's decorations had been dismantled, but there was still the odd piece of litter to be picked up. One volunteer unlocked the doors to the plaza and decided to give the area the once over, in case some people had been outside the previous evening. Sure enough, he immediately found a couple of cigarette butts on the pavement, so he knew the no-smoking signs had been ignored. Looking farther along the path, he spied another butt and went over to it, but before he knelt, he glanced at the pond and saw something in the water, close to the bank. It looked like a sweater or something, definitely clothing. He went closer, then saw a blouse as well. Aware of the previous incidents, he left and walked hurriedly back to the pavilion.

"There's some clothing in the pond. I left it there. What should we do?"

The woman also knew about the recent events, and she didn't hesitate. "I'm calling the police."

"You sure? It seems to be only a sweater and a blouse."

"What kind of party do you think happened here last night? I don't think it was an orgy!"

"Okay, good point."

The admin person at the VPD taking the call was uninterested in a report of lost clothing at first, then saw the call history, dispatched a patrol car to the Gardens, and called Robert at home.

Good God, I hope this isn't what I think it is, Robert thought, as he got into his car for the drive over to the Gardens. He had told his children that duty called, and that he might be awhile.

It was after eleven and the day was looking to be a fine one, cool but sunny. From the call, it sounded for all the world like the resumption of bad things at Eden. He drove slowly east, then south, Saturday being worse for traffic than a weekday rush hour in Vancouver. It was the day of the week when every driver with dubious driving skills got out on the roads—something to be fearful of. Robert took his time and eventually pulled up in front of the entry pavilion, where he left his car behind the patrol car that had already arrived. He realized the Gardens was open to the public already.

Robert went into the lobby of the pavilion, all the way to the guest desk at the eastern doors. The patrol officers were talking to a man and a woman wearing volunteer badges. Robert asked if Dominic was around. The reply was negative, Dominic having spent all the previous day and evening at the fundraiser.

"So, someone found some clothing in the pond?" Robert asked.

The male volunteer responded, "Looks like a sweater and maybe a blouse."

"Can you show us?"

"Follow me."

"Nice place," one of the cops said. The other one agreed. Apparently, neither had been to the Gardens to deal with recent events.

Robert looked around as he followed the volunteer over the wooden bridge to the north edge of Fraserview Lake to take a closer look at the open water and the waterlilies. They went further along the stone path beside the pond before Robert looked again at the water.

He spotted the blouse and sweater floating in the water amongst the flowers and lily pads. The clothing looked expensive, but he supposed everyone had been wearing their best outfits to a fundraiser. He looked around for something to snag it with, but there was nothing handy. He thanked the volunteer and sent him back to the pavilion to find a pole or broom. He asked one of the officers to accompany the man and bring back whatever was found. I think I'm going to be ill, Robert thought. The other cop looked worried.

The first officer came back with a broom. Robert fished the sweater and blouse over to the edge of the water and retrieved them. It was then that Robert saw the body laying on the bottom of the lake in amongst the grasses, a half-naked woman. He stooped down, rocked back and forth on his heels, and paused to gather his wits.

"Crap," was all he could spit out. The other two had seen the body by now and were visibly rattled. Robert sent one of them back to tell the staff to close the Gardens. He called the precinct on his cellphone to ask for a crime scene group to get down to Eden Gardens as well as some more police to control things. He then called Camille's cell and told her what was happening.

"You better get over here. We've found a woman's body at the bottom of the lake. It looks like Sam Greene's wife, but I'm not certain, I only met her the one time. See if you can get hold of Tony. He was supposed to have been here last night."

"Oh God," was Camille's reply. "I'll get over there as soon as I can." She dialled Tony's cell.

Tony answered, groggy, "Hey, what's happened?"

"Can you get over to Eden right away? Robert has found a woman's body in the lake. He thinks it might be Lydia Greene."

"What?"

"You heard right. Can you get over there?"

"Yeah, be there in thirty minutes or so." This wasn't good, he thought. Wait until the news finds out. He was starting to feel even worse than his hangover. He slid out of bed, got dressed and said goodbye to Chiara, who was only just waking up herself.

"Hey, I thought we were going out for lunch today."

"Looks like I have to cancel. I'll call you when I find out what this is." Tony yelled as he went out the door.

So maybe this is what it's like to date a cop. Although she had to admit, she had a pretty good time the evening before, even if it was a little out of the ordinary. Her head felt fuzzy, so she decided to go back to sleep.

Tony's car was still sitting in the Garden's parking lot, so he texted a ride-hailing car to get him back there. He asked the driver to hurry, so they were soon flying across the Granville Bridge over False Creek. This can't be happening, he thought. The hammers beating on his head weren't helping any. His mouth was dry, his hair was pointing in several directions, and he looked the mess he felt like.

***

Robert was talking to the administrator on site, asking her to get a hold of Dominic. Then he asked her to shut the whole Gardens down. She told a couple of volunteers to get carts to go out into the far reaches of the Gardens to round up the visitors. Fortunately, it was early enough that weren't many, and staff knew exactly how many people were still out on the paths.

"Is it possible to get some coffee?" This from Robert.

"Maybe. I'll see if there is any equipment left over from last night to make a pot."

"Thanks. There's going to be a whole bunch of police showing up here shortly. Probably be a good idea to send home any staff and volunteers you don't need." Robert added, "And if you could refrain from saying anything to the news people for today, we'd appreciate it. We'll issue a statement for them when we confirm what we have here."

"What did you find out there?"

Robert realized the administrator didn't really know

what was happening. "We think we have found a body in the lake again."

"My God!"

"Exactly. If you could just try to clear the public out of the pavilion, that would be a great help to us."

Robert asked one constable to get some yellow tape to rope off the area, then he sat down to wait. It was about now he realized what a mistake it had been to ask Tony to attend the event. Probably no one at the fundraiser had a clue about what happened the previous evening, including Tony, but when the press found out about the police presence at the event, and someone was killed anyway, well, it wouldn't be good. And then there was Sam to consider. He would need to be notified if it was indeed his wife. What a miserable weekend this was turning out to be.

After several minutes, Camille came down the hall and into the area where Robert was sitting. About the same time, two more squad cars pulled up. The officers brought gear to enlarge the roped off area, erect some screening and put up a tent. Tony wasn't far behind Camille. He did not look sharp.

"Where is the body?" Camille asked.

"Still in the pond over there," Robert pointed.

"Sure it's her?"

"No, but she's face up on the bottom. It's not very deep there. Tony, can you go over and check?" Robert added, "Did you see anything last night?"

Tony paused, looking pensive. "We were at the next table, a bit down from them, but I had a good view of Sam and Lydia all evening. They were both drinking like there was no tomorrow." He didn't mention his own drinking. "Near the end, Sam seemed to get in a short fight behind his table with a young guy, then came back."

Robert said nothing, waiting for more.

"Lydia looked pretty disgusted, so she got up and walked out onto the plaza. I think she took a sweater and her purse with her. I don't think anyone followed her."

"Did you see anyone else out on the plaza?"

"It was hard to see anything. The glass was basically like a black mirror. There wasn't a lot of light out there. I did see a couple come back in a few minutes after she went out. I suspect they were probably smoking."

"Maybe that's why Lydia went out there. We think that she smokes." Robert said, then he got up suddenly and went out the doors. He came back a minute later, a small smile on his face. "Found a cigarette butt by the edge of the path close to where Lydia is. We should be able to find out if it was hers, but it has lipstick on it."

"We need to find out who that couple was and talk to them. That's your first task, Tony. Don't worry about last night. I never should have sent anyone, it's on me." Robert added. He sat there, contemplating the picturesque view and gardens beyond the plaza, and wondered again why so much violence was being visited upon all of it.

Tony inwardly breathed a small sigh of relief. He had been worried. With a task to complete, he went back to being a police officer, although a very hung-over police officer. "I need some water."

"Go over and see if it's Lydia first, please. Don't try to hide the fact that you were here last night, either.

Dominic is on his way down, so he'll recognize you. It'll get out to the press somehow, it always does, just accept that it's going to happen. Someone asks you about it? 'No comment' is all you need to say." Robert knew this was a teaching moment. "One other thing. Was Lydia wearing a bra that you could notice?"

Tony looked sheepish. "Yes, she was."

Robert then thought about Steve, the fact that he was away on vacation. Small mercies, he thought, maybe we can get a handle on things before he returns. Fat chance, he thought. Robert sensed a few demerit points heading his way over this case. Then he dismissed this thinking and concentrated on what they needed to do.

Tony returned, nodding, "It's Lydia. That's her blouse on the path."

Robert made his way back to the hall and beckoned to Camille. "Let's take a walk outside."

Meanwhile, Dominic had turned up and was staring at Tony. Tony returned the look and made Dominic sit down. "I'm going to need a complete list of the attendees from last night's event." He then gave Dominic a summary of what was going on out on the plaza.

Dominic said, "I can't believe it. Once I get through this, I'm looking for a new job. My nerves can only take so much disaster."

Robert and Camille walked around the south side of the lake and on past the parterres to the expansive vistas of the Meadows. Robert needed to think, to clear his mind of the operation happening on the plaza.

He started in. "Whoever's doing this has taken it up a big notch."

"It may not be directly related." Camille was doing exactly what a detective should do, concentrate on the facts. Robert kicked himself mentally.

"You're right. Although it would be crazy if this is not somehow related."

"Agreed. But we should follow the evidence, right?"

Who was doing the teaching now, Robert thought.

"You are absolutely correct." He smiled at Camille. "Let's wait until the coroner has done her thing, and we get cause and time of death established. I can't help thinking that this is all getting closer and closer to Sam Greene. I'm going to warn him to be extra vigilant for the next while."

"Yeah," was all Camille could manage.

"How is the research on Sam's properties coming?"

"Slowly. There are more than a few layers of companies and shell companies involved. Might have some ideas by end of Monday if we're lucky."

"I think we should ask the Gardens to keep closed for a few days. I know they'll be angry that their Seasonal Lights Festival will be impacted, but that's just tough." Robert said. "We'll take our time with the crime scene. Let the other officers know they can go slow."

"Why did they take her top off? It doesn't exactly match the other things that have happened, does it?" Camille was thinking.

"Something sexual for sure. I think it'll be obvious what the coroner needs to check for. It's hard to imagine this all happening right outside a big event like last night. Anyone could have interrupted the murder. Very brazen."

"Hope Tony is successful. There must have been a few more smokers in that crowd, so we'll have to find them all and do interviews," Robert added. "Call the station and find out if Lydia has been reported missing."

Camille did as requested, but no missing person report had been filed. They stood for a while looking east at the forest and the higher hills of the German Garden areas to the east side of the Great Meadow. "This place is beautiful, isn't it, Camille?"

"Yes. Such horrible things happening in the middle of a paradise. It is bizarre."

"Let's get back. I have some more thinking to do."

They turned around and retraced their steps back to the plaza, where a multitude of officers were going through all the crime scene tasks required to document the scene of the crime.

Robert went back inside the entry to the hall and poured himself a large mug of coffee. For coffee put together on the fly, this is decent, he thought. Robert usually shied away from restaurant or hotel coffee, most of it being along the lines of acidic dishwater, but this was good brew. He signalled to the lady who had made it happen, thanking her with a smile.

He thought about the similarities between the first two events; including no real identifiable method of killing that could be definitively attached to any perpetrator. He wondered what the results of Lydia's murder and autopsy would bring to the case, and whether there would be connections or dis-similarities. Camille came inside and sat down by Robert. She looked at his coffee mug but declined the offer of any.

"I think we should have a meeting tomorrow, maybe around one. Can you let the team know?" Robert asked. "I think you need to get back onto the Sam research. I'm also wondering about whether we need to expand the research into his background, maybe get his phone records, things like that. I have to get back to the office later this afternoon, once the body is removed, so I can get Sam down for the ID confirmation." Robert added. "You might as well get going. There's nothing more you can do here."

"Right, see you tomorrow then." Camille got up and left the building. Clouds were moving in. Robert hoped the police would be able to finish their duties before the rain started, trying to ruin everything.

Dominic came over to Robert and asked him what the prognosis was for opening the Gardens again.

"We want to keep it closed for a couple of days in light of what has happened. Once we get autopsy results, we may be in a better position to advise you. I get it that the Seasonal Lights thing is starting. You'll just have to be patient."

"Ok. I'll advise the staff. Later in the week, you think?"

"Let you know end of Monday. I'll call you. I expect that the publicity of all this may also affect the lights thing. I wouldn't be shocked if you have an uptick in ticket sales."

Tony came over. "I have the list of people attending last night's event. I'll head to the office and get some help

THE CHAPEL OF RETRIBUTION ~ 199

to start calling them up. I'm guessing this is going to be all over the TV and papers pretty quickly."

"You can count on it," Robert said, then added, "We're going to have a team meeting tomorrow early afternoon. Anything you can find out before then would be good. See if you can narrow down the list to smokers and who may have been out on the plaza last night."

Robert had one more task that could not wait. "Do you have a phone I can use? A landline?" Robert asked the administrator. He didn't want this call to be interrupted or dropped because of bad cell coverage.

"In the office down here." She said, pointing down the corridor.

Robert went down the short hall and through the door. He checked his watch, looked at the office wall, steeling himself for the call he didn't want to make. Before he dialled, he made sure the door was shut, then called Mr. Greene.

A *basso profundo* voice answered, sounding like a croaking Barry White. "Hello?"

"Mr. Greene?"

"Yes, who is this? The phone says you're calling from Eden Gardens."

"It's the police, Mr. Greene, Robert Lui, detective on the Eden Gardens case. I am afraid that I have some terrible news for you. I am sorry to say that we found your wife in the Gardens this morning, and it appears that she may have been murdered." Robert didn't stop to take a breath. He just wanted to get it out. Although he didn't like the guy in the least, it was his professional duty to make this as easy for Sam as he could.

"What? We were together last night at the fundraiser."

"Did she come home with you?" Robert kind of knew the answer to this one.

"I really don't remember much. I know she wasn't here when I woke up this morning. I thought maybe she went out shopping."

Robert wasn't sure why, but he didn't sense any tears being shed on the other end of the line. "Do you think you could come down to the city morgue at Vancouver General Hospital later this afternoon? Come into the entry off West 10th Avenue. Leave your car in the parkade and walk across the bridge. I'll meet you on the hospital side. I trust that you know where that is, correct? The morgue is on the lower level. Our crime scene people are here and doing what they need to do. After they are done, Lydia's body will be brought down there for you to formally identify, if you are up to it."

"Oh God," was all Sam could say.

Robert had a feeling that things were sinking in on the other end. After you hit someone with news like that right between the eyes, it takes a moment.

"I'll give you a call later when I know what time you should come down. Please accept our condolences. Is there someone who could stay with you in the meantime?"

There was a pause on the other end. "My sister. I'll call my sister." With that, Sam Greene hung up, leaving Robert with a dead line in his hand. He slowly put the phone back onto its cradle and stared at it. I do not get paid enough for this kind of shit, he thought.

Robert then took a good look around, talked with the recovery team, and decided to head back to Cambie Street. Before he left the parking lot, he checked in with his kids and told them what was happening.

"We were wondering why we hadn't heard from you. Are you okay, Dad?" Sophie asked.

"I'm fine. I have to go back to Cambie and then to the hospital to meet with someone. I'll call you when I am done. If you're hungry, you may have to scrounge for leftovers." Then he drove off.

* * *

Much later in the afternoon, when Lydia's body had been finally transported to the morgue in the Vancouver General Hospital, Robert sighed and called Mr. Greene.

Sam Greene showed up at Vancouver General Hospital in the upper lobby just before six. Robert was sitting on a chair in the lobby, watching him as he entered from the second level walkway, and greeted him before leading him downstairs. Mr. Greene wore a long grey trench coat, with a black silk scarf draped around his neck and shoulders. He was not exactly walking tall. He looked stooped and had a defeated air about him.

"Mr. Greene, again, my sincere condolences for your loss." Robert started in, offering his hand to shake with Sam. "Please follow me. The morgue is on the lower level under us." Somehow, lower level sounded better than saying that your loved one was in a basement. Sam ignored Robert's hand, saying nothing. They proceeded in single file down the stairs, Robert leading slowly, Mr. Greene trailing with hesitant footsteps, grabbing his scarf with both hands. Even on a Saturday evening, the lobby was alive with people: patients, visitors, nurses, and other staff. It was like an airport, except that the flow of people was more constant, and there were fewer smiles to be seen.

They reached the bottom level, turned right, and walked down the hall, stripes in primary colours on the floor directing people to their destinations. Robert was steeling himself, ignoring the signs to the morgue, knowing the way far too well. They reached the door and walked into the waiting room with its fluorescent lighting rendering everything flat and grey. This is a place for death, all right, Robert thought. He went up to the reception window, had a quiet word with the receptionist and then led Mr. Greene through a door and down a rubber floored grey corridor.

They entered the room where Lydia was laying. She was waiting peacefully for her husband to come and say goodbye. She did not want to be waiting on the cold stainless-steel table with only a light sheet covering her, her temperature exactly the same as the table's. Lydia was past wanting anything, but she was still waiting patiently. The faint odour of formaldehyde lingered in the deadened air. A doctor dressed in light green scrubs was also waiting for them. He was not smiling, and he did not look patient. Perhaps that had to do with it being Saturday evening, and personal plans that had been suspended.

"Mr. Greene?"

"Yes."

The doctor moved to one side and drew back the top of the sheet so that Lydia's head was exposed. Her skin had a chalky pallor.

"That is my wife." Mr. Greene said in a slow monotone. Robert could barely hear what he said. The doctor moved to replace the sheet over Lydia's face.

"Who would do this to my wife?" His voice was stronger now. "How did she die?"

Robert noticed the lack of tears, the lack of any visible emotion at all. He answered, "We can't know much until the autopsy is conducted. I believe it is scheduled for tomorrow, so we may have some information on Monday. Don't expect too much, though. This is a murder investigation, and we'll be limited in what we can tell anyone, including, unfortunately, yourself."

Sam Greene's eyes blazed at this remark, Robert noticed, but Sam didn't say anything.

"You are free to leave, Mr. Greene. Thank you for this. I realize how hard this is."

"Do you?" And with that remark, Sam Greene turned around and fled the room.

Lydia was maybe disappointed that her husband had not thought to say goodbye to her, but it was hard to tell. Her expression had not changed the whole time the visitors were in the room, even under the sheet covering her.

Robert and the doctor stood there, looking at each other. Robert shook his head, then thanked the doctor, telling him that he would call tomorrow. The doctor said nothing, just turned and wheeled the body away to await its appointment with medical tools and the coroner.

Don't know if I could work in this place, Robert thought. Then he turned as well and left, thankful to be heading home, up from Hades into the world of the living. He got out his cell and let Sophie know he was on his way home.

~ 18 ~

Sunday broke with rain gently falling, bouncing off the glistening street pavement. It was only a few degrees above zero, so miserable outside. Robert woke up shortly after eight and lay there, contemplating the events of the day before. The thin light tried unsuccessfully to penetrate the blinds. He lamented the shortening days and hoped it would not snow. Snow in Vancouver was a special kind of nastiness for drivers that was best avoided, if at all possible. He lay there, hands behind his head as he tried to arrange his day in his mind, as he usually did before rising. There were no signs of life anywhere in the house. It was cold. The bed's pull was exceptionally strong today. He wasn't sure he could overcome it, so he remained there a while longer, not even trying.

Eventually, he was able to break free. After turning up the heat and showering, he got the kids out of bed and made French Toast for everybody. He lounged around, sipping coffee, reading the paper, flipping through the sections, trying to find just one uplifting or interesting story. But the paper's contents were like the weather, dour and gloomy. He was trying to avoid the inevitable, delaying his exit out the door back to the office.

"What happened yesterday, Pops?" Robin asked, while chewing on his breakfast.

"Can't say much, but it looks like another murder at the Eden Gardens. I have to go in this afternoon for a while, but I'll be home before dinner. In fact, I'll pick you up at your game."

He felt a bit more normal for doing breakfast with his kids, but he also knew he might not be seeing much of them for the foreseeable future. With Christmas looming, this would not be popular. Robert made a couple of calls to line up a ride for Robin to his game.

"I'll get to the game at some point before it's over. It's at Trout Lake, right? Don't score a goal until I get there, okay?"

"Sure Pops, I'll just rag the puck for two periods."

"You'll be okay today, Sophie?"

"Yup. May go out with Rose later."

"Just check your hockey bag Robin, make sure you have all your equipment. Hard to play with only one skate."

"Yah, yah, you always say that, Dad."

With that piece of fatherly advice dispensed, he gathered his wits and stepped out into the cold rain, got into The Silver Streak, and headed west to work.

* * *

On Cambie Street, five people shuffled into the case room. It was just past one-thirty. A recent addition to the team, Erwin, was ill and unable to make it. Seeing as it was Sunday, Robert thought maybe more people wouldn't show, but obviously the team felt the urgency brought on by the most recent murder. Tony looked much improved from the day before. Robert correctly guessed what Tony had been doing at the fundraiser but didn't raise the issue. Tony looked as though he had suffered enough on Saturday from what Robert had seen. Lawrence and Winnie were there as well.

Camille filled them in on what had transpired the day before. "So, you are up to date. We think we'll get autopsy results shortly. The coroner was working this morning, which is not normal. Hats off to her, I say."

"I agree. Above and beyond." Robert added. He then filled them in on the scene in the morgue the night before. "Kind of weird, I would say, if I had to sum it up. Does that description help any?"

No one responded, so Robert continued. "I thought not. I didn't know what to make of it last evening, and I still don't. There wasn't a lot of emotion present. Maybe it was shock, but I've seen shock before. This wasn't shock."

"I didn't see a lot of love spread around on Friday night between those two." Tony said. "They seemed to spend most of the evening ignoring each other."

"I watched the local news last night. The story led, but of course there was more speculation than fact." This came from Camille.

"Unfortunately, it looks like Lawrence was correct after all. Our perpetrator may have been waiting to take it to the next level, and I would say that this is the next level."

Robert added. Robert looked over at Lawrence, who was displaying a grin at this small expression of confidence.

"It's not a reason to smile, Lawrence," said Robert.

Lawrence immediately looked chastened. Robert continued. "I'll write up a press release once again. The press and TV have been hounding the station, looking for comment."

"That Bernard pipsqueak has left me a couple of messages as well," said Camille.

"Well, I can't tell them much, because we don't know much, do we?" Robert said. "Have you been able to learn anything from talking to the people who attended?" This was aimed at Tony.

"I found the couple who were on the plaza, probably the last to see Lydia alive. All they can remember was Lydia ignoring them and then she walked away over the wood bridge. They lost sight of her then and went back inside shortly after. They didn't see or hear anything out of the ordinary. Apparently, no one else was out there at that time."

"Except the killer," Robert added. "The guy, and I think we can say it's a guy, kills Lydia, then has the balls to take her tops off before dropping her in the water. A pretty cool customer, I would say. Either he is not too worried about getting discovered, or he has done this before. Lawrence and Winnie, I want you to go through past cases and see if you come up with anything resembling this. Camille, any results from that neighbourhood canvas done a week ago in the Greene's neighbourhood?"

"We only found one home that had a camera looking

at the part of the street where the van would park. We got a better picture of the van, but not the occupant or the plate number. We think it's an old GMC brown panel van, with some specific dents. I've got a picture and have circulated it to the squad cars. Maybe we'll get lucky. That's about it."

"How about the other canvass on Kerr regarding the cut tree?"

Tony answered this time, "Not many people home, but we did talk to one person who remembers hearing a chainsaw in the middle of the night. They looked out their window but didn't see anything out of the ordinary. The sound didn't last very long, and then it was silent. So really, a big bunch of nothing from that street."

"It may be a long shot, but I think the immediate neighbourhood around Eden should be canvassed to see if anyone noticed the brown van on Friday night, or if someone's security camera caught it." Robert looked at his watch. "Winnie and Lawrence, you can get going on that search."

After they left, he drummed his fingers on the desk. "Maybe if we go grab a coffee, the coroner's report will arrive. Doesn't look like it'll come to us if we just wait here. Let's go up the street and then we'll come back unexpectedly and catch it unawares."

Camille shook her head but rose and joined Robert and Tony for the walk up Cambie. The group stopped at Café Paulo and, after an exchange of pleasantries with the barista, sat down by the window with their Americanos.

Gilberto was absent, taking Sunday off per his usual custom.

"Our rate of non-progress on this case is getting a little depressing, I would say," Robert said. "What is it we're not doing right? There are multiple crimes, with lots of clues, and no progress. I can almost hear Steve giving me the gears when he gets back."

"Everything has been swirling around this Sam guy. Maybe he is the next victim. What do you think?" Camille asked.

"You could be right. I'll give him a call tomorrow, warn him, and see if he wants any police watching his back. I am going to guess that he'll tell us to take a hike, but we should try."

After this exchange, the group sat there sipping on their coffees quietly watching the other customers who seemed to be mostly staring at their mobile devices. If they were talking, it was into the devices, not to each other.

"Quite the society we've developed with those gizmos, isn't it?" The other two knew Robert's opinion of those 'gizmos,' as he put it, and tried to not use them overly when they were around Robert unless it was for communicating. "Let's get back. Maybe the report has arrived."

They exited back out into the rain. I wonder if Gilberto would let me buy shares in this place, Robert pondered, as they splashed back to the station, trying to avoid the streams winding their way down Cambie Street's sloping sidewalks.

* * *

Sure enough, the team's departure had caused the coroner's report to appear on Robert's desk. The group stripped off their wet coats and sat down while Robert ripped open the envelope and started to read.

"Not a lot. Lydia was not sexually interfered with, and the cause of death was strangulation—with hands, they believe. She was dead before she went into the water. Her neck was crushed by whoever did this and gloves were used, latex. The coroner's opinion is that the assailant was approximately the same height as Lydia. Time of death matches closely with the disappearance of Lydia from the party. And a footnote, she had over three times the legal limit of alcohol in her blood at the time of death."

The three of them sat there, considering the information they had just received.

"Different from Stan and the dog." This from Tony.

"Yes, similar, yet different." Robert said. "Again, with a body in the pond, yet slightly different," he paused, then, "At least she wouldn't have suffered much with all that liquor in her. Probably had no idea what was happening."

Camille wrapped up the meeting. "I'm going back to the research on Sam's past dealings. I don't think that we're getting anywhere after hearing this report."

"I agree Camille, let's meet tomorrow, say 9:00 am. I have to pick my kid up at a game now, so I'm going to get going." With that, Robert left, followed by the other two.

***

Robert drove slowly east across town to the Trout Lake arena, where his son was playing his hockey game. He walked into the rink just as two players were fighting, each trying to send the other to dreamland. The referees were trying to make them see reason, not very successfully. Some parents were yelling. All in all, everything as it should be. Robin was playing Peewee house level hockey, the age group where hockey transformed from a cute civilized kid's game into a teenage slugfest almost every game. Robert watched as a player took a swing at the referee. Perfect, he thought, here comes a suspension, or maybe worse. The trouble was that the referees were not much older than the players they were trying to keep in line. At least the parents were generally more reserved, unlike rep hockey, where in theory, everybody's kids were on their way to the NHL, the parents a little crazier because of it.

After things had quietened down and a couple of the players were banished to their respective locker rooms, the game finished, everybody happy. Robert waved at Robin as he left the ice. Robert waited patiently in the lobby of the rink for Robin to change and stow his gear, hopefully not leaving any of it behind.

"Hi Pops. You missed a goal! I couldn't wait for you, so I popped it in while the open net was staring at me."

"Jeez, I'm sorry. Getting kind of rough out there, isn't it?"

"Nah, our guys are just protecting the smaller players."

There was a whole code of ethics in this hockey stuff that eluded Robert, but he understood the protection part. At least Robin still had all his teeth. Small mercies, he thought as they headed home.

~ 19 ~

Monday morning, after successfully seeing his two children out the door to school, Robert saddled up in The Silver Streak and headed west to work, all the while wondering how his team was going to solve this mess. He also needed to check on the gang thing, see if Surinder had done his school visit.

When he arrived at the station, Robert noticed two reporters sitting in the waiting area. They tried to get his attention, but he studiously ignored them. The morning meeting was getting started, the group sitting in the larger case room. Some new pictures and lines had been added to the display board. At least the team is acting in an organized fashion, Robert thought.

When all six of them had all settled in, Robert looked around the table and nodded to the others. Winnie spoke first. "We've been looking at murder cases with a similar M.O. as you suggested. We have a couple that we found but are looking for more."

Not to be outdone, Lawrence chimed in, "Strangulation with sexual interference," as if they had all forgotten what had happened on the weekend.

"Cases solved or unsolved?"

"Both unsolved so far, but a suspect has been identified. They go back two years and five years, both in Vancouver." Winnie added. "Both women strangled, one of them raped, after the fact, it appears, if you can believe it. The other one had her blouse wide open when she was found."

"Cast the net wider. Look in the adjacent municipalities." This would complicate the search, as some cities surrounding Vancouver used their own police force and others used the RCMP. "Start close, like Burnaby and Richmond, the North Shore, then work outwards." Robert said. "Anything else?"

"I have a lawyer helping me with the title issues on Sam's lands that he developed. Might get some answers today." This from Camille.

"Anything on the van yet?"

"No."

"Speaking of Mr. Greene, I'm going to call and see if he wants someone watching him, like protection." Robert said. "Wanna stay and witness my call, please? Not taking any chances with this asshole." Camille stayed and settled in. The rest left the room, trying to ignore the questioning stares of the other police on the floor.

Robert sat for a moment, looking at the phone. He sighed, looked over at Camille with a small grin, punched in Sam's number, then put the phone on speaker.

"Yes?"

"Mr. Greene? It's Robert Lui from the Vancouver Police Department."

"I know who you work for."

This was starting well, Robert thought. "We're wondering if you would consider some police presence in your neighbourhood to watch your house. Whoever is perpetrating all these crimes seems to be getting closer and closer to yourself."

There was silence on the other end. "You there Mr. Greene?"

"I'm thinking. And what I'm thinking is that if you guys could do your job properly, then I wouldn't be in this mess, would I?"

"I'm not sure what to say, Mr. Greene." Robert responded.

"Yeah, no kidding. You guys are incompetent, is what I think. You should concentrate on catching this guy instead of baby sitting me." The line went dead.

"Don't you just love this job, Camille?" Robert paused, then said, "I tried. I have to admit, he didn't sound at all scared, did he, or sad for that matter?"

"A for effort. You're right, though, sounded pretty cocky. It all seemed to be about him, no mention of his late wife." Camille got up. "Think I'm going back to the research. Don't get back talk from history."

"Let me know when you come up with something. I need to work on a report for Steve. He's back this Wednesday, I think. Things are going so well I may need to polish up my resume."

Camille just smiled at him as she left the case room. Robert headed back to his room, locking the case room door behind him. Once he was inside his office, he had to contend with the fact that he needed some coffee. There was no doubt what he had to do, so he grabbed his coat. As he walked by the growing gaggle of reporters, he stopped and told them he would have some comments when he returned. Then he walked out of the station and headed up to Gilberto's establishment. When he entered, Gilberto, the maestro, was behind the gleaming La Cimbali machine where he was coaxing out another cup of God's nectar.

"How're you a do-in Roberto?" Gilberto asked.

"Never better, yourself?" then, "double long please." His cell rang. Robert excused himself and took the call. Norma was on the other end. Reporters were in the lobby of the police station, being persistent. They wanted the story about Lydia Greene.

"I'll deal with them when I return. I'm up at Café Paulo. I'll write out a couple of thoughts and then head back. Where is that liaison officer when you need him?" He then took his cup of joe and went over to a window seat to think out what he could say. After he ruminated, writing nothing down, he headed back to the station.

***

As he entered the lobby, he was beset by several reporters, all talking at once. Robert stood there, saying nothing, waiting for them to shut up. He produced a notebook and opened it to a blank page and waited for a question that he could understand.

"One at a time please, or I'll just leave," he started off.

"Is it true that Lydia Greene was found half-naked in

the pond?" A reporter from the *Vancouver Sun* newspaper asked.

"She was found Saturday morning in Fraserview Lake at Eden Gardens, dead." Robert continued, "She appears to have been killed. This was not an accident. I do not have anything further to say about how she was found or how she was killed." Then he added, "We are making our enquires and doing the work we need to do to apprehend whoever was responsible." It figured that the press would start with the most lurid aspect of the case, he thought. How else were they supposed to sell papers?

"Is this linked to the other events that have happened at Eden Gardens over the last several weeks?" This from a TV journalist, who was probably not quite up to speed on what all the other events were. Robert speculated that he was present to fill in his lack of knowledge before his employers found out how little he actually knew.

"It is too early to tell if there may be a connection, or what the nature of the connection may be if there is one." He consulted his blank page more closely.

"Hi, Bernard Lily from the *Province*. Don't you think all these events happening at the Gardens are slightly bizarre?"

"Well, Bernard, these events happening anywhere could be considered bizarre, but I would agree, a botanical garden is not a place where one would normally find someone murdered."

"Who are your suspects?"

"I have nothing further to say today, thank you." With that, Robert smiled and walked past the group as they broke into excited chatter again, yelling questions at his receding back, none of which he could distinguish, or would answer.

Back at his office, he closed the door and worked on his report for Steve. It was not going well, so in the absence of any other idea, he started praying. After an hour of ineffective writing and praying, he decided to break for lunch. Maybe a bowl of noodles would turn everything around. Why not? Nothing else was going right on this case. He grabbed his coat and waved at Norma as he went by her on the way out.

After spending an appropriate amount of time at Bountiful Noodles, Robert felt he must have generated some sort of luck; at least he felt full, so he headed back and started working again on his report. It still wasn't going well. The recent murder had plenty of clues, but so far, no progress. He could not escape the feeling that he would be fired or demoted because of this.

A couple of hours went by, with the report in no better shape than when he started, so Robert was about to call it a day when he heard a knock on his door. Camille opened the door and stood still with a smile that would put a Cheshire Cat to shame. Robert beckoned her into the office, and she quietly closed the door.

"I think we've found a link, Robert! We went as far back as we could into Sam's development past to when he got much of his land. From what we can tell, most of it once belonged to a Sonny MacDonald. It is hazy how Mr. Greene actually acquired the land, but we looked into Sonny's history, and found it didn't last very long."

"Meaning what?"

"Meaning he killed himself not long after Sam got titles to the land. Sonny descended from one of the early Vancouver railroad families that exploited the natural resources of the area to help build Vancouver. In doing so, the MacDonalds had acquired a good number of properties around Vancouver and here is the good part: he had one son, whose name is David MacDonald. Apparently still in Vancouver, but his location is unknown." Camille's voice was getting louder and louder.

Robert started grinning. "I knew it would work."

"What would work?" Camille didn't understand.

"The noodles. We needed some case luck, so I went up to Broadway for some lucky noodles. It worked!"

"You know you're crazy, right?"

"Okay. Maybe. I recognize that name. I think it is on the list of employees at Eden Gardens. So, this guy could be our perpetrator! I would even go so far as to say it's quite likely you have busted this case open." Robert considered what this meant. "Now all we have to do is to find Mr. MacDonald. Great work Camille."

"You were right all along. It's all about the land. We are looking a little further to make sure we have the correct MacDonald before we go chasing him."

"Hopefully, we can get a home address from Eden's records. They are probably closed by now, so we should head over there first thing tomorrow to talk with the people there. We need to nail this guy before anything else happens. I'll try them now, in case they are open." He dialled Eden's number, but the call went to an answering service.

The sentiment was correct as expressed by Robert, unfortunately it was also late. David MacDonald was already embarking on the next act in his revenge drama.

~ 20 ~

One Year Earlier

A lone gull glided over the fir trees and screeched its familiar cry of hurt. David MacDonald didn't bother to look up. He stood with hands folded on top of a rake handle, resting his chin on them as he watched the Vancouver airport, across the north arm of the Fraser River. The silence and calmness of the golf course where he worked was broken only by the sound of the machines that were needed to keep the grass in perfect trim. Somehow, the airport sounds seemed to head the other way, south. Must be the wind, he thought.

He looked down and inhaled the scent from the recent cutting, all the blades of grass uniform in height, just as the club members desired. He had perfectly raked the sand trap. There was not a grain out of place. The parallel furrows curved round and round, not unlike a Japanese garden, at least until the next duffer blundered through and left a mess. It was mid-fall, so the deciduous trees were missing half their leaves. The ones that had taken their exit from the branches swirled around the edges of the fairway in vague clumps, attempting to form their own structures. He would have to deal with them, eventually. Club members hated messes, and this was what the leaves were trying their best to be.

David was tall and tended to the lanky side. His hands were weathered, callused, and scarred from years of outside manual labour. His face was long, with piercing green eyes. His years in the sun and wind had added a crackled pigskin patina to his skin. Flaxen hair framed his face, the hair descending to his shoulders in ragged tangles. He resembled the scarecrow from *The Wizard of Oz*, but no one would dare say that to him. With his unkempt appearance and perpetual frown, he would never be playing Santa at a mall for Christmas; the children would either run away or be nightmare ridden for life.

He detected a hint of smoke on the air. Someone must be burning leaves nearby, something outlawed decades ago. His thoughts drifted to his youth and the smouldering piles of leaves that he and his father would gather every fall. Then his mind slipped down a darker corridor as he revisited how he and his mother had moved out of their house after his father had died and the banks did the inevitable, forcing them to leave the neighbourhood where he had spent his childhood. His mother had been forced to go on welfare, along with all the attendant sacrifices required of the situation. He remembered the awkwardness of their friends, the looks from the other children at school, even those at the new school after they had moved. It didn't take long for the stories to follow the family. He didn't want to be pitied but he was bitter, and the bitterness had only grown with time, not diminished, after he had eventually thought he understood what had happened. That his mother blamed Sonny only increased the anger inside him.

His childhood had been a mess after his father had killed himself, and he didn't stick with the education system very well after that. Once he was old enough, he landed some part-time work as a greenskeeper at a couple of local golf courses. He found cutting, trimming, and fixing things more enjoyable than sitting in a classroom. Eventually, he was able to parlay his experience into a job at VanDusen Gardens. His mechanical abilities led to a promise of a full-time role, when one of the older workers suddenly passed away. No one had suspected that his death wasn't accidental. David was a problem solver first and foremost. Rat bait had other uses than just killing rats, and lord knows Vancouver has a lot of rats.

David was turfed out of VanDusen after an argument with his supervisor but joined Eden Gardens soon after. He didn't last longer than three years at Eden before suffering the same fate as had happened to him at VanDusen. The inability to get along with people got him fired from the Eden job. Which was a shame because he really enjoyed the work and the Gardens themselves. Given a different set of circumstances growing up, he may even have gone into horticulture and given himself a brighter future. That is, if his intellectual tools were sharp enough. The jury was still out on that one.

David didn't know it, but the golf club he was now working for was the same club that formerly inhabited the site of the present day VanDusen Botanical Gardens in Vancouver. The golf club had moved in the early 1960s to its present location on Musqueam First Nations land along the Fraser River. The Southlands Golf and Country Club was at the west end of an even wealthier part of Vancouver than Shaughnessy Heights, an area of mansions on huge land parcels near the Fraser River. The horsey set played there, at least the people who had not been pushed out to Langley, a suburb where horses were bred for racing and land was less dear.

More than a few dollars had been made during Prohibition by people running booze out the river to thirsty Americans down the coast in Washington State from some of these 'reputable' mansions. The land in this part of Vancouver was part of the river delta that had somehow not been zoned for industrial use, something to do with it being on the wealthy west side of Vancouver.

David liked the golf course because of its proximity to the river, making it easy to get rid of things. Another attribute was its lack of hills. David hated hills. They were hard to walk up, and machines didn't like them either—they had a bad habit of rolling over if the incline was too steep. The greatest thing about the course in his eyes was the trees, the opposite of what golfers thought.

Golf courses generally had many tree varieties, but some courses had so many types, they were like arboretums. David had increased his already extensive knowledge of tree species and their different attributes gained during his tenure at the two public gardens. He knew how long each tree was likely to live, the hardness of its wood, and whether it might become a hazard due to age or storms. Among David's tree favourites were the Arbutus and Ginkgo trees. The Arbutus tree was exotic looking, he thought, and he had learned that it was also medicinal. He liked the name, Ginkgo, and he had found out that the species, *Ginkgo biloba,* was over two hundred million years old. Plants helped soothe the savage beast, he had heard somewhere, but he wasn't feeling very soothed these days.

Late fall at the course involved a lot of tidying things. Leaves fallen from the deciduous trees had made their usual impact on the grass and needed to be corralled and composted. Grass didn't grow nearly as quickly, but the golfers didn't stop coming, there were just fewer of them. The fair-weather golfers stayed home or sat in the clubhouse sipping their lattes or Rob Roys, depending on the time of day. The course used winter greens most years. These had to be set up just short of the real greens, which were left alone during the winter so they wouldn't suffer unnecessary damage by golfers during the bad weather. One of the advantages for a golfer living in Vancouver was the ability to play year-round. The other advantage was to be able to brag about it to just about anyone else in Canada, as if the rest of Canada needed any more reasons to hate the people living in Vancouver.

The sound of jet engines brought David back to the present. The wind had shifted. He turned, dropped the rake, and grabbed a hand saw from the back of his Gator. He started trimming some lower branches from an offending tree near the ninth fairway. Somehow, a golfer had managed to hit the branch with her club on a backswing the day before, and she was not happy about it. Words were spoken and passed along. After he completed the task, the branch cut up and stowed in the back of his Gator, he moved back over to the traps around the green. David knew that making the course easier to play every time a golfer had a problem of their own making was not a recipe for luring competitive play. If this kept up, the golf club would quickly acquire a reputation as a social club, and tournaments would no longer want to grace its fairways.

He again looked south out through a break in the forest lining the fairway, over the log booms lolling in the mouth of the Fraser River, toward the airport. He watched one of the larger jets taking off, heading west, probably to some exotic holiday destination. David put those thoughts out of his mind. He had more pressing things to attend to.

In addition to avenging his father, there was payback due for his friends who had suffered through a bankruptcy resulting from a deficient condominium. They had purchased their home from a development company run by Samuel Greene. David's recent conversation with them confirmed their financial collapse. They were sure they were going to leave Vancouver because of it. This was just more grit in the wound. David didn't have many friends, so losing a couple of them wasn't good. It was time to even the ledger.

~ 21 ~

Present Day

After drinking tea most of the day Monday with Carol, his sister, who had come over to offer comfort, Sam decided he needed something more substantial, so he hauled out a bottle of scotch and poured himself a healthy shot. Friday evening was a distant memory now, and he was back on the horse. He settled in front of his laptop in the kitchen and went to the website of the dog breeder from Langley. He scanned over a few of the more famous breeds to check out their temperaments and requirements before settling on the Rhodesian Ridgeback. This was a dog bred in Africa to hunt lions—just the type he was looking for. He would at least go out to Langley to check it out and maybe look at a couple of other breeds as well. After another half-hour on the breeder's website, he poured himself some more scotch and moved onto other websites. His sister continued surfing on her cellphone in the living room.

An hour drifted by, and he realized he hadn't eaten much all day, so he got up and checked out his fridge.

He couldn't see much in there: obsolete looking greens, an older looking pork chop from a past meal, and cheese. He opened the freezer. Bingo, a frozen pizza was looking back at him. He hauled it out and set it on top of the stove to thaw.

"If we aren't going to talk, then I'm going to head home." Carol said, as she entered the kitchen.

Sam looked up, but only nodded. With that confirmation, Carol knew it was time to leave, so she grabbed her coat and left by the front door without another word.

At about the same time, a beat-up brown van slowly made its way down the darkened back lane behind Sam's house. One or two security lights flashed on, then dimmed as the van idled past garages of neighbouring homes. David was driving and was grateful for how handy Sam's home was to the golf club where he worked. He had stayed late at the work barns to rip a mower apart, lubricating and then re-assembling it. What he was really doing was killing time until the clock read 7:00 pm, a time when he figured people had already arrived home from work or had already gone out to whatever event they would be attending that evening.

He was the last one to leave the barns, and after locking up, arrived at Sam's house ten minutes later. The homes on either side of Sam's house were dark, the owners being away in some warm place far from Vancouver, so he parked behind the garage of the adjacent house. The lights were on in Sam's house. David could see Sam walking around in his kitchen.

David grabbed a broad short piece of lumber, his bottle

of ether, a rag, and got out of his van. He hastened to Sam's carport, to the driver's side of an Audi, and swung at the mirror. The wailing of the car alarm was instantaneous. David hid behind the adjacent wall for Sam to make an appearance.

He didn't have long to wait. Sam came out, no coat on, and stood in front of the broken mirror. David walked up behind him, gave him a good smack on the head, and then grabbed the ether bottle and rag to complete the job on the prostrate man laying on the pavement. He put the bottle and rag into his coat pocket, grabbed Sam under the arms, and dragged him to the back of his van. Two minutes later, Sam was taped up, and the van moved down the lane out onto Crown Street, driving off north then east. The car alarm kept wailing for ten more minutes before re-setting itself. No one bothered to come out from any adjacent houses to check on the noise. That would have required a neighbourly concern not present along the street Sam lived on.

* * *

Sam woke up slowly, retching as he came to full consciousness. It was cold and wet. It was also totally black, no sign of light anywhere he looked. He was sitting with his back against a concrete pillar, his arms and legs bound in front of him. He flexed against his bonds, but they were snug. His head ached something fierce. He tried to remember where he had been before the blackout. He could hear the dripping of water, but that didn't help him. Water dripped everywhere in Vancouver. He felt sick to his stomach, and had a foul taste in his mouth, but couldn't figure out why.

His memory drifted back. The last thing he could remember was walking out to his carport where his Audi was parked, seeing the smashed side mirror dangling from the driver's side and the car alarm wailing to beat hell. Sam hadn't bothered to check the security feed on his computer before venturing out—a decision he was now ruing. He also remembered that he hadn't eaten in a while, and despite feeling ill, he also felt hungry. He twisted his arms to look at his Rolex, surprised that it was still on his wrist. The luminous hands showed 11:03 am on Tuesday. He had been out for over fifteen hours.

* * *

Tuesday morning saw Robert and Camille heading over to Eden Gardens to meet with Dominic and Marty. The detectives arrived just after nine and Robert parked in his usual spot out front. After entering and talking to the volunteer, they were directed down the hall to Dominic's office. Marty was already there, sitting across from Dominic, looking over a file that contained personnel information.

"Dominic tell you who we are interested in?" Robert asked, without saying hello.

"Yup, a David MacDonald. Got his information here. I had to fire him for insubordination. He turned out to be a piece of work, that one."

Insubordination, thought Robert, where are we, in the army? "How long was he employed here?"

"Three years. I fired him two years ago."

"Do you have a picture of him?"

"Not in the file here, but on our computer system somewhere, I believe." This from Dominic.

"Address? And do you know what he drives?"

"Here is the address."

Camille took the page from Dominic and copied it down in her notebook.

"And he used to drive this old brown van."

The smallest of smiles glimmered on Camille's face.

Robert thanked them. "We are going to track this guy down. We'd appreciate it if none of this left this room until we catch this guy. If you could forward his photo to us by e-mail, that'd be great. Could you send us a copy of his resume as well? Assuming he had one."

Dominic and Marty both shrugged and assented. They just wanted this whole thing to be over. But Dominic hadn't forgotten that crack from Sam about vetting employees. Who wasn't vetting people now, Dominic thought. Marty, the little general, was responsible for the gardeners.

After Robert and Camille left the office, Robert got on his phone and called Norma at the station. He gave her the address for David MacDonald, and told her to send a couple of cars, with a warning that the suspect could be dangerous. They then went out, got back into the Crown Victoria, and returned to the station feeling better than they had felt in months. They were grinning at each other as they drove back.

As it turned out, the grins were slightly presumptuous. They returned to the floor, and after getting off the elevator, Norma called them over.

"The cars called in. David MacDonald hasn't lived at the address for two years, and they couldn't get a forwarding address from the building manager."

"Check your e-mail, Camille. See if that resume came in with the photo. We need to track down where this guy may be working. In the old days, when everyone had a land line, you could find people using a phone book. I guess that era is long gone." With that said, Robert needed to contemplate how he had managed to get this far in the day with no coffee. He couldn't come up with a reasonable explanation, but he knew that he better do something about it before he started suffering. He decided to go grab a drip coffee and bring it back to the office, just in case they found this MacDonald guy.

***

Earlier that morning, Carol Greene had phoned Sam to check in on him. No answer. She tried his cell. Again, no answer, which she found strange. She tried both numbers again an hour later. With still no response, she drove over to his house to make sure Sam was okay. After arriving, she called 911. The technician told her to stay put and a patrol car would be there in a few minutes. The call taker called the VPD, passing on the sparse information he had been given. Robert was quickly contacted, as most of the station personnel knew Sam Greene's name at this point.

Robert wasted no time in calling Carol.

"This is Robert Lui with the Vancouver Police. Sam is missing?"

"I think so. When I didn't get an answer on the phone,

I came over. I went in the front and it felt cold, as though a door had been open for some time. I went to the back where the kitchen is and sure enough, the back door was open. There's an uneaten pizza sitting on the counter. In the carport, the mirror on his car is damaged, like someone had bashed it."

"Were you with him yesterday?"

"Yes, but I left around seven in the evening. He was just getting ready to heat up the pizza."

"Okay, a patrol car should be there shortly. I'm sending one of my assistants over as well." He ended the call.

Camille called over to him. "The patrol officers are securing the scene. Tony is on his way to interview the sister and see if there is any evidence to be found." She added, "Nothing has been called in as yet. No ransom demands or anything like that."

"Well, I don't know who they would send a demand to, do you?"

"No."

"This isn't about money, it's about revenge, if what your research tells us is true. Based on what's happened lately, I don't like Sam's chances right now. Can you find out where that information from Dominic is? Call him if you haven't received it." Robert added, "Let's get the team together when you get it, in the case room."

Five minutes later, Camille was signalling for Winnie, Lawrence, and Erwin to go to the case room. She bobbed her head around the door frame and looked into Robert's office. "Ready to go."

Robert followed Camille to the room where the rest

were waiting. Camille started, "We have his picture, so we are sending it out to all the patrol cars, in addition to the van description. David's resume lists a few golf courses in his past, so maybe we start there?"

"Not maybe—definitely. Good work Camille." Robert said. "Can the three of you get a list of golf courses around town and divide it up? Ask for the manager and find out if any of them have our man as a greenskeeper. Right away, please. Sam has been taken, and my guess is that Mr. MacDonald has him. We may not have much time." With that, the other three left quickly and started their search. Robert's cell rang.

"It's Tony. I'm at Sam's house. His car is damaged in the carport, mirror broken off, and we have a piece of lumber with a bit of blood on it. Guessing it was used to whack him with, not much else to report. We're doing a canvass of the neighbours again, but I'm not hopeful. We'll check the lumber for prints when I get back. There is a security camera in the area of the car as well. We'll see what's on it." Tony rang off.

Robert looked at Camille. "Craps, craps, craps," as if saying it three times would make everything right. Robert was going over everything in his mind, wondering if he had screwed up somehow. They seemed to be one step behind this guy at every turn. Camille was about to say something when Winnie ran into the office, her face flushed.

"Found him! Southlands Golf Club down on the Musqueam lands, just off Marine Drive. He works as a greenskeeper there, and I have a home address as well.

The manager checked with the head greenskeeper, and apparently David is there today."

"Great work Winnie. Get a couple of ghost cars over there, quiet - no sirens, and make sure the officers know what they are getting into. Tell them there may be a kidnapping victim involved and to be very careful. Come on Camille, we're going for a ride." Robert added, "Can the club tell us whether David is out on the course or in the service barns?"

Winnie answered. "I'll call back and check."

"We may need a few more cars in case this guy makes a run for it. We need to cut off the perimeter of the club. Ghost cars to the barns, patrol cars to the edges—no sirens, and get a canine unit just in case. Let's move." The calls went out, along with the photo of David MacDonald. "Anyone got a plan of this place?"

"I'll print a map off of the computer," said Camille. "Meet you at the car downstairs."

Robert remembered something. As he went by Norma, he asked her to dispatch a couple of cars to the address noted as where David was supposed to be living.

Robert drove as quickly as he dared down the south slopes of Vancouver, then west across to the golf club, afraid David was going to slip away from them. In the end, he needn't have worried. When they arrived, driving into the parking lot of the service buildings, several police cars were already there, and David MacDonald was in handcuffs in the middle of a group of officers. Robert and Camille sat in the cruiser for a moment, watching, savouring the moment.

"The scarecrow," Robert said.

"What?"

"You know, from *The Wizard of Oz*. The guy looks like the scarecrow, and not in a good way, either."

"Let's go Robert."

Robert and Camille got out of the Crown Victoria and walked over to where the group of officers were standing. Some greenskeepers were standing by their barn watching the scene, talking amongst themselves. Robert looked across the parking lot. The brown van that had eluded them for so long was sitting under some cedar trees.

Robert walked up to the suspect. "Hello David."

David remained silent, staring at Robert.

"Where is Sam Greene? What have you done with Sam?"

This was met with more silence.

"Right. Can a couple of you check the brown van over there? That's the suspect's van." Then he yelled over to the men by the barn. "If you want to still use your cars, you better move them. Tape is going up around the van."

"We'll need an organized search of the course and all the buildings. Camille, can you go over to the clubhouse and inform the manager that the club is closed for today? You can tell them we are conducting a search for a kidnap victim on the premises, and we'll need their cooperation." Robert caught the faintest of glimmers from David's eyes. Then it was gone. "Put the suspect in a car and take him down to Cambie Street. We'll need to get that van taken in as well after photos are taken."

Robert grabbed Camille by the arm, and they backed up

while David was being loaded up into a cruiser. "He's not here. We still need to go through the motions, but my bet is that Eden Gardens is where we'll find Sam. Everything that has happened has centred around that place since the beginning of this mess."

Robert stood, looking around the parking lot while Camille walked over to the clubhouse. A couple of greens mowers were sitting quietly beside a large gang machine that Robert guessed was used for cutting fairways. He looked south and could glimpse what looked like tennis courts beyond the branches of the intervening trees. Nice place, he thought, way out of my league.

A co-op car rocketed into the parking area and slid to a stop, gravel spraying in a fan. Out stepped Bernard, the newly minted *Province* reporter. He looked around, recognized Camille, and walked over. Before he could open his mouth, Camille said, "No comments yet. We are in the middle of a situation. We have a suspect in custody. That's pretty much it."

"Is it the Eden Gardens restaurant guy?"

"Can't say anything more at the moment."

Bernard stood looking perplexed. He could see all the cars and officers and that they weren't leaving, so he figured something was still up. He couldn't see anybody who looked like a bad guy. Bernard didn't know Sam Greene was missing—but that would change soon. Sam's house was going to be his next stop. It was on the way back downtown anyway. As he was about to get into his car, a local television van pulled up and a reporter with a camera crew jumped out. He waited to see if they knew something he didn't, as if that were even possible. No one was more on top of this story than Bernard—at least that's what he kept telling himself. He rolled down his car window and listened, but it was plain that they were just fishing, so he left for Sam's place.

When he drove up Sam's street, he saw a police cruiser. Something was going on, so he stopped and watched. He couldn't see anything, so he drove around to the lane side, at least as far as the yellow tape would let him. The police had the carport and back of the house taped off. Bernard got out and walked up to the tape line. No cops were in sight. All he could tell was that something had probably happened to Sam Greene. His next gambit would be to check the local hospitals.

***

Back at the golf club, Robert slid into the car and got on his cell. "Norma? Can you organize some cars to go over to Eden Gardens? We need to conduct a thorough search of the entire property. I have a feeling that this is where we'll find Sam Greene."

"Ok. How many officers do you think?"

"The place is one hundred and forty acres, so maybe thirty or so if we can manage it?" He added, "Better call Dominic over there and warn him. The place needs to be closed again. Try to get the cooperation of Marty, the supervisor. He knows the Gardens, I would think."

Robert waited for Camille in his car, watching the officers begin their search for Sam. He watched the TV crew standing there, talking amongst themselves, and he knew the police were shortly going to be dogged by many more reporters. When Camille returned, they left to head back to Cambie. Robert couldn't wait to question David.

~ 22 ~

Sam Greene was making progress. His mouth had not been taped, so from time to time he yelled for help. All he heard back was his own voice echoing. Except for the hands on his Rolex, he still couldn't see a thing. However, because his hands were taped together in front of him, he could work on the tape binding his ankles together. After a half-hour of this, and tearing a couple of his fingernails, he was finally able to rip through the tape and free his feet. He stood and immediately needed to relieve himself, barely getting his fly open in time. He was dizzy and immediately fell over, not being able to balance himself with his arms. He smacked his head on the concrete floor and saw stars but didn't black out this time. After he managed to sit up again, he could feel something dribbling down the side of his face. He stuck his tongue out and tasted the rich metallic flavour of his own blood. He let loose with a few curses and felt somewhat better after doing this.

* * *

Robert asked Camille to arrange an interview with David. When he had been placed in a room, Robert and

Camille went down to the cell block area to talk with him. They both entered the room and took a seat. David was sitting bolt upright, posture perfect, as if he were in a military academy waiting for dinner service. He was shackled to his chair.

"Can you please read him his rights, Camille?"

After this was done, Robert launched in, "You want a lawyer present?"

"I don't care."

"Do you know why you are here?"

"Because of that asshole Sam Greene."

"Correct, amongst other things, such as murdering an east side resident, chopping him up, cutting a tree down, murdering Sam's wife, kidnapping Sam and killing his dog."

"Sam's wife? What are you talking about? I never killed Sam's wife." His eyes blazed.

"Doesn't matter right now, she is dead. I hope Sam is not dead for your sake. Where did you put him, David?"

David smiled this time, with no attempt to hide it. "You won't find him. He's going to get what he has coming to him. It's time for Sam to pay."

So, Sam was still alive, Robert thought. He looked at Camille. She had picked it up as well. He signalled to her, and they both left the room. "Don't go anywhere," Robert said to David, as they walked out.

"You can be a real jackass, Robert." Camille was grinning as she spoke.

"I know. Okay, let the guys know out at Eden that Sam is most likely still alive, but they need to be thorough in their search. If he is not at the Gardens, then the likelihood of finding him, let alone alive, is pretty slim. I am betting he is there, somewhere," then he added, "Sounds like he is going to agree to all the other stuff. A little strange about Lydia, don't you think?"

"I agree. Maybe he really didn't do it, but at least we should go back and get him to agree on the other stuff. We can grille him later on Lydia, correct?"

"Yes. Call the site and then we'll go back in." A couple of minutes later, they returned and resumed the interview.

"We know what Sam did to your family, David." Robert was fishing with the sympathetic phrase, but he was also trying to find out how it had all happened years ago.

"If you know that, then why am I being arrested? He's the one who should be arrested." David was plaintive.

Robert looked at the wall above David's head, thinking, "Well, we'd have to find him first, wouldn't we?"

"Nice try."

"Does this mean you did the other stuff, leaving out Sam's wife?" Robert was going for it, all in, as they say in poker circles.

"Maybe."

"What about Miguel? How did you find out his story?" Robert was again making some assumptions.

"He is a stupid one, that guy. We went out for drinks one day and he let slip the story. He didn't really want to tell me, but after a couple more beers, he did. And I remembered."

This last came out triumphantly, as though he routinely forgot things such as this.

"Interview is over, for now." Robert was ticked at himself. What did he do wrong? He was certain that David was going to confess his sins. He signalled to Camille. They both left the room, went up to their floor, and into Robert's office. He closed the door and they both sat down.

"Let's let him stew a bit in his cell. Maybe we should get out to Eden to monitor the search. What time is it, anyway?" It was dark already, the time of year when the foggy shroud of drizzle closes in on the coast, driving people indoors.

"Four."

"I'm hungry. I haven't eaten all day. Think I'll call home, then we should go up to Paulo's for some sustenance before we head back out there." Robert said. He phoned and told Sophie where to find the leftover Bolognese sauce in the freezer, and that he would be home late. These were the days when he worried about his kids, when he had serious things happening at work.

As he and Camille walked past Norma, he stopped and thanked her for her help in coordinating the personnel. She smiled back at him, but he also noticed a hint of the stink eye at Camille. Good gravy, he thought, there is no winning anymore, there's just staying even, if you were lucky. The two of them walked out of the building and up the street to Café Paulo.

After Robert and Camille ordered the last paninis out of the glass display case and sat down, they started discussing the events of the day.

"It is a lot to take in for one day," Robert started. "I'd say David is our guy. But the Lydia thing is troubling, to say the least. Somehow, despite all things David has done, I don't feel that lying is one of his sins. Tomorrow, first thing, we need to meet with Winnie and Lawrence to see what else they've uncovered regarding similar cases. Maybe we have a different killer on the loose. But with what motive?"

"Then there is the missing Mr. Greene."

"The missing Mr. Greene indeed." Robert paused. "I am still betting the Gardens is where he'll be found." The server brought their paninis over to the table. "I hope they find him soon, because I definitely got the idea that he is still alive from David, didn't you?"

"Yes." They started in on their food. "Assuming he's not in a pond, because that's where most of the other things have ended up." Camille said, as she bit into her sandwich.

"Let's finish up quickly and get over there. Don't know what we'll be able to do effectively in the dark, but we should check the search progress."

* * *

Sam had tried and was successful in standing without toppling over again. The bleeding from his head had abated. He had been working on the tape around his wrists but had only limited success in trying to chew through the edges of it. He shuffled around to figure out where he was, but had to move tentatively in order to not bump into walls or trip over things on the concrete floor. He still tried to yell occasionally, but his throat was hoarse from the effort. Sam wasn't used to screaming. That much was clear. He checked his watch again. It read 5:08 pm.

* * *

Camille and Robert drove back over to Eden Gardens, the car almost driving itself being so familiar with the route. They checked with the officer in charge of the search, who had set up a table in the hall looking at the plaza outside the glass wall. The darkness made it almost impossible to see anything. Robert guessed it would be slow going out in the reaches of the Gardens. He asked if Marty was about and was told that he had just left.

Dominic came over to them and explained that about one-third of the place had been searched along with all the staff areas at the north side as well as the eastern service buildings.

"Is the light display ready to go? It would help the officers." Robert asked.

"Unfortunately, no." Dominic responded.

After a few more minutes discussing the process with the officer in charge, it became plain that Robert and Camille had nothing to contribute to the effort. They said they would return at first light tomorrow, and then left.

After changing cars at Cambie, Robert was relieved to be heading home to get re-acquainted with his children. He turned on the radio and drove out into the darkness. He was happier than he had been in a while, maybe not in spite of Sam's failure to be found, but because of it.

* * *

Sam was back to sitting down and getting colder. He was trying to conserve his energy, but was going through shaking fits as hypothermia set in. He was facing the fact that he might die in this place, wherever he was. He was getting thirsty. He could still hear water dripping, but also scurrying sounds, exactly the sounds rats would make. What if no one came for him? Sam was trying not to panic, but the more he tried, the more frightened he became. He didn't want to die in here, being eaten by rats, but he was having trouble imagining any other outcome. He screamed again. The blackness was a death shroud over his head, as he screamed and screamed until his vocal cords were useless.

***

Wednesday dawned, the sun not making its appearance until close to eight, and even then only faintly. Robert saw his children off, then drove over to Cambie to collect the Crown Victoria and Camille for the trek to Eden Gardens. They had not been there for more than a half-hour when Marty made an appearance. He came into the hall, excited about something.

"I just thought of a place that we haven't searched yet. Next to the reservoir, out at the east side, there is an underground service room, built to handle all the additional water lines to the remainder of the Gardens and the fountain displays. It is normally locked, but we should check it, I think."

"Let's go then, round up some carts please," Robert asked. He beckoned to a couple of uniformed officers to come along with some equipment. When a couple of Gators were commandeered, the group got in and took off, Marty leading the way. It took over five minutes to reach the reservoir.

Dew clung to the grass across the Great Meadow, and water dripped from the branches of the oak trees near the German Gardens, their brown leaves still refusing to fall. The group drove around the still body of water to a small hut-like building sitting in the middle of a copse of beech trees, where Marty slid to a stop. He beckoned the officers to follow him as he made his way around to the east side of the hut to its service door. Un-trampled brush indicated that it had been a while since anyone had visited the area.

He yelled. The group listened, but no one heard anything in return. Marty pulled out his extensive set of keys, eventually finding the correct one, and opened the door. He reached past the door frame and switched on a light. Robert followed Marty into what was essentially the top of a circular metal staircase descending into the depths of the earth. There was no room for anything else. A line of men slowly descended into a concrete room that seemed about one hundred square metres. Large pumps were arrayed along one wall, with associated black pipes flaring out in all directions, both at ankle level and above head height. It didn't take long to figure out that Sam was not in the room. Marty shrugged. "It was worth a try."

Robert nodded, turned, and started back up the stairs. When everyone had exited the hut, Robert turned to Camille and suggested they return to the pavilion to talk to the head search officer. After a discussion with the officer, revealing nothing except that the north half of the Gardens had been thoroughly searched, Robert was at a loss.

"Perhaps you need some coffee," Camille suggested.

Robert's eyes sparked. "I believe you have nailed it." He looked around, and sure enough, there was an urn on a table by the wall. He was wary as he sipped at the cup, but it was serviceable. He and Camille sat at a table trying to put themselves inside the mind of a vengeful gardener. After he had finished, he had a thought, rather basic, but he wondered why he hadn't come up with it before.

"Is there a map of the whole Gardens? A detailed map?" This was directed at the search captain.

"Of course, here is a copy."

Robert grabbed the paper and sat back down. He ignored the north half for the moment and looked for any structures in the south half. It didn't take him long to discern that there weren't many. There were three clustered together in a meadow in the southeast quadrant of the Gardens but had nothing naming them or even indicating what they were. He looked over and beckoned to Marty.

"Marty, what are these structures?"

"They are small chapels."

"Why three? Are they named?"

"I don't know why there are three, but the names are The Chapel of Passion, The Chapel of Retribution, and The Chapel of Redemption. We have already checked them out once early in the search."

"Are you kidding me?" He looked at Camille and yelled,

"Let's go look at these chapels. Even if they have been searched, I want to see them for myself."

Once again, the group mounted up on Gators and headed out in a column, Marty in the lead. As they headed south, they passed first through a meadow of statuary, then one where topiary was on full display. The group entered a third meadow where three compact stone buildings stood about thirty metres from each other. They were ornate and had a Baroque look to them. Robert knew they couldn't be that old, as people had been golfing on this land only twenty years earlier. Looked to him as though some instant history had been added to Eden Gardens.

They stopped, killing the engines, silence descending once again onto the meadow. Robert yelled at Marty, "Which one is the Chapel of Retribution?"

Marty pointed, and the group headed toward the small building. From the outside, it had the appearance of a small church one might find anywhere upcountry north and east of Vancouver. But these were always built of wood, whereas this one was of stone, blackened granite, or basalt, it seemed. Robert was first to the door and entered, the others crowding in behind him. The layout was simple, with six rows of dark wooden pews on each side of a narrow central nave. The group was staring at a font and small altar sitting in front of a rather impressive piece of leaded glass at the rear of the apse. It seemed evident that there was no one in the building, but Robert let loose a yell anyway. "Sam?" The group was silent, but no reply was heard.

"Is there a basement under here?" Robert directed this at Marty.

"I don't think so, but I seem to recall running some water lines in a service tunnel under one of these chapels when they were built, to supply irrigation to the south end."

"Well, does anyone in your crew know which chapel it was?"

"I'll check." Marty then called Nate on his radio. After a moment, he looked at Robert. "He says it was under this chapel. It was used as a relay junction. We should look for a floor hatch."

The officers spread out and examined the floor, most of which was stone and tile. Robert went behind the altar. Close to the rear wall, in front of the stained-glass window, was a scuff of mud. The only thing he could deduce from this was that someone had been in there recently, but he couldn't see any signs of a door or hatch. He knelt to study the floor closer. Nothing. As he put his hand down to steady himself before rising, a small piece of tile under his thumb moved. He pushed at it, and the tile moved again, revealing a grommet. He stood up and asked for a glove, not wanting to queer any evidence if possible. After gloving up, he poked his index finger through and pulled slowly. A heavy section of stone tilted up, revealing a dark hole.

He looked in while yelling, "Hello?"

A faint reply came from the depths.

"Anyone there?"

An officer with a flashlight came over, giving it to Robert.

A croaking voice answered, "Here."

Robert looked up and smiled, then manoeuvred through the hole and down a metal ladder. His light shone out and was swallowed by the gloom. The tunnel was larger than the chapel above, that much was evident. Robert flicked his torch around, looked over and there Sam was, sitting against a wall in a puddle of water, not very far from the ladder, his arms bound in front of him. He was squinting at the sudden influx of light. It must have been terrifying to be in the total darkness for a couple of days. It was cold and wet, not a scenario for survival. He moved over to Sam as a couple of other officers descended.

"You're safe now. We'll get you out of here and to the hospital," Robert said. He yelled up, "Got him. It's Sam!"

Camille called for an ambulance to get over to the Gardens. After confirming that Sam was not injured, other than the cut to his head, they tried to get him standing, but Sam was having difficulty. Robert decided to get Sam out of the service room, rather than wait for the paramedics. They fashioned a harness out of rope and cinched it around Sam's torso under his arms. They manoeuvred him over to the ladder and pulled him up carefully through the hatch. Robert looked around the service tunnel once more before climbing back up and dropping the hatch in place. After they exited the chapel, one officer checked Sam out and loaded him onto a cart, then the rest of the group mounted up for the trip back to the entry pavilion. Another officer remained to place tape around the area.

Sam had the grace to at least say, "Thanks."

Robert asked, "Who did this to you?"

Sam could only croak, "Don't know. I was out for a while." He then remained silent for the return journey. Camille called ahead and told them Sam had been found, was hypothermic and would need blankets and some water.

Back in the pavilion, Robert stood next to Camille. They were both looking at each other, not resisting the urge to smile. Sam was being rolled out on a stretcher to a waiting ambulance, looking better for getting some water, warmth, and first aid for his various cuts.

"All of a sudden, I feel a lot better," Robert said.

Camille grinned. "Yeah, we should celebrate somehow."

"We'll figure something out on the drive back to Cambie Street. Meanwhile, let's get the search wrapped up and a crime scene group out to the chapel. Where is Dominic?"

The arrivals hall in the pavilion suddenly got busy, with some officers coming back in from the gardens, getting ready to leave, most with smiles on their faces. Always good to be part of a successful rescue, especially in a kidnapping case. Robert thought of something and called Norma.

"Norma, could you possibly give Carol a call, Sam Greene's sister? Let her know that we found Sam alive. We also have a suspect in custody, and that Sam should be safe. We didn't have time to let Sam know before he was carted off to the hospital. I doubt if they will keep him in overnight. He didn't look to be in terrible shape when we discovered him."

"Excellent news Robert."

"Yes, the best possible outcome." With that, he rang off.

At that moment, Dominic walked up to Robert, smiling. "Great work Robert."

"You can also thank Nate. He was the one who remembered the service tunnel below the building. I think you could now safely open up the whole Gardens tomorrow. We'll have a team over at the chapel for the rest of today, but they should be finished after that. If they aren't, we will leave the area taped off." Dominic looked visibly relieved to hear this news. He turned and beckoned Robert as he made his way back down the corridor to his office.

"I forgot about something that you may be interested in. After the dog incident, remember you said something about security?"

"Yes."

"We actually did something about it. We had the security company we use plant a bunch of mini cameras in the woods, along some paths, and at a couple of the gates. They're not tied into anything, essentially they are stand-alone as we got the cheapest models available, but they might have something on them. I didn't know if they had been activated as yet, which is why I forgot to mention them after Lydia's murder. But it turns out that they were activated when they were installed."

"Really? So, they were working the night of the fundraiser? Can we get the recordings?"

"I'll get someone to do the rounds and send them over to you later today."

"Thanks." Robert shook Dominic's hand and together

they walked back into the hall where officers were continuing to leave except for the ones at the command table. "Can I ask a question?"

"Of course."

"How did those chapels come to be, and who named them?"

"Well, one of the directors on the board has a Catholic background, Spanish heritage, I believe. He thought it appropriate to build some small rooms for prayer out in the reaches of the Gardens. He had names for them but someone whose name I can't reveal, but whose initials are Samuel Greene, changed the names. The chapel where he was found is by far the most popular. What does that say about our society?"

"Maybe it reflects people's true concerns. There seems to be a lot of popular culture built around the idea of getting even for real and imagined slights, or all-out revenge, the bloodier, the better."

"I suppose you might have something, unfortunately." Dominic stood, shaking his head.

Robert walked over to Camille. "I think we can leave now. Things are under control. Apparently, Marty and Dominic had their security company plant some cameras in the Gardens a while back. Dominic is going to get us the files by tomorrow. We need to get back and have a meeting to figure out where we are in this big mess, and how to deal with David MacDonald. We'll have to charge him with something pretty soon."

"Yes, boss." Camille was still grinning. They both

turned and walked out to their car for the return trip to Cambie.

* * *

After the two intrepid detectives walked onto their floor and were met by clapping and grins by both admin staff and the few officers on the floor, Robert decided a trip up the street was in order. He knew he didn't deserve all the credit, but he also wasn't above accepting accolades. The job was so shitty most of the time, these moments needed to be savoured. He asked Norma to get the team together in their case room in an hour.

"Steve is looking for you." Norma offered. "He got back today."

"Excellent, be back in half an hour." With that snappy retort, Camille and Robert departed for their well-earned shots of caffeine. For a change, it wasn't raining as they walked up and entered Café Paulo.

"Gilberto," Robert yelled.

"Roberto," Gilberto yelled back, then for good measure, "Camilla!" The officers ordered long espressos and pastries, then sat over by the window. When Gilberto brought the coffees over, which was frankly outside the normal service parameters for Café Paulo, he couldn't help noticing the smiles on the officer's faces. "Things are a go-in' good?"

"So good, we can't stand it." Robert laughed. He'd like to tell Gilberto more but decided against it. He knew Gilberto would not share it anyway, even though he talked daily with a wide assortment of caffeine fuelled individuals.

Robert looked at Camille. "We're going to need some evidence from Tony's searches if we are going to be able to lay charges. David looks a little crazy, so let's hope he was also a little sloppy."

"We'll also have to figure out the Lydia murder," Camille said.

"Not much of a celebration coffee, is it? More like a 'we still have a lot to do' coffee."

"Yeah, but the best thing is that the bad stuff is behind us."

"We hope. Say, did you ever talk with that developer? Nicholas Ng?" Asked Robert.

"I did. He wasn't very complimentary about Sam Greene. He said that the dispute with Sam happened after he had found out that Sam was behind the Eden Gardens development, and he let the development community know. Sam wasn't happy, it seems."

"Maybe that's when David found out and started his revenge drama. No wonder Sam wasn't happy."

He got up, went over to the counter, and paid for a bunch of extra pastries for the team meeting, and Norma, of course. He wasn't sure whether Norma was ticked at him or not, but a sweet wouldn't hurt. "Okay, got to go say hi to Steve. Let's move."

~ 23 ~

Back in the office, Robert readied for the audience with Steve by trying to figure out what Steve had missed. In summary, he had missed a lot. Robert composed himself, walked slowly down the corridor, and knocked on Steve's door. After being asked to enter, he walked in and saw a face so tanned he wanted to throw up. Steadying himself, he took the offered chair, sat, and opened his notebook.

"What did I miss?" Steve asked. No small talk for this man, Robert thought. He also realized that it appeared that Steve did not keep up with the news.

"A murder, a kidnapping, and the arrest of a suspect." Robert didn't mince words. He then laid out the sequence of events from the last week for Steve to digest. He stared at his notebook, but the pages were mostly blank.

"I knew you could do it. I think I should obviously take more vacations."

Robert silently agreed with his boss, but said, "We got lucky. We still have a lot to do. Lydia's murder also does not quite fit. We're not sure if MacDonald did it."

"Of course he did. The guy is a wacko. Just clean it up, talk to the prosecutor, and get all the charges laid."

If this was the way Steve worked, it was a wonder anything he touched went to trial, Robert thought. He just smiled and excused himself, thanking Steve for his time, saying that he had a team meeting to attend.

Robert went back to his office, grabbed the bag of pastries, and walked down to the case room, where he placed them on the table in front of the assembled group. Erwin produced a large plate and laid the sweets out. Everyone seemed to be in a good mood.

Tony spoke first. "Great news, you two." The others nodded as they sat chewing on their mid-morning snacks. "We were able to lift some prints from the piece of lumber used to whack Sam Greene on the head in the carport. They match David MacDonald's. There wasn't anything else to find out there. A bit of blood on the lumber was a match for Sam's. We expect the security camera to have some footage as well."

"Excellent," said Robert. "We can charge him with assault with a weapon, and probably kidnapping. It's enough to keep him around while we do our work. The crime scene people are out at the chapel right now, hoping they get some more prints off the access hatch." He added, "It seems that David was getting less and less careful the more things he did."

Camille asked Winnie and Lawrence about their progress on cases similar to the Lydia Greene murder.

"We found two more unsolved murders that fit the profile, one a year ago in Surrey and one four years ago in Burnaby." Lawrence said, then added for good measure, "Sexual interference and strangulation," just in case again, that everyone had forgotten. Robert was beginning to wonder about Lawrence.

"I assume that all these cases are still open?" Robert asked.

"Yes." This from Winnie. "The officers on the cases have a suspect in mind but are lacking the proof needed to arrest. It's frustrating, I think, from talking to these officers."

"We should get some video from Eden Gardens later today. They planted a few cameras around the Gardens after all the goings-on lately. We'll see what they can tell us, particularly from last Friday night." Robert said, then added, "We'll formally charge David MacDonald in the meantime, and wait for any more evidence. Let's meet again tomorrow morning, say ten." With that, the meeting disbanded.

* * *

Robert spent the rest of the day writing up the reports that needed to be done for all the events of the last week. He called home around four and talked to Robin about dinner. After some conversation that was going nowhere, Robert decided he would make a choice at the store. Sometimes people didn't know what they wanted to eat. He called it a day and walked up to the grocery store where he wandered the aisles before buying chicken breasts, a bag of potato tots, and asparagus, along with a few other accessories. With this in hand, he headed home, more relaxed that he had been in several weeks.

Once home, he yelled up at the children and received

answers, so he headed to the whisky cupboard and stared at its rather limited selection, finally selecting one from the land of Nippon. He got out a couple of knives, garlic, lemons, and proceeded to beat the chicken breasts flat. He got the asparagus ready to be dropped in boiling water, slipped the tots into the hot oven, and then started sautéing the breasts. Half an hour later, the lemon butter sauce completed with capers, dinner was plated, and they all ate in silence. The food didn't stand a chance.

"How's school?" Robert asked as he was finishing the last of his meal. He had found out that Surinder had indeed made a visit, but he hadn't heard the outcome.

Sophie answered, as Robin's mouth was full of potato. "Pretty good." She knew what Robert was really asking about. "That gang guy visited the school. We haven't been hassled since then, but I don't know whether it's over or not." It appeared that Robin was not going to add anything, so Sophie continued, "He looked pretty tough, and I think he made an impression."

"That's because he is tough. He is an ex-gangster, so he knows what he's talking about, and doesn't fool around." Robert said. "You be sure to let me know if anything happens again, okay?" Robert was pretty sure this wasn't going to be the end of the problem, but it sounded as if things were better for now.

"Sure Pops." Robin suddenly found his voice, admittedly garbled by the tots still in his mouth. "Good meal Pops, thanks."

It was enough to melt your heart, Robert thought. Or maybe they were buttering him up so they wouldn't be asked to help with the cleanup. His kids could be very cagey.

He capitulated, "I'll do the dishes. You go do whatever it is you do in your hideaways." They did not need to be asked twice. They both smiled and headed upstairs. Robert poured himself some more wine and went to relax on the couch. Wasn't it the rule that whoever cooked didn't have to do the dishes? Something was wrong with this picture, he thought, as he sipped the wine.

'You shouldn't let them get off so easy, Robert.'

Robert looked over at the stairs as he answered Susan. "Things are going so well at work. I am feeling charitable tonight."

"You softie."

Later in the evening, he flipped on the local news to see what the chicken heads were making of the Eden events. One of the stations had figured out that David MacDonald was in custody, and that he was likely responsible for all the mayhem over at the Gardens, including several murders. They had not apparently found out the back story, which wasn't surprising, as they couldn't even get the present-day events correct. He flipped over to the people's network. These newscasters were more circumspect, but again, they didn't have the whole story correct. Well, it wasn't his job to correct them. That's what the media people down at the station were for. He wasn't sure how young Bernard was doing, but figured he'd be leaving the *Province* newspaper soon when he figured out how well print was doing these days. Eventually, Robert got the dishes into the dishwasher and went upstairs to sleep the sleep of the dead.

***

Thursday morning dawned on Southlands and Sam Greene got out of bed with an aching head. He had arrived home the evening before, promptly poured himself a huge scotch, ordered in some food, and thanked his lucky stars he was still alive. Speaking of Lucky, he was going to have to prioritize that trip out to Langley for a new watch dog. The nurses at the hospital had made sure he was re-hydrated and had some food inside him before discharging him. They had stitched up his head where David had whacked him with the lumber, and from when he had fallen on the service room floor. Sam didn't consider what they had fed him to be real food, but he was just being Sam. The nurses were happy to see him discharged.

The police had left his residence earlier the previous day, taking all their yellow tape with them. He went out the back door and looked at his Audi. He would need to fix that as well. What a pain in the ass this was. Good thing that guy was locked up. He would have to check that David remained behind bars. Couldn't have crazy people roaming around threatening respectable citizens.

Sam was drinking his first coffee, looking at the dog breeder's website again when his doorbell rang. None of his neighbours were friendly, so it wouldn't be them. He opened the front door, and a short wide man with a flattened nose came in and promptly drove a gloved fist into Sam's face, breaking his nose, and toppling him back into the foyer where he smacked his head on the stone floor, bouncing once. Blood was flowing liberally from his nose and the back of his skull. The man came over to Sam, looked down at his wrist, bent over, then slipped off Sam's Rolex Daytona and looked at it closely.

"That'll teach you to stiff me. Don't try that again, or it'll be a lot worse next time, asshole. This better be the real thing." With that, the man turned around and departed, leaving the front door wide open. Sam was definitely not having a good week, medically or any other way.

* * *

At the Cambie police station, Robert pulled into the parkade and got out of The Silver Streak with a spring in his step. He hadn't felt this good in weeks. It was a lot more to do with how his children were doing than anything else. Family always came first, as far as Robert was concerned. He decided to go straight up to the coffee place to grab a coffee to go, all to help with the paperwork that had still not filled itself in on his desk.

He walked slowly up Cambie, watching all the people heading east and west along the cross-streets on skateboards, bikes, and just plain walking. It was getting more and more crowded all the time, like a real big city, he thought. Then there were the dogs. Every third person seemed to have a tiny dog pet, not really a dog in the normal sense, but more like a small plush toy. These apparently sometimes could not walk, but were carried around in purses, or more annoyingly, in strollers that used to be reserved for baby humans. Robert couldn't figure out if it was a funny or sad commentary on modern urban life.

When he walked onto the floor, he waved to Camille, who was hard at work on something. He went into his office and sat down, looking out the window at East Vancouver, sipping his coffee.

Minutes later, Camille came into his office. Robert almost always left his door ajar. Most people thought he was encouraging guests, but he was really keeping an ear on things.

"Morning Robert. I'm still doing research on Sam Greene, and guess what I found out?"

"What?"

"He purchased a life insurance policy on Lydia about two months ago. Three million dollars."

"Indeed. Jeez, I guess then that when I called Mr. Greene slimy a while back, I was being nice. You think he bumped off his own wife? Or rather, had it done?" Robert was shocked. "I think we need to get Mr. Greene's phone records, all his phones."

"I was just going to suggest that." Camille said. "Remember, he had two previous divorces. Maybe he didn't need a third."

"They were at that fundraiser together the night of her murder. That is pretty cold if it's true. What kind of society are we living in?" Robert contemplated this new information, then asked Camille if the camera records had come in yet from Dominic.

"I'll check the admin desk right away."

"Is there anything else we're missing?"

"We should interview David again soon."

"Yeah, let's wait until we've reviewed the camera stuff from the site. We might learn something we can use." With that, Camille left his office and Robert settled down to more of his paperwork.

He realized he would need Steve to sign off on the court order request to get Sam's phone records. He puzzled a while how to do this. Steve was convinced that David was the culprit behind all the events at the Gardens, and he seemed to be protective of anyone with social standing from the west side of Vancouver. Robert wondered if this was where Steve grew up or lived now. Maybe he had social connections that dictated how he acted. Robert had to admit that he didn't know much about Steve's background. He only knew what a pain he was to work for.

The best thought he could come up with was to use Camille to do it. Robert knew Steve would probably accede to the request from her. He'd be too mesmerized to say no. She wasn't likely to be happy doing this, but he'd keep his options open if he couldn't come up with something better.

~ 24 ~

It wasn't until early afternoon that the video recordings came over to the station from Eden Gardens. In the meantime, Steve had announced to Robert that he was taking away the three officers that he had given Robert, since the case was solved. Robert had been expecting this but could have used the help. In his mind, the case wasn't closed by a long shot.

Robert went out into the bullpen. "Camille, can you grab Tony and go through these recordings? Concentrate first on the Friday night, see if you can find anything. The three amigos have been taken back by Steve, no longer on the case."

Camille did the requisite slight eye roll, then walked off to fetch Tony and find a room. Robert suspected Sam was being himself, an opportunist to the bone. He saw a chance to pin something on someone else, in this case David MacDonald, and he took it. Apparently, the idea of killing someone, let alone someone you were married to, was not an impediment. What was society coming to? Robert had not got all the details of what happened to the MacDonald family yet, but he would have to fill in the gaps in his knowledge quickly before his second interview with David.

The smaller group reconvened in the case room. Steve had forgotten to take back the room from the team, at least for now. Camille had connected her laptop to the wall screen and waited for the other two to settle.

She started once they were ready. "We have only reviewed the Friday night footage so far, but we have something. There was a camera fixed to a tree near the third service gate along Kerr Street. It was looking inwards, or west." She scrolled through the images, then froze one. "You can see the back of someone walking along the path toward the German Folly. It is hard to tell, but he does not look that tall. Kind of squat, not what David looks like. It is the return trip that nails him, however." She scrolled forward to 11:50 pm and there was the person again coming toward the camera. "No attempt to hide his face at all, and he appears to be carrying something white in his hand. Looks like a bra." Camille finished triumphantly.

"Holy smokes," was all Robert could say.

"Indeed, and he looks Asian to me, not like David."

"We need to get this picture over to the officers working on the other similar cases. See if this matches who they have been trailing. We need an identity, and then we could pull the guy in. What do you think?"

"I think yes. Tony, could you take the photos and ask Winnie or Lawrence who the officers were who were working the other cases? Ask them first who their suspect is before showing them the photos," Camille asked.

With that, the meeting broke up. Robert wanted them

to review the rest of the footage, but he wasn't optimistic anything else would be found. The cameras had been installed after most of the events had taken place. The only things they'd likely see would be squirrels and racoons with the odd coyote skulking around. He asked Camille into his office for a moment.

Robert had decided it would be best to send Camille in to make the phone log request to Steve. They were only going to get one chance at this, and Robert figured Camille was their premium option for success. He would need a good excuse for why he wasn't making the case as the lead detective, but he'd come up with something. He prepped Camille on what she could say and then sent her off to the lion's den. Before she departed, she looked Robert squarely in the eyes.

"I know why I am doing this, Robert. It is going to cost you when I am successful." Robert nodded as she left.

Camille knocked on Steve's door.

"Come in." Camille slowly opened the door and entered. She noticed Steve's eyes light up just before they dropped a bit to check out her breasts. Nothing's changed in this office, she thought, not with the decor, not with the occupant.

"What can I do for you, Camille? Please have a seat."

Camille sat and looked Steve squarely in the eyes, letting loose her most fetching smile. "We're making some progress on the Lydia Greene killing, and we think we need a phone log of all the Greene phones, including Sam's just to be thorough. I have a court order here ready for signing."

"Why do you need Sam's?"

She smiled again. "We think there were a few calls placed to Lydia by David, and there may have been some placed to Sam as well. We want Sam's records to exclude him." Camille thought she had never lied so blatantly or so convincingly.

"Where's Robert? How come he's not asking me for this?"

"Robert is preparing to interview David MacDonald a second time, and he wants to make sure he gets it correct this time, so we can nail him." This caught Steve's attention, and in doing so, muddled his thoughts. Which ever way Steve's brain had been heading, his thoughts took a side track, like empty freight cars being shunted off the main line.

"Ok, sounds good." He signed the document, then a pause, before asking, "What are you up to for lunch tomorrow?" This gave Camille a pretty good idea of where Steve's thoughts had been all along.

"I'm having lunch with Robert. We're prepping the case in order to get it to the prosecutor and want to make sure nothing is omitted." The disappointment was palpable on Steve's face. "Thanks. We should be able to wrap up the case with this." With that, she turned and left his office, walking leisurely, so Steve could get a leer at her very good-looking ass. Sure enough, as she turned slightly to close the door, she saw Steve's eyes and they were not looking at her head.

Camille walked down the corridor, not sure how she was feeling, but one thing she was sure of, and that was the lunch that Robert was going to be buying her tomorrow. She stopped by Robert's office and went in.

"That was creepy. Here is the court order, signed. You are taking me to one nice lunch tomorrow. You're buying."

Robert smiled. "I knew you would come through. You pick the restaurant and I'll make reservations. What did you tell him?"

"I lied through my teeth. He has no idea that Sam is a suspect. He just thinks we're getting his records to exclude him."

"Brilliant. As I said before, you are going to be running this place some day."

"I'm thinking of that Italian restaurant in Yaletown, you know, the one in the hotel."

"It's a date, Camille. Now I'm going to go see a judge. When I get back, we need to meet about David's history before we interview him again." Before he left, he called the restaurant to make a reservation, knowing if he didn't do it right away, he would forget.

***

Later that afternoon, Camille and Robert met again in Robert's office to review the case against David MacDonald.

Camille began, "Let's start with Stan. We don't have proof that David killed him, and we have really nothing that shows him sawing off Stan's arm. We do have a set of keys to all the locks on the gates and service barns. We have a print from the service gate at Kerr Street after the tree was lopped off, and prints on the note from David, so circumstantial evidence, at best."

Camille added, "We found dog hair in his van that matched Lucky, so we could get him on the dog. The van also had a bottle of ether, some rags and duct tape, a lot of duct tape."

"The big one is the kidnapping and assault on Sam Greene. That would put him away for a while, forgetting all the other stuff." Robert considered the options. "If we intimated somehow that we are looking at Sam for Lydia's murder, without actually telling him, he may plead to some of the other stuff. Knowing that Sam could be going away for life would probably be exactly what David wants."

"Let's wait until the phone records come in. Sam may have been stupid enough to talk to this contract killer on his phone." Robert concluded. "Let's call it a day and regroup tomorrow."

* * *

At Vancouver General Hospital, the emergency department was lucky enough to have a second visit by Mr. Greene. As he had a reputation by now, he was made to wait several hours before a doctor finally looked at his nose.

"It's broken," was the doctor's diagnosis. "Do you want me to try to straighten it out for you?"

"Yeth."

"This may hurt," he said, and yanked Sam's nose to the centre of his face. Sam screamed, then started in on the cursing. The doctor wasn't phased by this because a couple of nurses had warned him. He wiped up Sam's face, gave him some free drugs, and said he could go. The nurses came up to the doctor and thanked him for getting rid of Sam so efficiently.

"It's nice that you can inflict pain as well as heal," one of them said. He just smiled and went along to the next patient in line.

* * *

The next day dawned with rain dropping gently. There was a grey leaden nothingness to the sky, individual clouds impossible to distinguish. Robert arrived at the station and went to his office, where the task of the morning was waiting, the court order having come through. Tony now had some phone transcripts to go through, and it was going to take a while evidently. There was still nothing back on the suspect in the Lydia killing. Robert looked at his paperwork while contemplating how he would interrogate David the second time around. Then there was lunch with Camille, which he was eagerly anticipating.

He sat there, not thinking about any of those things. He was staring out the window at the rain, thinking about his decision to leave the gang task force and where it had brought him. On the negative side, he had not avoided the threat to his family. On the positive side, he had met Camille, who, it must be admitted, he was very interested in. The case he was currently handling was one that would leave people puzzled, no matter how it turned out. It would need a psychologist or psychiatrist to sort through the machinations of revenge with all its ugly results.

Robert decided to leave the second interview with David until the team knew a bit more about Sam's potential involvement in the case. In the meantime, he would talk to the prosecutor about laying assault and kidnapping charges. He worked on his reports before lunch.

* * *

Lunch turned out to be one of the best meals he had eaten in a while, as he had hoped. After getting on the train for the trip across the Creek, the walk to the restaurant was short. They both decided on the minestrone soup, then some scallops with a lemon risotto. It was not everyday fare for police officers, who were lucky to get lunch at all some days. The two of them talked quietly about the case for a while, then things got personal. Each of them had been hoping to reach this stage in their relationship without admitting it.

"I understand you have two children, Robert," Camille led off.

"I do, Sophie who is fifteen and Robin, my son who is twelve. I suppose you have heard about my wife as well?"

"Unfortunately, yes. I'm sorry about that, Robert. Cancer is evil and seems to affect everyone at some point. I lost my father three years ago. Lung cancer."

"That's terrible, Camille. Is that when you came out west from Montreal?"

"No, it was about a year and a half later, leaving a relationship which was not working out. I still remain in constant touch with *ma mere*. Luckily, my brother and sister are still in Montreal to be with her if she needs it."

"What do you think of being a police officer in Vancouver?" Robert asked.

"Different, yet the same. I like Vancouver, and the winters are easier to take. The mafia is kind of a fact of life in eastern cities. Out here, things seem more fluid and less entrenched, probably to do with the young age of Vancouver as much as anything."

Robert considered his next question carefully before asking it. "Maybe when this is over, I was thinking of taking my kids to go see the Seasonal Light Festival at the Gardens. Would you care to join us?"

Camille smiled. "I'd love that."

Robert smiled back at her, then changed gears. "Maybe we should get back and see what Tony has come up with." After an espresso, he paid, then they walked out and over to the train stop to head back under the Creek.

* * *

When Robert and Camille got back to the office just before two, Lawrence was waiting for them.

"The photo of the midnight strangler is a match for the same person the other officers have been chasing for years. His name is Bobby Minolta. He goes by the name of 'Big Bobby' on account of how short he is," Lawrence added.

"Do they know where he can be found? Let's bring him in and give him the business." Robert said. "I think we have enough to charge him with murder, I'd say, premeditated."

"I'll check with the others and see if we can get him picked up. I think they will be totally on board, having been after this guy for so long."

"Do it then." After this, Robert went to look for Tony. He found him in a small office, going through the information from Samuel Greene's phones.

"How are you doing?" Robert asked.

"Slow going."

"Are you looking at the week of the fundraiser?"

Tony looked sheepish and shook his head. Good grief, thought Robert. Who was teaching these people? Maybe it was up to him to do the teaching. Quite probably, this was the correct answer. "Well, start with that week, Sam's cell and home phone. Better see if he has an office anywhere as well if you don't find anything."

With that, Robert's week appeared to be at an end. He was trying to avoid Steve until they had more definite information concerning Sam, so he stayed in his office shuffling some paper around until he felt he had been all he could be. He bid goodbye to Camille and headed for his car. She watched his ass as he receded down the corridor toward the elevators. She was smiling inwardly, contemplating the future.

~ 25 ~

Saturday arrived and Sam Greene decided that a trip to the dog breeder in Langley was in order. It was quiet around the house after Lydia had gone and got herself murdered, especially with the absence of Lucky. After the kidnapping episode and recent visit, it looked as though he needed a guard dog. He went to his garage and got into his seldom used BMW for the trip out there. He would have preferred to use the Audi, but if he was fortunate enough to be able to get a dog, the SUV would be the better choice for getting it home. The Audi still needed to visit the car doctor, anyway.

His head ached from all the abuse it had suffered, but some pills helped to mitigate that. He had exchanged a few e-mails with the breeder, so they knew he was coming and what he was looking for. After the lengthy drive out to Langley, made worse by the Saturday traffic, he pulled up to the kennel's office and went in. The usual din of yelps, growls, and even some barking was all he could hear. He noticed what looked like a llama out in the pasture as he entered the office.

The kennel owner greeted Sam, took him into the area

where the new dogs were kept, and showed him some Ridgebacks that weren't more than a month old. Sam smiled and explained that he was looking for something a little older.

"We have a Ridgeback that was returned to us a week ago that you might look at."

"What's wrong with it?" This must be what it's like buying a used car.

"Nothing. The new owner couldn't handle it. Too aggressive for their taste. These dogs need to be trained correctly when they're young. I don't think this owner knew what he was doing."

"I'll take it."

"What?" The breeder wasn't sure she had heard correctly.

"I'll take it right now. Does it have a name?"

"Ringo."

"Really?"

"Yes."

"Ok, good to go. I don't want the rustproofing." Sam chuckled at his own humour, however, it was lost on the breeder. After the paperwork was completed and the dog moved into the rear of Sam's vehicle, he stood there, eying it. Ringo looked back at him, his eyes showing some fire. He got into the driver's seat, hoping that the dog wouldn't shred the rear interior on the return trip to Southlands.

***

After a weekend spent by Robert at home stocking up on food and meals for the coming week, he was ready to see the backside of his case. As he arrived on the floor just before nine on Monday, Steve spied him and beckoned him into his office. Shit, thought Robert, this won't be good. Steve was sporting his less than beautiful new suit. Sure enough, Robert's worst fears were realized.

"Have a seat, Robert. Good work on that Eden Gardens case. I've got a new one for you to handle. Someone has been embezzling money at one of the west side clubs. I want you to investigate, seeing as how you seem to know how to handle these society types appropriately."

It appeared to Robert that Steve had the memory of a gnat. Robert hadn't even sat down; he just smiled, asked for the file while thanking Steve, then left the office.

When he got back to his own office, Tony was leaning against his door frame grinning.

"Got him boss. Sam sent a text on the Friday afternoon of the fundraiser to someone named Bobby, telling him it was on for that evening, probably around eleven or so. Bobby responded, 'consider it done'. Then he asked for payment to be made to his account. We are confirming that the phone number was Minolta's."

Robert leaned out a bit and signalled for Camille to join them inside his office. Once they were inside and the door closed, Robert started, "This could get messy once we bring Sam Greene in. Does anyone know if this Bobby guy got arrested? We'll need to check Sam's bank records to confirm the payment."

Camille responded, "They picked him up yesterday in Surrey. Get this, he had a Rolex on his wrist, and when the officers took it and logged it in, whose name do you suppose was on the inside? That's right, Sam Greene!" She didn't even give them time to guess. "It's a Daytona version. I looked it up and it's worth a cool thirty-five thousand dollars."

Robert grinned. "For a watch? Wow, it's incredible how stupid these people can be. Let's go interview this 'Big Bobby' right away." Camille then called down to the cell block and asked if Bobby was ready to be interviewed. He was not in the mood to talk without his lawyer present, so a time was set for after lunch.

"Has his place and car been searched?" Robert asked.

"Yup. They found some women's underwear, including a bra. We're having it checked now to see if we can match it to Lydia." Tony said.

"Trophies." Said Robert. "This is turning out to be quite the week for cleaning up Vancouver, isn't it?"

Camille and Tony just sat there, nodding.

"I don't think we will wait on the bra match before our interview. I'm just assuming it was Lydia's. Someone should let the other officers know about the other women's underwear. They'll hopefully link back to the other killings."

* * *

After lunch was over, Camille called down to the cell area and asked if Bobby's lawyer had arrived yet. She was told that he was running late. Typical, she thought, anything that could be done to disrupt the authorities would be done, all in the name of defence for the accused. It was no different in Quebec. Two could play at that, as they would find out.

She went up to Robert's office and told him of the delay. Robert just shrugged. "We have all day, if that's the game they want."

Eventually Camille got a call back from the cell level. The prisoner and his lawyer were in the interview room, ready to go. She went over and told Robert, who suggested they go up to Café Paulo for a quick fix. Camille smiled, and they left the office. Robert wasn't in a hurry as they made their way up Cambie Street to the café.

After they received their espressos, they stood at the end of the bar discussing the pending interview. "I think I'm just going to hit him between the eyes, see what he says. We have a strong case against him, enough to hold him on murder one. The lawyer will just have to choke on it once he finds out how stupid his client is."

"That sounds fine, Robert. I don't see anything wrong with that approach. Maybe he'll cough up Sam in the bargain." After downing their drinks, they meandered back to the station and down to the cell level. Robert nodded to the officer outside the room, then they entered, went over, and sat on the opposite side of the table from Bobby and his lawyer. Bobby's large hands were on the table, and he was checking out Camille, so Robert knew his mind wasn't where it should be.

"Hello Bobby. I hear your nickname is 'Big Bobby'. Who gave you that name?"

There was silence from the other side. The lawyer looked pretty frosted at having to wait twenty minutes.

"I have a new nickname for you, Bobby. How about Bobby the Strangler? Because that is what you are going away for."

The lawyer came to life at this. "You have no evidence that my client had anything to do with this Lydia Greene's death."

"Really? Is that what you think?"

"Yes, and I'd like you to release my client now."

"Sorry, no can do. We are charging Bobby Minolta with a premeditated contract murder. He's going away for life. We have evidence of him at the scene, leaving with a piece of the victim's clothing, we have a phone record of him texting to the victim's husband the day of, we have recovered the husband's expensive watch from Bobby, and we have the victim's clothing in Bobby's possession."

The lawyer was looking at Bobby, clearly not in possession of all the facts.

"Those pieces of clothing are my girlfriends'." Bobby spoke before his lawyer could stop him.

"Well, we don't think so, because you don't have a girlfriend, do you? Who would bother to hang around a thug like you? Someone with a death wish, perhaps?"

"It was Sam Greene's idea." Again, before the lawyer could stop him.

Robert felt a warm glow start within him. Bingo.

"My client is not admitting anything." The lawyer said.

"Well, he just did, so the interview is over for now. And I'm doubting bail will be coming your way for this one. He's going to swing for this." With that, Robert and Camille stood up and left the room. The lawyer was talking quickly in a low voice to a worried looking Bobby as they left.

Camille was laughing in the corridor. "Swing for this? What movies have you been watching?"

"Couldn't resist. He's probably stupid enough to have some doubts now, who knows. If you can't have some fun doing your job, what's the point? Let's get Sam Greene in here for conspiracy to commit murder one. I'll go warn Steve because things will go crazy when this gets out." Robert said as they went up the elevator to their floor. "Make sure we check his bank records. Bobby must have received more than a watch for his work."

When they were back on the floor, Robert strolled down to Steve's office and knocked on his door. Nothing. Robert walked back to where Norma was and asked about Steve.

"Steve left for the day, Robert."

"Okay, too bad. He's going to miss the excitement."

"What excitement?"

"We are bringing Sam Greene in and charging him with murder." Norma's eyes flashed at this development. "I'm going to get a couple of cars out to Sam's place right now. Maybe you could call downstairs and warn them they're getting a visitor." Robert added.

* * *

Two cars went out to Southlands that afternoon. One car went up the lane to cut off any rear door exit that Sam Greene might have contemplated. The pair of constables at the front door waited after ringing the doorbell. Sam eventually answered along with a Rhodesian Ridgeback who wasn't exactly trained up. Ringo and Sam had agreed on one or two things, but it didn't take long for Ringo to decide he had had it with Sam, so the open door was an opportunity not to be missed. The officers quickly backed up a couple of steps, anticipating being attacked, but the dog raced by them, escaping Sam and all his problems. The officers watched as the dog hit the street and headed west at a gallop toward the forest, then returned their attention back to Sam. After eventually getting the other officers to the front, they handcuffed Sam, who didn't seem thrilled about the whole process. This time one or two neighbours did take notice, coming out onto their front landings to watch as police took Sam into custody.

***

Bernard was monitoring the police frequency, so he heard about the kerfuffle out in Southlands as the police requested an SPCA vehicle out to capture the escaped dog. He immediately suspected who it involved but, unfortunately for him, by the time he got a car and made his way out to the neighbourhood, Sam had already been packaged up and was gone. Bernard had no choice but to head back to False Creek to the police station to see if he could get a comment for his paper.

At Cambie Street, Sam was read his rights and shown to a cell. When he was told why he had been arrested, he spluttered a bit and let loose with a string of curses. His head looked so bad at this point that Frankenstein would have been a big step up in appearance. Camille advised they would be interviewing him the next morning, so if he wanted counsel present, he better make a call. With that, she went back upstairs to Robert's office, pushed the door open and went in. After she took the offered seat, they just sat there, grinning at each other.

"I believe that a celebratory dinner might be in order very soon," Robert said.

"Agreed. I can't believe this whole thing is over."

"Well, I am sure that all the lawyers will be making their deals, but we've done our job. Very well done, Camille." Then Robert added, "I think we should talk with David once more. Could you arrange to get him in here from wherever they are keeping him? I imagine he's at one of the remand centres."

"No worries, I'll arrange it tomorrow. Now, I think I'll let you attend to your paperwork. I know it's one of your favourite things." She got up. "Of course, you realize that you'll need to explain all this to Steve tomorrow, right?"

"Gee, thanks Camille. That just took the shine off the day. See you in the morning." This time it was Robert watching Camille's rear end as she left the room, and Camille knew it. Robert's thoughts reluctantly turned to how he would handle Steve.

~ 26 ~

Tuesday dawned at the police station, and as the officers made their way in for the day shift, there was significant chatter after the previous day's events. Robert arrived just before nine and was expecting the 'Steve effect' right away. He was not disappointed, however Steve spotted Robert before he had a chance to get some caffeine into his system.

"Can I see you in my office, Robert?" Steve asked. Robert followed Steve in and took a seat, waiting for the blast. As soon as the door closed, it was immediate, Steve not having armed himself with any facts.

"Are you crazy? You are going to get yourself fired for this. Do you realize what you've done?"

Robert waited a moment, looking at Steve's eyes, then let loose. "As a matter of fact, I do. I know exactly what we have done. We have arrested a man who orchestrated the murder of his own wife. We have the guy he hired to do it in custody, who incidentally told us it was Sam behind the killing. We have Sam texting the killer the day of, and we have the killer in possession of Sam's Rolex. In addition, Sam had the foresight to purchase a life insurance policy on Lydia in the amount of three million dollars a couple of months ago. Do you want me to go on?"

Steve sat there, his mouth open, but nothing was coming out.

"If you don't mind, I am due for an interview with one Sam Greene in a half-hour. May I please get going so I can prepare?"

"Sure." Steve said weakly. Robert got up and exited the room, gently closing the door behind him. If he could have, he would have locked it from the outside, but sadly, that hardware option was not available. His first thought was not the interview, however, it was coffee. As he walked back to his office, he signalled Camille, and they both kept going down the corridor to the elevators.

After a rousing discussion with Gilberto about when the rain might end, Roberto and Camille took their cups to a small table by the window. Most detectives would be nervously preparing their questions before an interview. Robert had a different plan. He would be claiming the moral high ground, and the questioning was going to be more philosophical in nature. The police didn't really need anything from Mr. Greene. Robert just wanted to look him in the eyes.

"Anything you want to ask him? Robert asked Camille.

"Something about Lydia I suppose. What she did to deserve being killed. I get it that sometimes people don't get along, but murder?"

Robert stared out the window, not seeing anything, playing out the interview in his mind. "Ok, I'm ready. Let's do this." With that, they walked by Gilberto, Robert winking at him and then out into the rain. "It's a perfect day for what we are doing. It is not a day for sunshine and flowers."

"I suppose not." Camille agreed.

When they arrived back at the station, after it was confirmed that Sam and his lawyer were in an interview room, they made their way downstairs. As they entered, Robert couldn't help noticing Sam's black, blue, and ochre skin surrounding and complimenting his squashed and slightly crooked nose. He and Camille took a seat. Philosophy quickly took a back seat when Robert started in.

"Rough weekend Sam? You didn't look this bad when we pried you out of that service room." This was met with silence from the other side.

"They haven't been mistreating you in here, have they?" More silence.

"Is there anything you want to discuss, Sam?" The lawyer shifted in his chair ever so slightly after Robert asked this.

The lawyer broke his silence. "He would like to know why he has been arrested."

"I thought that was explained to him when he was brought in and read his rights. Do you need it repeated? Did you not take any notes?"

"There's no need to get snarky here." More from the lawyer.

"I'm sorry, I get that way when people pretend to be stupid. I also don't like my time being wasted. I can understand Sam here wanting to waste time, because that is all he's got now, time. Except it won't be nice time, it'll be crappy time. Who knows, maybe he'll end up in the same place as David MacDonald, and they can reminisce together."

"Who is David MacDonald?"

"You really don't know very much, do you? How are you going to defend this guy, using magic?"

"Are you going to charge my client?"

"As we are sitting here. Conspiracy to commit murder, namely hiring a thug named Bobby Minolta to kill his wife, Lydia Greene. Is that clear enough?"

"You don't have any evidence that Sam did this."

"Again, I don't think Sam has shared everything with you. We have plenty of evidence and Bobby, who is in custody, has already fingered Sam for it. We just have one or two more questions before you go to try and arrange bail. Camille?"

Camille looked Sam directly in his eyes. "I'd like to know why you would want to murder your wife? What did she do to you that made you want to end her life?"

Sam Greene's hands twitched on top of the table, then he looked down and didn't say anything. With that, Robert and Camille stood up and walked out of the room.

"Well, that was depressing. He didn't even say one word. His lawyer should be happy about that." Robert said. "When is David due here?"

"Just after one, I believe."

"Lawyer as well?"

"Don't know. I expect a court-appointed lawyer may be present, not sure."

"Good, let's meet after lunch." Robert concluded.

***

The second interview with David was done to see if he would confess to any of the other malfeasance that he had been behind. He wasn't in a confessing mood, however, maybe having listened to his lawyer, although Robert didn't get the impression he would listen to anyone who wasn't thinking along the same lines as David. At any rate, there was no lawyer present for the conversation.

"I don't know if you get the news in remand, but you may be interested to learn that we have arrested Sam Greene for murder." Robert said.

"Murdering who?"

"His wife, Lydia. I expect that he probably thought it would get pinned on you."

David smiled.

"Maybe you two can spend some quality time together when your trials are over and you're in prison." Robert concluded. He could almost see the wheels turning behind David's eyes at this thought. Suddenly, Robert wearied of the farce, and signalled Camille to leave the room.

After they left, he said, "I'm tired of this. It's up to the prosecutors now. I think we can rest." He smiled at Camille, and she smiled back. "Let me know what evening is good for that trip to Eden to see the Christmas lights. How about this Friday?"

"I'd like that." With that, they walked over to the elevator and rode back up to their floor.

Robert called Dominic, who was now staying on with the Gardens as the general manager. One of the board members asked him to reconsider after he had expressed thoughts about moving on.

"Hi Dominic, Robert Lui here. It's not business this time. Thought I'd bring my family over to see the lights this Friday evening."

"That's a nice thought. Of course, it's on us. I wasn't always a fan of how often you shut us down, but thanks for all you've done for Eden over the last couple of months. You'll enjoy the visit. The lights are spectacular."

"Appreciate it, Dominic. And as a gesture to express how my respect for you has grown, we'll park in the regular lot this time." Robert heard laughing as he hung up.

* * *

A few days later, in the Surrey Remand Centre, where people from all over the Lower Mainland awaited trial, David MacDonald was eating his lunch. The group area in which he was sitting was at the centre of the range of cells three stories tall. Tables and chairs were all fixed securely to the concrete floor, ergonomic considerations not on offer for extra tall, fat, or short customers. He ignored the other men at his table but looked up after studying his meat loaf for a moment. He could not believe his eyes. Samuel Greene was sitting at a table on the far side of the seating area. He was looking down at his meal, with his back mostly facing David, but David had no trouble recognizing him. Either bail had yet to be arranged, or maybe it had been denied.

David was sure that Sam did not know what he looked like anyway, so he had that advantage. He smiled to himself as he also looked down and started picking at his food. Wheels started to turn in his head; not very smoothly, his whole thinking process being out of sync after his arrest. His thinking had not been a model of clarity before this, but the prospect of being so close to his tormentor was pleasing and challenging to David.

He had not been happy to learn of Sam's release from the place where revenge was seemingly sanctified at Eden Gardens. Apparently, the gods were not pleased either and had seen fit to give him another chance at retribution. He watched Sam using furtive glances, and from what he could discern, Sam did not appear to be enjoying his taxpayer funded meal. David finished his food quickly, returned the tray and plates to the serving trolley, which was watched over by one of the 'guests', and went back to his cell for some thinking time.

* * *

Methods by which to kill someone in a lock-up were rather limited, but this was what David thought about. David had listened to some of the other people inside, and drugs could be an avenue, but David was almost certain that Sam was not a sampler of such pleasures, even though drugs seemed to be available if one had the need. He had no weapons, of course, and was uncertain if he could fashion one out of whatever was readily available, which wasn't much. He remained perplexed. David had no experience in hand-to-hand combat, so taking on Sam in a fight was probably out of the question. Perhaps he could surprise Sam and get the upper hand that way. He sat on the edge of his cot and studied his cell wall, but it was not giving up any clues this day. After another hour of strategizing, coming up with nothing, he grew frustrated and returned to a thin book that he had managed to cadge from another inmate. It was a novel translated from French and set in North Africa. While he didn't think much of the story so far, he could readily identify with the main character—he seemed to be a bit of a loner on the outside, just as the title indicated.

The next few days didn't provide any revelations to David. He was talking to another inmate during lunch one day. He listened more than he spoke, as he had noticed that most of his fellow inmates had a story to share. Everyone loved talking about how they had been shafted and shouldn't be in the remand centre at all. The other inmates' stories sounded like his own, if he was honest with himself.

The man talked about the value of striking fear into the heart of your enemy, how it put the person on edge. This pleased the man he was listening to, that he had become someone to be afraid of and maybe respected. David doubted the respect aspect, as the man was spindly, and had a twisted face, as if he had swallowed a lemon whole. However, David grabbed onto the fear factor as he nodded knowingly at his table-mate's story. His thinking about Sam changed slightly. Now maybe he would reveal himself to Sam, and promise that an early death was coming Sam's way. He didn't put too much further thought into what he would do to carry out the threat, but figured the menace would suffice for the moment.

***

Back at Cambie Street, after the success of the Friday evening Light Festival visit with his children and Camille, Robert was priming up to see if Camille would go out on a real date, and getting nervous at the prospect of asking. Then there was his position on the force.

If he was going through with this, then common sense dictated that he resign or shift to a different role, leaving Camille to be the detective she wanted to be. He was confident that if he asked Thomas Harrow, he would be let back onto the Anti-Gang Taskforce. It wasn't a perfect solution, but it was the best he could up with to avoid resigning from the Vancouver force altogether. He had yet to test the idea with Thomas, but he wasn't going to wait on that before asking Camille out.

Robert decided to get Camille up to Café Paulo to ask her—keep it out of the sight of nosy officers. He looked outside his office over to Camille's bullpen station. She was there, so he went over and beckoned her with his coffee sign language. She was slightly puzzled, as they were no longer working on any cases together, but coffee was coffee, so something must be important.

As they settled into their window seats at the café, Robert smiled nervously, "Did you enjoy last Friday evening?"

With that opening, Camille was pretty sure what was coming next. "No, not really." She sat, stone-faced until she couldn't keep it in any further, bursting into laughter, "Of course I did! You should see the look on your face."

Robert had been on the edge of turning purple with

embarrassment. "Okay Camille, you're good. You had me." Gilberto called over to them that their orders were ready. After returning with the espressos, Robert didn't waste any time. "Would you like to go on an actual date with me? No children this time, just to be crystal clear. I know of a really fine French restaurant over near Burrard Street in Kits that I think you'd enjoy; Parisian, not Quebecois, but fantastic food."

Camille's eyes glittered as she nodded. Robert smiled, and they remained silent as they sipped at their cups, looking at each other and speculating about something they had each been thinking about for some time.

***

A day later, in the Surrey Remand Centre, David thought it was about time to introduce himself to Sam. He picked lunch time as the strike point. He waited a bit, then strode slowly out of his cell, watching ahead to see where Sam would sit. After fetching his tray, he walked over to Sam's table and sat directly across from him, staring at him. Sam looked up. His immediate reaction was a muttered curse. This was why he needed bail, to keep away from the crazies which seemed to abound in this jail.

David smiled as he softly said, "Do you know who I am?"

"Another wacko or pervert?"

David laughed. "You should be so lucky. Remember Sonny MacDonald?"

Sam stiffened. He said nothing.

"I'm his son, asshole." David smiled again, and coming from his face, it wasn't the smile of a friend. Then he continued, "What are you doing here? Have you been cast out from the Garden of Eden for some sin?" When Sam declined to answer, he added, "I also have a couple of friends who went bankrupt because of a leaky condo that you built for them. I think you are in serious trouble."

With that, he got up, grabbed his tray, and went to another table to eat. As David ate, he glanced over at Sam from time to time, smiling his unpleasant smile. The effect was exactly what he had been hoping for. Sam did not look comfortable.

***

It was lunch time, a few days later, and David thought he'd visit Sam's table to rub it in a little, but it was Sam who spoke first as David sat down. Sam seemed to have settled down after the discovery of sharing a facility with David MacDonald, and he no longer seemed afraid of David. Maybe Sam thought he was safe in remand.

"There is something you should know about your dad. Your father had a gambling problem. Sonny didn't agree, of course. He thought he knew a good bet when he saw one, so it was easy to take advantage of this. We had been visiting the horse track up at the PNE a few times. The key to doing well in the betting game at the track is to get some inside information. I supplied him with a couple of very good tips for previous races and presented myself as being pretty knowledgeable about the horse game. How I gained this knowledge wasn't a question that your dad ever asked. He was focused on the racing information, never wondering why I was providing it to him."

"So, why were you doing it?"

"Had to keep up with the Joneses. My friends were starting to develop projects in Vancouver, and I needed to be in the game. Land is the key to success, and your dad had a lot of it he wasn't doing anything with. It wasn't hard. He was already in debt from his past gambling. I just offered him a way out in exchange for a guarantee based on the land that he owned. And then I upped the ante. I told him I had knowledge of a long shot that was going to pay off hugely. In order to make it big, you had to bet big, which he was preparing to do. He already had so many loans and mortgages on his home and a few other properties that your head would spin."

Sam continued. "He was putting his money on a horse called Fancy Feet, which had been showing poorly for its last several races. These results were purposeful—at least, that is what I told Sonny. He believed me. Fancy Feet was slated to race in the sixth race of that afternoon. A stakes race with a purse of thirty thousand dollars, if I recall correctly."

"Sonny didn't much care what the purse was, as long as the odds were long for Fancy Feet to win or even place. The track was dry for a change and Sonny hoped Fancy Feet wasn't confused by this after being run in the light rain most of her young life. I told him that the training runs were good the previous week. And they had been holding her back, so no one was expecting this horse to do anything but lose the race. Somehow, your father was still not following the logic. He only had one thing on his mind, and that was winning big."

"When we went down to do the wagering, I seem to remember the odds were around thirty-eight to one, which was better than what Sonny was hoping for. Then he asked me to help him place the bets. Sonny seemed oblivious to the fact that I wasn't planning on putting very much of my own money down. We finished our drinks and went up to the wickets in the betting area."

"Sonny went going all in, Fancy Feet to win. It was the dumbest thing I had seen in a while. Without the show or place added to the bet, the odds significantly went up in Sonny's favour, but only if he won. Of course, to a sane person, it also made the odds of winning any money at all significantly worse, but Sonny was a little past sanity at that moment. After setting the bets, the odds dropped as the market adjusted to the influx of extra money. Then we went back up to the bar where we could watch the race with a scotch in hand."

David was gripping the sides of his lunch tray so tightly that his fingertips were turning white. His eyes were riveted to Sam's face, rage slowly building.

Sam continued the tale, "At the start, the line broke cleanly. Fancy Feet, not frightened for a change, eventually settled into fifth place as they bounced down the straight toward the first corner. Rounding the long bend, as I recall it, a horse named Night Commander led the line into the back stretch. No whips, just twelve ponies running for all their limited worth. Fancy Feet dropped a place on the back stretch but wasn't fading. In fact, she seemed to be running comfortably. At the last turn another horse tried to overtake Fancy Feet, but she wasn't having it—actually gaining on the field as the rider took her wide while breaking out the whip. Fifteen lengths from the finish Fancy Feet was eating up the ponies one by one. Sonny was so excited he was spilling his scotch. I was also getting nervous. From fourth, to third, then second, trailing Night Commander by a length as they rumbled to the line. In the end, Night Commander edged Fancy Feet by that one length at the finish."

But Sam wasn't finished, unwisely adding, "And that is how dumb your dad was. It was like taking candy from a baby. About racing, a horseshoe had a better grasp of things than your dad."

David lost it. He pointed up, and as Sam raised his eyes uncertainly, David took his lunch tray, the macaroni entrée scattering everywhere and swung it for all his worth into Sam's exposed throat, smashing his larynx and sending Sam toppling backwards. The only other person at the table sat still, eyes wide. David stood up but did nothing else to Sam as the room exploded.

Guards were watching from their perch in a control room overlooking the central area, but none were on the floor where the assault had taken place. A button was pressed, and a blaring alarm sounded. No one immediately attended to Sam as he lay on his back, slowly suffocating from his crushed windpipe, his left leg still hung up on the fixed chair he had only just been sitting in. Some inmates were running around. One knelt beside Sam but didn't know what to do to help. The others continued eating their lunches, not willing to miss a single meal no matter the circumstances, but only after pounding their tables several times in support of whatever violence was on offer and whoever was so bold as to offer it up as noontime entertainment.

The veterans who knew what was coming choked back the rest of their meals, certain that lunch would be aborted by the guards, with no chance of seeing the dessert trolley making its rounds—not that they had ever seen one in all their time spent there.

Sure enough, as one guard tried to attend to Sam while a doctor was making his way over to the range, the other guards rounded up the rest of the prisoners and sent them back to their cells. The exception was David. He was led away to a different holding cell, for people who had not exhibited the best of behaviour.

***

A day later, on Cambie Street in Vancouver, Robert was having the utmost trouble concentrating on his work. After an extremely successful date with Camille the previous Friday, it was impossible to think about anything else. They were no longer working the same cases, but having her sitting just outside his office door was not conducive to efficient anything. He knew what he had to do, so he left his office, walked down a floor to Thomas's office, and made his request about returning to the gang task force.

"I will consider it, Robert. Favourably I would say." Thomas paused, secretly pleased at the return of someone with slightly more intelligence than most of his officers.

"Have you heard about Samuel Greene?" Thomas asked.

"What?" Robert wondered how Thomas knew something about his last case.

"In the hospital. Got into a mild disagreement with another man in remand over lunch. Crushed windpipe, maybe some brain damage done before they could free his airway. It's uncertain."

"Do you know who the other man was?"

"David something or other, don't remember the last name."

Robert shook his head. "An eye for an eye." Then he added, "What was that chapel called, Retribution? Where would we be without it, Thomas? Probably selling insurance or working for a bank to make a living in this world."

The End

Glenn Burwell was a registered architect who practiced in Vancouver, British Columbia, for almost forty years. He's seen all sides of the local development industry and how it affects the lives of people living in the region. This is his first novel. Now retired, he is working on more stories of detective Robert Lui, manages a small tomato and herb garden, and continues to keep an eye on the never-ending saga of housing problems in Vancouver.

You can contact Glenn through the Somewhat Grumpy Press web site, www.SomewhatGrumpyPress.com.

Help independent authors and small presses by leaving reviews at your favourite retailers.

CPSIA information can be obtained
at www.ICGtesting.com
Printed in the USA
LVHW030923310323
742574LV00001B/1

9 781777 689865